MW00800979

JEANNA ELLSWORTH

Pemberley's Heir

By Jeanna Ellsworth

Check out Jeanna Ellsworth Burrill blog and other books
by Hey Lady Publications:
 https://www.heyladypublications.com
Follow Jeanna Ellsworth Burrill on Twitter:
 @ellsworthjeanna
Like her on Facebook:
https://www.facebook.com/Jeanna.Ellsworth
Connect by email: Jeanna.ellsworth@yahoo.com

This book is a work of fiction and any resemblances to
actual events or persons, living or dead, are purely
coincidental, because this work is a product of the author's
imagination. The opinions expressed in this manuscript are
solely the opinions of the author.

DEDICATION

To those who do not know their divine heritage
—keep searching.

ACKNOWLEDGEMENTS

I cannot help but think of my mother who never knew she was a daughter of God until someone told her more than 50 years ago. Because of the way my mother raised me, I never doubted my heritage. Just as importantly, my father taught me through his powerful example that patience and understanding are key elements in a happy marriage.

My own journey to discover my missing piece—and a happy, stable life—took far too long and included many detours. Thank you, Richard Burrill, for lifting me on a daily basis and for being my partner in the many projects I take on. I have the creativity, confidence, and will power to be an "accomplished" woman, but it is you who makes me truly succeed.

I'd like to thank my editor, Kellene Adams, for being so flexible and efficient with her work. From the first time we met, I could feel your enthusiasm for Jane Austen was equal to mine. I could offer no better compliment than that.

The cover is an original work by award-winning local Utah artist Heather Olsen, @heatherolsenart. Her talent and ability to bring the characters to life made it impossible not to truly see where this book was going. I'm indebted to my graphic design artist, Austin Beckstrom, who took Heather's painting and, with one glimpse, sold me on his exceptional talent.

CHAPTER 1

Wickham slapped William on the back in a way that spoke of more than simply colleagues. "William, it is good to see you are loosening your stoic nature a bit. I was beginning to think you were too good for the likes of us. I should warn you that the new rank of lieutenant will attract a great deal more women."

William shuddered, and knew the correction could not be held back. Regardless of where he came from, it was poor form to speak of the gentler sex in such a way. "I prefer to think of them as *ladies*."

"William, William, the day I lay down with a woman and she turns out to be a lady is the day I wake up a rusty penny that is worth a pound."

It bothered William that Wickham never used his surname, as was customary when addressing a peer, unless Wickham was formally introducing him to others for the first time. It was always William, never Daniels. It would be interesting to see if he would start calling him by his new rank, lieutenant.

The other soldiers gathered around William and Wickham howled with laughter, hooting and banging their cups on the tables of the pub.

One bold gent called out, "More like you lay down with a lady, and she wakes up a *woman*."

William turned to leave. He had low tolerance for company at the moment. Solitude was what he sought, not more foul gaiety. Most days, solitude was always the remedy for his social agitation. He had no true excuse this night, for he was generally familiar with all in the company; however, his mood was somber, more so than normal.

Wickham nodded acknowledgement of the crass remark about ladies vs. women with admiration, but then he turned back to William, causing William to stop.

Seeing that he had William's attention, Wickham began. His lip curled into a half smile that made his thinly trimmed mustache fully straight. "Are you too prideful to share a pint? Or will you force us to revel in this opportunity to celebrate without you again? All this is for your honor, William. Do you not understand? Sit for a moment; let go of the iron posture you carry, and drink with your peers." Wickham turned to the rest of the militia who had been dipping rather deeply for more than two hours already. "What say you? One more drink for Meryton and one more for the militia that will help it rise from the ashes! Raise your glass to the new lieutenant, William Daniels!"

William allowed the men to continue in their imbibed enjoyment. After all, he had seen this behavior for several years now—five, to be exact.

For a moment, William Daniels worried he would have to stay with the half-sodden soldiers; however, as Wickham started spouting old Scottish drinking songs—none of which William knew—William realized just how foxed his companion was. He waited patiently, positioning himself closer and closer to the exit. He had learned the art of being invisible in a crowd.

Before long Williams saw his opportunity to escape and slip away like so many times before. He knew he would not be missed.

Indeed, this celebration had been in his honor. After five very long and lonely years, Williams had finally risen to the rank of lieutenant.

Even though being in the militia meant he was always in someone's company, he still described the time as lonely years because he didn't know what or whom he should be missing. One must know his ancestry or even birthright to know those things. He could not even provide his birthplace.

Or last name.

He had risen from nothing—from no one—to someone.

As a lieutenant, Williams could now afford to support a wife and family with his income, although meager it would be. He knew it would take many years to have the monetary means he desired in order to look at a lady with a marital perspective.

As the singing rose to new levels, William knew the moment was upon him, and he slipped out of the lively pub, intent on reaching his quarters.

William deeply desired to return to the book, *Sense and Sensibility*, that had been his balm for the last few weeks. He had read it three times already and could not fathom why Marianne Dashwood never saw the love of Colonel Brandon until she suffered, so terribly, the loss caused by John Willoughby's mercenary senselessness. The signs were there all along regarding the colonel's intentions and deep affection. Was it her youthful age that limited Marianne's vision?

He feared it was the colonel's temperament.

Unfortunately, William Daniels shared the colonel's same reserved and taciturn temperament. It was one of the only things about himself of which he was sure.

As William bowed his head and left the pub, he caught the watchful eye of Samson, one of the few men he tolerated enough to call a friend. He would have to atone for his early departure tomorrow, but William did not enjoy large groups, regardless of the fact that he was fairly well acquainted with most of the men in the pub.

With one exception. William did not enjoy Wickham, a man whom he hardly wanted to know. He especially detested how the man made sport of him.

*****

Mary Bennet was as outraged as she had ever been. "Elizabeth Bennet! How dare you mock the christening and baptism of a babe!"

Elizabeth suppressed a giggle and continued to spar with her sister, her favorite, second only to Jane. "It seems only fair that we should not make them join a church when they are only weeks old. How do they know if they believe in the Church of England? Can we not ask them first?"

"They cannot decide for themselves if they must be baptized any more than they can decide what or when to be fed. A parent must help them when the choices are complex or vital."

"My dear Mary, that is just the thing. What if we are wrong? I am not disputing that every man and woman must be baptized. The Bible indisputably says they must. I am supposing that we should not force any religion on anyone who does not want it. Otherwise the parents have made covenants in their baby's behalf. It would only be logical that the parents will be held responsible for that covenant, not the infant. Imagine that," Elizabeth said, glancing up at the ceiling momentarily before continuing. "Imagine that our mother would be accountable for each and every thing her five daughters did in their lives when they strayed from Christ's path. There would be no amount of smelling salts to help calm her tremblings and nerves when she meets her maker. That much I am sure."

After a beautifully rewarding and prolonged moment, Mary closed her gaping mouth.

But then, to Elizabeth's surprise, Mary timidly whispered in a low voice. "I doubt she could bear the weight of her own transgressions."

As always, Elizabeth had hoped to shock her sister, but Mary had done the shocking. Even with her black and white thinking, Mary still found her usual way to liven up the conversation.

Both girls were still giggling, perhaps Mary was only sheepishly smiling, when Jane entered the sitting room of their home, Longbourn. "These two sisters of mine are not hard to find. I just wait to hear raised voices or these lovely giggles, and then follow the sound. Have you been debating some grand moral topic again? Do you not get bored of these passionate oratories?"

Elizabeth stood to fill her teacup again. "Jane, you are too reserved and kind and rarely stand firm in your opinions, unless they are good opinions. But I am afraid my good opinion, once lost, is lost forever. After all, Jane, whom else can I debate with when Papa is busy, besides Mary? I must have my share of the conversation. My dear sweet Jane, now that you are here, you must tell us more of Mr. Bingley," she said.

Jane dipped her chin and turned slightly away. "He is. . . he is . . . kind."

"Yes, Jane," Mary said with a steady and low tone. "But will he be a good father?"

Jane's face turned crimson and said, "Please, Mary, I dare not imagine that far in advance."

Heavy on the impertinence, Elizabeth added, "Mum nearly has your wedding breakfast planned. You might consider it soon. After all, he makes five thousand a year!'"

True to her reserved nature, Jane ignored Elizabeth's mocking of their mother. "I have only danced with him once and had tea twice. And both times, he was very, shall I say, kind."

"Kind," Mary and Elizabeth both said in unison with Jane, bringing smiles to all three sisters.

"Very well. He was not just kind but solicitous to my needs. Three times he filled my punch glass at the Assembly. I felt I must drink it or appear ungrateful. Luckily it did not pose a problem later. Oh, dear. Did I just imply . . .? But enough of that. I have news. Very intriguing news!"

Jane had always had a low threshold for teasing.

Recognizing that she had likely teased her favorite sister far too long today, Elizabeth turned to Mary with raised eyebrows and a single shake of the head indicating to her to allow the conversation to shift.

Jane had a knack for steering pointed conversations away from herself, especially when they involved their newest neighbor, Mr. Charles Bingley, who had taken a fancy to the young Bennet girl. His attraction was no surprise, nor something to lament, as Jane was the fairest Bennet daughter.

Both Mary and Elizabeth waited on Jane to disclose her news, and she finally whispered, "I am afraid that Lydia and Catherine will find out soon enough that the militia has come to Meryton. The soldiers arrive tomorrow."

Elizabeth laughed and said, "I am afraid, sweet Jane, that is not news at all!"

"She is correct," Mary chimed in. "For we have known about it for a full nine and a half hours."

Elizabeth furrowed her brows, quirked her head inquisitively, and asked, "Mary, you knew before I did? But how? Oh, dear. You have been tasting sweets with Papa again in the wee hours of the morning!"

Mary lifted her chin as she replied. "I shall not feel remorse for maintaining family ties. And I will say that if you were not traipsing around the countryside at dawn without an escort, Papa would have told you first. But I will add truth to your gossip, Jane, and tell you that Colonel Forster already paid Papa a visit yesterday afternoon. He had a particular need for his troops to dig trenches. As you know, our canal has filled in over the years. The real scandal is that the militia will be working on our very grounds."

There comes a time in a young lady's life when shock warrants a gasp.

But when one becomes truly mature, silence is the only appropriate response to the truly scandalous.

Jane and Elizabeth both felt they had matured at that exact moment.

*****

Of course, there was no keeping the news from Lydia and Kitty. The three eldest Bennet sisters and Mr. Bennet were indeed proud that they held the secret as long as they had.

But when the redcoats started marching past their garden windows the next morning, the secret was no longer theirs to hide.

The militia was easily one hundred meters away. However, without forehand knowledge that fifty eligible bachelors in brilliant uniforms would be visiting their grounds, Kitty was still in ribbon curlers.

And regardless of not being visible, the youngest Bennet sister, Lydia, fainted from the excitement.

Of course, Jane hurried to her side along with Mrs. Bennet. Elizabeth simply looked at Mary, who never restrained how she truly felt. In truth, she doubted she would be any good at it if she tried. There were equal parts disdain and pity on her face.

Mary began to share her opinions verbally. "What are men to rocks and mountains?"

Between wails for her Lydia, Mrs. Bennet hushed her middle daughter.

As Lydia feigned coming to, with her head in her mother's lap, she mumbled breathily, "Redcoats. Hundreds of them. Hundreds of redcoats."

"Oh, Lydia! My sweet daughter." Mrs. Bennet hugged Lydia to her bosom. "I nearly lost you! Mr. Bennet! Mr. Bennet, there are officers outside! How could you admit them to our property without warning poor Lydia? What is this nonsense?"

"I should ask you the same thing, my dear. My silly girls faint at the drop of a hat." Seeing that his youngest daughter's eyes were completely fixed on him, Mr. Bennet knew he could cause a speedy recovery of his supposedly feeble youngest with his next statement. "Goodness, if only it were just hats that were dropping. They cannot be called redcoats any longer the way they have thrown their coats to the ground. Maybe burgundy, or crimson."

Lydia indeed appeared to be fully recovered as she and Kitty ran to the window, screaming, pushing, and pulling the other in attempts to be the first to see the now coatless men.

Elizabeth held her breath momentarily then shook off the girlish tendencies. She admitted that she saw the logic in the soldiers' efforts to disrobe in the gardens. It was much too warm to be digging ditches in late August without anything other than a vest and shirtsleeves.

"All of them . . . bare," Kitty said in awe.

Lydia's voice was sweet and sensual. "I wish it were true. Is it? But I shall believe! For my eyes could never imagine such handsomeness. Indeed, I want that one with the broad shoulders who is working so hard. And him over there. Not the short one. La, I shall take all of them except the hairy one on the end. You can have him, Kitty. And the short one, I suppose."

"Mama! Mama! Lydia says I should only get two while she picked the best for herself! Mama!"

Elizabeth stood and walked from the room towards the front door, away from the militia, and away from the frivolities that they brought.

As much as Elizabeth loved her sisters, there were times she didn't much like them.

Pushing her hair away from her face, she opened the front door. Then noticing she would need her bonnet today with the Hertfordshire wind, she turned back.

Jane acknowledged her departure with a dismissive wave of the hand as Elizabeth retrieved her bonnet, then started backing out the door.

"Pardon me, Miss, do you . . ."

She stopped abruptly, then turned around quickly, learning rather suddenly how close the man was. Both took a proper step back.

As Elizabeth watched the stranger, he appeared to grow uncomfortable. He was tall but not too lean. He suddenly stood taller, broadened his shoulders, and took a breath.

He bowed the briefest bow, hardly respectful in Elizabeth's mind.

They stood there looking at each other. She was expecting this soldier to re-address her or at least finish his request.

Instead, he stared at her with slightly narrowed eyes and a look of incredulity.

She returned the inappropriate and rude glare as he took visual inventory of the front vestibule in which she was standing.

She took a breath and hoped this contest of wills would end soon. The wind picked up behind him, almost blowing his own hat off his head, but he was quick to secure it.

He continued to glare at her person from head to toe, although she doubted he meant to have her notice him doing so.

How dare he scrutinize her in her own home! Was there some lack of morals on his part?

She had thought him handsome, at least briefly, but now he was not handsome enough to tempt her.

Her temper may not have been her weakness, but it most definitely was not her strength.

"Sir, do you have a request? Otherwise I believe you should be in the west gardens, as that is where the trench for pigs resides. I am to understand that it must be amended."

His head tilted momentarily, but then he squared his shoulders further and said, "Is there a Mr. Bennet here? My name is Lieutenant William Daniels. Will you please tell your master that I am here?" She could have sworn he had winked, but his stern eyes and lips did not move from the taciturn position they held from the horrid beginning. His tailored beard, worn slightly too long for her taste, covered two-thirds of his face, hiding any clues that he had any humorous intentions.

But she knew very well that he was intentionally mocking her. "Well played, sir. Come in or the whole of Hertfordshire will blow in, and our servant, Mrs. Hill, will blame me. I shall lead you to his study. Do you know what a study is? A study is where true gentlemen gather to discuss things of importance. Have you seen one before?"

The only response was a slight clearing of the throat.

Elizabeth walked far enough in, hung her bonnet again, and led the strange man into the study. She motioned to the cushioned chairs and said with a stern, corrective tone, "I have no master, sir."

She sensed that he was not entirely shameful for the earlier jab, so she added, "I won my freedom by making the finest chocolate sponge cake. It would not have worked in the Americas, for they do not enjoy sponge as the British do. The recipe is worth a great deal."

The finely groomed, dark-brown beard twitched just enough for her to know that he recognized she was speaking tongue in cheek.

She turned to leave, but he spoke two very predictable words. "Thank you."

He bowed again, this time slightly lower.

*****

William Daniels was too puzzled to take a seat. There was plenty in his life that puzzled him, but he considered himself sharp and quick. However, this lady—whom he just now realized did not introduce herself—was not just sharp but quick-witted too.

She was not too tall, although taller than average, and had untamed brown curls flowing freely around her shoulders. Society would have turned their noses at such vulgarity, and part of him felt that draw too, but the deeper part of him felt differently. At minimum, it was a surprise, but he couldn't fight the intrigue, nay, temptation, either.

Colonel Forster had wanted him to make contact with the owner to confirm that the work the soldiers had commenced and was according to the colonel's standards.

Unfortunately, he did not have a good view of the "pig trench," as the young lady had called it, so he could not monitor the militia while he waited.

Over a quarter of an hour passed. Leaving untrained militia without supervision was never a good idea.

He took out his pocket watch again, but that did him no good. The time was nearly the same as it had been the last time he had looked.

That is not to say he wasn't entertained while waiting upon Mr. Bennet. The wails and giggles that came from further inside the house made him question whether Colonel Forster had actually met Mr. Bennet, or at least raised the question that Mr. Bennet was a gently bred gentleman who taught his daughters proper decorum and decency.

But what did he know about raising gentleman's daughters?

Why were these types of thoughts imposing on him all the time?

He understood a great many things that he couldn't explain. He had learned that he could calculate revenue from the visual inspection of a barley field's yield as it browned. Granted, it was an estimate, but a darn exact one.

He even had gone as far as to test himself. He had been training in a town just outside of Brighton and asked a landowner what yield he was expecting. The man guessed high, perhaps a moment of inflated ego at his tall and perfectly browning field. Daniels asked him if he felt that it was a high estimate, and the owner shook his head confidently, his bottom lip protruding for emphasis.

However, William Daniels knew he guessed high. He was sure of it. As sure as you knew which foot was your left one.

As the weeks went by, Daniels had followed up with the man, and the farmer admitted that the guess had, indeed, been high. Daniels's private prediction, made weeks earlier, was within two bushels of yield from the final harvest.

But it was more than random knowledge about farming. He knew his past was more than being a farmer.

Perhaps he was just hopeful that it was more.

No, it was more.

It was the complexity of his knowledge, the management itself, that tipped the scales of logic and curiosity that he had once been a man of means. Deep down, he knew he hadn't been a farmer prior to the ship sinking five years ago.

His ability to ponder any more on his favorite topic—who he was before five years ago—halted as the door to the study suddenly opened.

A very short man, with plenty of abdominal girth, waddled in then leaned on the back of the armchair. His protuberant abdomen heaved and gasped. "Oh, pardon me, are you waiting for Mr. Bennet too?"

William Daniels suppressed a smile, grateful that this gentleman was not the one who had asked the militia to do the work he and his sons should be doing.

"Indeed, I am Lieutenant William Daniels."

"Pleasure to meet you." The man continued in a breathless way, as if he had walked from London. "I am Mr. Phillips. My wife and Mrs. Bennet are sisters by birth. I suppose I should start calling Fanny my sister too. After all, it has been twenty-three long years. Dear me, I think I need to sit down. That is a very long time." Mr. Phillips did just that on the very chair he had originally leaned on. It was the closest chair available.

The gentleman took several more deep breaths while William observed his slightly disordered state. His cheeks were ruddy, and his nose a bit bulbous. He licked his lips twice before he asked, "Do you wish for a drink while we wait? Thomas shall not be long. Never is far from his study."

"No, sir, I do not drink much and usually not without the host." Not to mention that it was only the middle of the morning. William assumed this man had not broken his fast yet but planned to break it with drink.

Phillips looked to the decanter, then to Daniels, and back to the decanter. There was no doubt there was an unspoken request to serve a guest liquor in an estate that did not belong to him. In fact, it was a home of which he had yet to meet the owner.

Luckily, he was spared the requisite offer to oblige as another man walked quickly into the room, then slowed when he noticed it was occupied.

He was much more intriguing than Mr. Phillips, as he had four books tucked under one arm and his eyeglasses bridged on the tip of his straight nose. He had the same brown eyes as his daughter, whom William had met earlier. Those eyes were bright and playful, yet also ready to spar.

William bowed, then took a step or two forward with an outstretched hand.

But his introduction was interrupted.

Mr. Bennet did not offer his hand but jovially exclaimed, "How delightful! You must be here to have the first pick of my five daughters. I knew one of you would turn out smarter than the coat implies."

William didn't have time to request an explanation before the ruddy-nosed man, with an unquenchable thirst, started hooting laughter. The laughter shook his abdomen dangerously, threatening to bust the tightly fastened buttons on his vest.

Mr. Phillips spoke loudly. "Tom-tom, always the jester! Did you see the confusion on his face? Pure mortification at that accusation, yes, it was. Why I'd like to hear what he would have said."

Daniels ignored the contraction in his speech, as this man was still his better. He was a gentleman, while William Daniels had no idea what or who he was other than what he had become over the last few years.

The room quieted.

Did they actually expect him to respond?

Mr. Bennet smirked slightly, imperceptibly, for it was only noticed near the eyes. Yet he did not rescue Daniels in any way by retracting the question.

Instead, Mr. Thomas Bennet strode over to the decanter and poured three fingers of brandy, handing one to his brother-in-law. Mr. Phillips took it most gratefully.

Mr. Bennet then turned his full attention to William Daniels and waited.

William tucked his chin slightly in doubt, furrowing his brows.

Mr. Bennet's eyebrows rose sharply. He continued to wait, saying nothing.

"Sir, my name is Lieutenant William Daniels," he began.

He was interrupted by Phillips. "I know that, Mr. Daniels. Answer Thomas's question."

He was not sure which direction to proceed. The majority of him desired to depart through the door he had come in, but he was better trained than that. And somewhere in the back of his mind, he knew that it hadn't been the military training that had taught him how to handle this unique situation of husband-hunting parents.

Daniels turned his gaze back to Mr. Bennet, took a breath, and said, "Forgive me, I am not acquainted with any of your daughters. I have no doubt that they are quite accomplished and would make many men happy. I, however, have nothing to offer at this time."

"Very diplomatic, Lieutenant. I shall look forward to continuing this conversation when you do have something to offer. I shall be delighted to know which daughter you choose. Now let us travel to the west side, and we can discuss matters other than my heirless estate."

"Thank you, sir."

Heirless estate? So there were no sons on the Bennet estate? It was likely that it was entailed away. How would it be to raise five daughters, knowing that the estate you have worked on all your life would fall to some nephew or cousin?

That understanding shamed him a bit when he reflected on his earlier judgment of the owner as perhaps a bit of a slacker for not maintaining his own trenches through the years.

There was even more understanding when he noticed the right hand of Mr. Bennet, the same hand that had not reached for William's when it was offered. The hand was badly burned and badly scarred, with two of the outside digits amputated. William had only caught a glimpse of it as Bennet reached for his hat, but almost immediately, the hand was tucked into his waistcoat pocket, preventing further scrutiny.

How had he missed this observation? Normally, William was excellent at noticing detail. But he realized that Bennet had been carrying the books with his right hand, the good thumb in view. He had even poured with his left hand, an oddity therein, thus shielding the scarred right hand from William's visual field. Bennet had also folded the right hand under the left elbow when William failed to answer immediately.

The men exited the study and, while they walked, Thomas Bennet continued to share the oddest details about Hertfordshire, Meryton, and Longbourn, which was apparently what the Bennet home was called.

However, no further mention was made of any of the five daughters, especially no comment about the brown-eyed nymph William had not been properly introduced to.

That night, even though he was physically fatigued from assisting with the trenches, William's body struggled to succumb to sleep, all because he didn't know her name.

"Miss Bennet," he whispered to himself as quietly as he could.

CHAPTER 2

"Lieutenant Wickham was the most handsome of the three officers," Lydia announced.

Elizabeth agreed with Lydia, but there was a charisma about him that intrigued her. "He certainly was not the hardest worker yesterday," she stated.

"I heard he has an old shoulder injury, and he must moderate his activity to prevent it from getting aggravated," Jane added.

Lydia nodded and said wistfully, "A war injury. How charming! Maybe it was a bullet. One can survive with a shot to the shoulder."

Mrs. Bennet nodded profusely. "You can survive! A distant cousin, although much older than me, suffered greatly due to the injury he sustained in the rebellion in the Colonies. Oh, heaven help my nerves. I will have five daughters married soon! Bingley and Jane. Elizabeth and . . . an officer. Mary and . . . well, you know how it will go. All the way down to my Lydia and Wickham. Mrs. Wickham. How lovely that sounds."

"I shall be married first," Lydia declared. "Then you will have to let me go to dinner first. I will be first in everything now and always. Not last! Ha! I shan't be last anymore! Wickham even told me he was nearly introduced to the king last month when he was granted the privilege of escorting a soldier to receive his accommodations of bravery. The king! I bet, when I am Mrs. Wickham, I will be serving all the king's favorite foods from my fancy dishes."

Elizabeth sometimes wished she could rein in her tongue, but this time she was happy to remind her younger sister of a minor political detail. "Lydia, King George is unwell. He never leaves Buckingham Palace except on a weekly carriage ride through Hyde Park."

"You are just jealous! The only officer who looked at you was the awful Lieutenant Daniels! You can have him. Lord, you can have everyone but Wickham."

Jane briefly met Elizabeth's gaze then looked down at her lap demurely. Of course, Jane would not come to her rescue. And Elizabeth knew her sister Lydia well enough that to say anything at all would have been adding fuel to the fire.

"I believe I shall retire to my room for a spell," said Elizabeth instead.

Mrs. Bennet mumbled something about how that meant Elizabeth was going on another walk in the country when ladies should be resting in the afternoons.

Elizabeth smiled as she passed her. Ignoring her mother had become habitual over the years, even entertaining.

Elizabeth climbed the stairs to retrieve her half boots because the housekeeper, Mrs. Hill, was always too quick to put them away. She had just used them that morning, and Elizabeth had a longstanding tradition of trying to hide them near the door for easy access. Hill had a knack for finding them, dusting them off, and returning them to the foot of her bed on the right side.

Windows, boxes, and closets were the typical locations where Elizabeth stashed her boots. But last June she hid them behind the freshly cut spring bouquet, which enraged Hill the most. "Not by my peonies!" she had wailed. But it was all in jest for both of them.

At one point, Elizabeth had hung the boots from the chandelier in the entryway. That only passed by Hill's notice for three days; however, it was the longest her half boots had stayed on the main level in four years.

In no time at all, the boots were laced, and the Bennet daughter was moving through the brush to one of her favorite paths: the meadow. The afternoon sun warmed her from the inside out.

Perhaps it was more that she found peace with the wooded area. Sometimes, like today, she took a walk more than once.

Her mind pondered the events in Meryton lately. Their little town was generally predictable, a characteristic that wasn't all that favorable with Elizabeth. Some people avoid change or, at minimum, prefer knowing the pattern their days will bring.

But Elizabeth found it wasn't that difficult to adapt to new changes. She enjoyed traveling, even if she did not have her usual comforts from home. "But this," she exclaimed aloud, "this is too much change."

"Pardon?" A male voice spoke.

She startled and turned to search for the voice. She had a nagging suspicion that she knew who it was, as it held a strong element of disdain. As she located the source of the voice, directly from her right but near the ground, her suspicion was confirmed. "Good afternoon, Lieutenant Daniels. Pray tell, what are you doing in the grass?"

"Reading, of course."

She couldn't help but smile in surprise. "One of my favorite pastimes. Dare I ask what you are studying?"

"Studying? How I wish I had access to resources as you suggest. My current attention today falls to a novel. A romance, in fact. I am afraid I am only minimally interested in this particular book."

He closed the book with his finger holding his place, which led her to believe he may not have entirely meant the latter part of what he had said.

It was intriguing. Most intriguing. Why did he not want her to know he liked the book?

She let that pass for now and instead chose not to tease him. The decision was not a hard one to make. After all, a gentleman who reads love stories alone in the hills, hidden in brush and grasses, likely has other secrets.

"May I sit down?" she asked.

His brows rose slightly and nodded. "Certainly. I do not own the land."

"No, at the moment a gentleman named Charles Bingley owns this particular hill," said Elizabeth.

"I probably should have asked permission."

"Oh, yes." She felt the tingle of her wit bubbling inside. He seemed slightly less reserved than earlier. "You most definitely should have. If poaching is a hanging offense, I can only imagine the punishment for irritating and disrupting the grass. This particular patch took years to be so thick and lush."

She knelt down a few feet from him, casually trying to catch the title of the book, but he hid it just enough to prevent detection.

His mustache twitched slightly, and he said, "I see that now. And would Mr. Bingley be forgiving of me disrupting the grass? Perhaps merciful to a fellow book lover?"

"I highly doubt that. He did not even know that the Netherfield estate had a library until last Tuesday when Jane and I were invited for tea by his sister. I am partly in jest though. He is a forgiving man but not because you are a book lover. You must have other talents, do you not? Any that would stand as good testament of your character as you are sentenced?"

His deep-brown eyes brightened a bit, and she saw his mustache twitch slightly once again. "Talents. Do you mean like accomplishments?"

"Yes, let us start there. What have you accomplished? What are you most proud of in your life?"

"Pride is a dangerous foe. Vanity too," William Daniels replied.

"I cannot disagree more. For it is a common misconception that pride taints a soul. My personal opinion is that where there is a real superiority of mind, pride will always be under good regulation."

He nodded, with his head tilted a miniscule amount, as if he was passively agreeing.

Apparently she was wrong.

"May I use the very phrasing you just said to debate the statement?"

She blinked briefly but then gathered herself from the shock of the counterattack. Her heart picked up briefly. His speech was refined, with the subtlest Northern accent. The smoothness and the quality had not been noticed in any way with their first encounter at Longbourn. She evaluated its tones a bit more as he shared his thoughts.

"The very words themselves, 'superiority of mind,' drive me to consider that superiority is an essential element to your personal definition of pride.

To label or create distinction between one person and another, other than a lateral distinction, is hypocritical and contrary to humility. The fallacy of your belief is that it suggests there is a classification system of the human race, implying there are those who are deemed more superior than others. The moment a vertical distinction is formed, suggesting a hierarchy of any form, a superiority if you must, then that is the very moment that one's pride is not under good regulation."

Elizabeth was speechless for a moment. She couldn't help but think his comments interesting. She shifted her kneeling position enough to get more comfortable and, now fully sitting on the grass, tucked her feet tightly to the side under her skirts. Her half boots were much loved, which meant they were well worn too.

It was a unique and surprising retort. How ironic it was that her initial opinion was that the lieutenant was no stranger to pride. "And am I to assume that you, Lieutenant Daniels, had no distinctive vertical thoughts, ranking those you have met in the last forty-eight hours? For that is how long the militia has been in my pretty little town of Meryton."

Lieutenant Daniels bowed his head and then tucked a long blade of grass in his book as a bookmark. Setting the book down, he admitted, "I am afraid I am not the example to follow in this. I have poorly regulated my pride in the past, as well as less remotely. And sadly, I have no excuse for it. There have been many moments in the recent hours where I have encountered new faces, new places, new habits or customs, and judged without hesitation."

She tried to mask her blatant surprise at his frankness, especially at the clear truthfulness.

She responded in kind. "I am afraid that I am just as guilty."

He looked up at her and smiled. His look was genuine and contrasted greatly to the initial cool greeting. She was pleasantly surprised with the way his eyes smiled too when he allowed himself, which appeared to be an extended minute.

Gratefully, the moment stretched without becoming awkward.

"Lieutenant, dare I ask what you are thinking at the moment?"

His shoulders bounced as he chuckled. "I almost asked the same of you. Ladies first."

"Oh, no, I was first out of the 'asking gate,' so you are obliged to answer."

Chuckling again, he smiled and then nodded in agreement.

He took a breath to speak but then exhaled. He cleared his throat a few times as he made attempts to answer, but nothing came out.

She waited.

It seemed an inordinate amount of time as he gathered his thoughts. But there was no doubt he would answer.

Perhaps he is ashamed of what he was thinking, Elizabeth wondered. Perhaps he was distracted momentarily? Perhaps she didn't truly wish to know what he was thinking!

"I was thinking. . . forgive me, I have never spoken this way to a lady before. My thoughts were along the lines of . . ." He exhaled a bit loudly and then quickly finished. "It was actually a very distinct thought. I was trying to sketch a lady's character."

She couldn't help but smile. "Many men have tried to sketch the character of ladies, but I shall warn you, it cannot be done. I happen to have constant full access on my own thoughts, yet there are times I cannot truly comprehend my own mind!"

"No. Perhaps that did not come out as I intended. I desire to sketch one particular lady's character." He had been looking at his hands, which were rubbing the corner of the leather book, but as he made the last statement, he looked up and their eyes locked.

She whispered under her breath, "Oh, dear, I do not have a witty remark for that. I should thank you. Yes, that would be in order. Forgive me. It is just the way you said it. It was so genuine."

He just looked at her, seeming to offer confirmation of what she had implied.

Her cheeks began to heat, and her heart started to pick up its pace, not drastically, but just enough for Elizabeth to notice.

"Well, thank you again, Lieutenant Daniels. I do not think I have had the pleasure of such a compliment before. "

She began to feel awkward with the lack of verbal response from him after that. She realized that a good deal of time had passed since she had left Longbourn, and she began to gather her skirts to stand. He was quick to assist her in standing up.

His hand reached for her elbow and stabilized her while she rose. She lost her footing briefly but did not lose balance. The reason, however, was not of her own accord but rather from the steady support offered by the gentleman next to her.

"May I escort you wherever you are going?" Daniels asked. His voice was deep, yet soft. The last word hung in the air, as if he feared her answer.

She laughed briefly. "Sir, it might be wise to determine my destination prior to offering to accompany me."

"It does not matter. You chose to rise and leave, yet I dearly wish to hear the other half of the conversation."

She cocked her head in confusion. "Other half?"

"Yes, Miss Bennet, you are required, by statute, to disclose your thoughts from a moment ago. I disclosed mine, as you requested, now you must do so in turn."

She hadn't been this diverted for some time.

Hoping to tease him further, she said, "I usually do not stutter in my thoughts, nor when I choose to disclose them. However, in exchange for my thoughts, I ask that today you allow me to be my own escort."

They had begun to walk already; however, he paused briefly, weighing her offer.

"Very well," he replied.

Elizabeth delivered her earlier thought with confidence. "I was thinking that you had fine eyes." She smiled brightly, knowing the brief reply would startle him.

She turned to leave, feeling a natural thrill from her courage to share such a scandalous remark.

Looking back over her shoulder, she winked then picked up her skirts and ran home towards Longbourn.

CHAPTER 3

"Aye, Pemberley has not been the same since the children . . ." Mrs. Reynolds paused, still finding it painful to talk about. ". . .were lost to us."

Mrs. Anne de Bourgh Darcy nodded. "Do not lose hope. My husband and I have not. Fitzwilliam Darcy is not lost to us. I know it in my heart, and so does his father. When Mr. Darcy and I pray at night, we feel a peace come to us. We have searched up and down the Falmouth coast, and you know Mr. Darcy is there again at this very moment renewing the search. I personally believe the search has been what sustained Albert Darcy. It has given him purpose, perhaps even keeping the master of Pemberley alive these past five years."

"Thank you kindly for the reminder. I shall hold out hope a little longer. But at least he has you now. And your two young'uns."

"My husband may have a great deal of faith that his son—and true heir—is still alive, but he was required to remarry. I shall never replace my Auntie

Anne Darcy, but if we never find him, Pemberley needed an heir. And I am convinced the true heir, Fitzwilliam Darcy, is alive."

Mrs. Reynolds's eyes filled briefly, and she nodded silently, then curtsied and went on her way.

She was not quite prepared to address the rest of the serving staff in the servants' quarters, so she took a small detour to the art gallery.

Once there, she looked up at the portrait of the young Fitzwilliam Darcy and the beautiful Miss Georgiana Darcy, taken two full years prior to the shipwreck on the Falmouth Coast. She admired the strong jaw on William, a Darcy trait, and the fine brown eyes that had a way of smiling when he was truly happy.

Young Fitzwilliam Darcy was practically raised by Mrs. Reynolds, Pemberley's housekeeper. And she had experienced enough death and loss in her life that she had felt the death of William and Georgiana immediately. The remains of Miss Georgiana had been recovered, but Mrs. Reynolds hated to even contemplate where young Master William might be.

One thing she knew in her heart, however; there was no true reason to hope he was still alive. None at all. No God in Heaven could raise the dead, and Master

Darcy and his new wife were delaying their grief for no reason.

Mrs. Reynolds was a kind and loving woman but did not offer trust and faith in a God that had taken so much from her, nor did she trust in mankind in general. She knew her role, but her skills in observation meant she knew a great deal more than anyone else in the household. There had been no proof at all that Fitzwilliam Darcy had survived.

Having no tangible proof meant there was nothing to believe in.

As Mrs. Reynolds studied the portrait, her heart ached to hold the children she essentially raised. She was as responsible for the successes in their short lives as either of the parents—and certainly more than the last three governesses or nursery maids.

She could understand the pull to hope that the young master had survived.

For the first time in more than ten years, she whispered a silent prayer, not to God but to the Universe in general, perhaps Mother Earth or whomever would listen to her aching heart. "If he *is* alive, help him come home."

*****

His foggy, sleepy mind tried to process the noise he thought he had perceived.

Silence. Then the sound came again.

He was quite sure he heard something this time. He startled awake and felt unnatural movement of the bunk.

He blinked wildly, trying to focus on what was stationary, but in the fragile seconds he stole to do so, he still failed to find anything in eyesight that was stable.

Confusion filled him entirely. Why was the earth moving? What had he heard? What woke him up? Where was he?

Had someone just screamed? Or had he dreamt it?

His chest felt tight with the strain of trying to make sense of what seemed impossible to understand in the fraction of time that had passed.

He heard it a third time, and he knew with certainty that a young girl had just screamed.

And that young girl was directly above him in the top bunk.

He bolted up from his supine position and jumped to the floor, staggering as it shifted aggressively, first one way and then another. He reached out for the upper bunk to stabilize his balance but encountered nothing solid in the first three attempts.

With exerted effort, he lunged forward, landing not just his hand on the bunk but his shin and shoulder as well. He screamed with pain as his body made direct contact with the safety boards of both of the bunks.

His eyes had clenched with the grimace and groan that escaped with the impact. Forcefully exhaling, he continued his attempt to assist the girl.

Her white gown was hardly white. Not anymore.

The plaited flaxen hair was an unnatural shade, at least not for hair. The crimson blood dominated the scene.

Sucking in a breath, he began to understand why the scream had sounded like the world was ending. The critical and desperate tones were dead-on for the nature of the emergency.

The roof of their cabin had caved in.

There was no hope for this little girl.

She had to have only been nine, possibly ten at the most.

He couldn't understand the rush of emotion he was feeling. She was very important to him, that much he understood. He also understood that he loved her desperately. But who was she?

With one hand grasping tightly to the side of the upper bunk, he reached to touch her face. She was gasping audibly, making an unnatural sound that came from both her mouth as well as from lower in her chest where the bulk of the beam had landed.

Was it possible for the heart to speed up to an immeasurable rate while at the same time feeling like it completely stopped?

Overwhelming love and compassion filled him, and he tried to breathe, but her painful, agonal gasps were indeed the only breathing occurring between the two of them.

Finally, he felt a choking sob escape his chest as he wiped the saturated hair from her eyes.

What skin color this beautiful girl had had seconds ago, was fading at a radical pace.

Their eyes locked. The fear in her deep blue eyes tormented him as he understood that rescuing her was a hopeless endeavor.

Even in her innocent youth, she too was fully aware of her fate.

She reached out her hand, exposing her palm, her petite fingers wiggled just enough for him to understand what she wanted.

Her name came to him in an instant.

"Georgiana . . ." He took her hand as gently and securely as he dared.

"It hurts, William . . ."

"I know. I know, Georgiana. I will stay with you."

Only two more gasps escaped from her chest before it fell for the last time.

Her eyes had never truly relaxed into the post-mortem absence of expression.

The fear in her youthful azure eyes was captured permanently on her face as well as etched forever in his mind.

His mind couldn't have held a thought or two more before he crumbled with grief. The emotion rocked him harder than the movement of the floor beneath him.

But just like every time he relived the emotion of that moment five years ago, he drew in a steady breath and forced his sleepy mind to awaken.

He was groggy, but he knew the dream was over, leaving him just as breathless as he had been in the dream.

William Daniels tried to take another steadying breath; however, the grip in his chest was excruciating. Slowing he gained control of his body and mind. At least this time he was handling it better.

For the past year, he no longer woke from this reoccurring nightmare with frightening screams that he had to explain to those around him. It was one thing to have a nightmare as a grown man, but to expose oneself so openly to fellow militia often led to merciless teasing from stoic soldiers. Three times in the past, the irreverent and unkind teasing had been cause enough to change battalions.

But who the hell was Georgiana?

How he wished he knew. He loved her. That was all he was certain of.

She had called him William . . . but was that his name? It had to have been. At least he was confident enough of the fact to use it when he started life over, with no reliable memories of his past.

He rehearsed in his mind the instruction he had regularly given himself, words that had seemed to help in the past: You may not know much of the past, but you can create any future you desire. Move forward, always.

With that, he pushed himself off his militia-issued cot and tried to shake off the grogginess and the weight of the tragedy from five years earlier.

The cool breeze that flowed in from the flapping tent entrance was a tender mercy because it cooled his damp brow.

After a week of rain, the clouds appeared to have finished their torrential downpour. The rain had slowed, and nearly stopped. That was another tender mercy, as he was more than ready for the confinement that rain enforces, to end. The militia's meager options for activities of late had confined the men to their temporary tent camp.

Absentmindedly, or perhaps not, Daniels wondered if the trench the militia had cleaned out had filled in at Longbourn.

In the last week, he had finished his book yet again and played chess more times than he could count—and won every time too. He had learned he was pretty good at the game, not even needing to be taught. It was as if he had loved the game in the past, or at the very least had a great deal of practice with someone more skilled than he. But after at least ten games in a row of winning, the challenge lost its savor.

He had hoped to take a moment to himself while his tentmate, George Wickham, was visiting another tent, most likely gambling again.

How did Wickham still have money to lose? While it wasn't of any concern to William personally, he did take deliberate measures to make sure his own pocket money was safely hidden.

He felt the cool breeze freshen the air again and looked back towards the tent flaps.

He did not know how long he stared in that direction, but it was longer than he should have done. He sighed and looked away, reminding himself to shake the nightmare off.

Time these days held one of two flavors, either refreshing or nightmarish.

Today, he was failing to keep his mind from reverting to that stormy night five years earlier.

That night was clearly where he lost his memory, but why was he on the ship anyway? And who was Georgiana? She was so young, at least ten years his junior.

He wasn't daft, long ago concluding that she was most likely his sister.

But the facts were few, suspicions were many, and intuition was plentiful. The only thing he knew for sure about Georgiana was her first name.

Perhaps that was not entirely true. He knew the feelings he felt as she died in his arms, and the memory of her pained azure blue eyes would forever be his.

Yet he had no memory of why he was on the ship with her or where they were going. The fact that the two were sharing the narrow, modest quarters certainly implied a close relationship. Being the eldest, as well as the male, one would think it would have been appropriate for him to be on the top bunk, for both safety and propriety.

But Georgiana had been on the top bunk, not him.

He must have been asleep when the crash happened, because that was the only time the repeated memories, or dreams, began. Thankfully, they had lessened over the years, now haunting his sleep only several times a month rather than. Depending on how deeply William was sleeping, one of two things would take place. He would either start remembering what happened and wake up, or relive it entirely like he had done today.

But after five years, the only concrete facts he had to show was a racing heart rate and that same blasted memory of scrambling to get to Georgiana on the top bunk.

When the memories were strong and vivid like they had been today, he could almost hear the storm worsening all over again, lightning and thundering seconds apart all around them, and then . . . flashes of William yelling Georgiana's name.

The only words she had whispered back were "William, it hurts," before Georgiana gave the subtlest squeeze of the hand, and then, less than a minute later, the horror of that disturbing look plastered on her face, stealing her fragile youth.

He exhaled again forcefully and started removing his cravat. William nearly had it off, at least completely untied, when Wickham entered the tent.

Glancing at Daniels' disarray, Wickham startled a bit, and his gaze landed on Williams neck.

"Nice ring," he said. "The militia can be devastating on a man's desire to wear jewelry. "

"I suppose." William tucked the ring, and the chain it was hanging on, under the opening of the neck of his shirtsleeves. He deeply desired to take the cravat off, but it had always made him uneasy to be dressed so casually, even with a fellow officer.

"Too bad, I suppose. It is a nice ring."

"Yes, you said that." William wondered if the gambling had gone badly.

The man appeared more anxious than usual. Not necessarily anxious, perhaps it was just less . . . false, as if he had let his theatrical performance slip a bit. At least that was how Daniels had come to see Wickham; he always had something to sell or a performance to be praised. He seemed to be constantly play acting, and his character was not a man with whom William wished to associate.

Wickham's performance offered nothing for William other than plenty of two distinct feelings. Unexplainably, William felt a sense of homesickness and, with it, a desire to be open with him.

However, William's feelings of distrust for the man were even stronger. Therefore he shared little with Wickham. And kept his distance.

Wickham also had a way of making you feel like you weren't being fair to him, or that he got the short end of the stick in many ways.

Wickham was lazy, that was what it was.

Oddly, the frequent yet genuine looks of coveting, or jealousy, were familiar too. Perhaps William was being hard on Wickham. Yet there was no better way to explain those sideways glances Wickham cast his way. They weren't quite sneers, for that would have been stretching it. But William somehow sensed that he should not be entirely open with his tentmate.

But it was more than just distrusting him.

There were times over the recent three months since Wickham had bought his appointment—the same appointment that Daniels had to earn—that William Daniels could actually sense when Wickham had entered the room. He felt as if someone was watching him, yet when he looked up, he never caught Wickham actually looking at him. Which made him feel like he was not being fair to Wickham.

It was a vicious cycle of those two feelings: homesickness and distrust. Nevertheless, William Daniels remained steadfast in keeping his distance and privacy.

At the moment, as he looked at Wickham with the nightmare heavy on his mind, William Daniels had an inextinguishable desire to groan audibly, but he managed to suppress it.

At least he thought he had.

He always had a hard time shaking off the weight of the nightmare, but this time seemed worse than usual.

William shook his head and attempted a bit of conversation once again. "How did the cards treat you?"

Wickham half smiled, and an eyebrow rose as he said, "Quite well, quite well. It should not be long until he is begging back for what ends up in *my* pocket."

William nodded, trying to agree with Wickham, but inside he fully understood that Wickham was still losing.

"Did you finish that lady's gothic novel already? You read way too much!"

William felt slighted somehow and came back at Wickham with passionate words. "Reading is a pastime that has been my constant friend. Any person, be it gentleman or lady, who has not found pleasure in a good novel must be intolerably stupid. Regardless of whom I meet or whom I leave behind after meeting them, my books—and the characters in them—stay with me."

"Whoa, Dar . . . Daniels, I do not need an insipid monologue or lecture on your loneliness. I say, a grand idea just came to mind. Shall we ride to Longbourn since the rain has finally abated?"

Even though he had become slightly unraveled, William spirits soared suddenly; and his heart rate increased appropriately.

William tipped his ear upward, hearing more silence than he had for some time, and said, "It appears the stars have aligned. The rain has stopped."

William looked back at George Wickham and gave a single nod.

"Brilliant! You might want to put that cravat back on and cover up that fancy ring hanging from your neck," Wickham said. "It looks costly. Women tend to have an eye for money."

Feelings of disgust rose again at Wickham's reference to the Bennet sisters being not only women, but mercenary women. "The *ladies* of Longbourn are definitely a draw. I am happy to accompany you."

Winking, Wickham replied, "Ladies? I think not. Miss Lydia has found her way to me twice through the rain!"

William stood quickly, his hands fisted at his side.

"Hold on now, stay the trouble you are about to start," Wickham was quick to defend himself. "For one, I doubt you could take me, and for two, she had her sister as escort. I have done nothing other than share an extended minute or two. Good Lord, Daniels, you are wound tighter than usual."

Perhaps it was the rain and the feeling of being trapped. William sat back down.

But intuitively William knew it was more than that.

It was more than the nightmare too.

It had been over a week since he had seen Miss Bennet. More than a week since she had winked and run from him in the meadow, leaving him completely speechless.

And heaven help him, he had begun to crave those saucy remarks and intelligent debates.

You hardly know her, he reminded himself. He didn't even know her Christian name.

How does one find understanding in the irrational desire to have what one doesn't actually have?

And Daniels knew it was irrational.

But neither could it be described as anything other than desire.

*****

Mrs. Hill announced the gentlemen as she entered the parlor. "Mr. Samson, Mr. Dennison, Mr. Wickham, and Mr. Daniels are here. Should I let them in?"

Lydia giggled and started to primp her bosom. Kitty sat up from her slouched position on the chaise and nearly threw her reading glasses off.

It had only been the three sisters and their mother this afternoon because Jane was visiting Netherfield, where the "kind" Mr. Charles Bingley and his sister, Caroline Bingley, were offering her a chance to sketch the hills by his pond. Mary had gone as chaperone instead of Elizabeth this time because Elizabeth had some mending to do.

Elizabeth tucked her mending to the side, placing a pillow over the undergarment.

Smoothing her skirts, Mrs. Bennet replied with a plastered smile. "Oh, yes, please present the officers." Then she turned to her daughters and whispered far louder than necessary for all three daughters to hear. "Make haste! Pinch your cheeks, and plump the ladypairs in your corsets!"

Elizabeth did no such thing with her breasts, but of course, her two younger sisters did; Lydia had done so without prompting. Her younger sisters and mother were exasperating! Elizabeth was caught rolling her eyes and smirking when the gentlemen were ushered in.

They all entered, bowing respectfully.

She stood and indulged the gentlemen with a proper curtsy.

Wickham provided the two youngest sisters with a charming grin then turned to properly greet Mrs. Bennet. "Forgive my fellow officers and I for intruding, but the boredom in camp was overwhelming, and the unanimous consensus was that the Bennet household would provide the best diversion, a most delightful diversion. So here we are."

Elizabeth restrained herself from rolling her eyes again but was delighted when she saw that behind Wickham, William Daniels too had failed to restrain himself and had taken an extraordinarily deep breath.

What made it even more delightful was that Daniels glanced at her just at the right time to witness her observing him. She quickly looked away but could not help but think to herself that either Daniels thought Wickham a fool or he did not quite agree that the Bennet household could delight them the most.

"Oh, Mr. Wickham!" Her mother screeched. "You flatter us. Are we not the prettiest family in Meryton? All except my middle daughter Mary, but she is not here."

Elizabeth quickly took a step forward, bringing all eyes on her, distracting attention from her mother, which, of course, was her intent. "Please come in, gentleman. Mrs. Hill, please bring hot tea and refreshments."

*****

Wickham did not need Mrs. Bennet's help to direct himself where to sit. Lieutenant Dennison followed Wickham, and William felt his pulse speed up when he saw that the only remaining seats in the parlor were by Miss Bennet.

Lieutenant Daniels and Lieutenant Samson both preceded in that direction and casually flipped their coattails, taking the loveseat nearest to her.

"I see you possess marked intelligence," she said, with a twinkle in her eye while looking at William.

He was pleased she was in a teasing mood. His mood had been poor prior to coming because of reliving the entire nightmare from start to finish. "Miss Bennet, I am afraid I have always possessed marked intelligence. What, pray tell, has enlightened you to this knowledge? Are *you* now trying to sketch *my* character?"

Samson interrupted, asking, "Now pause right there, Daniels. What makes you think she was addressing you? She does not have the slightest idea that you whipped my backside in chess six times in a row. Miss, Lieutenant Daniels tells me I play chess shortsighted and that I should plan my next several moves prior to moving a single piece."

Elizabeth giggled and replied, "That does indeed help to win the match. Forgive me, Mr. Samson, but I do not think the fact that he won six times is the indicator of intelligence, although it could be. But the fact that you returned for a fourth loss, or fifth, or sixth loss for that matter, might just sway one to believe the opposite of *your* intelligence. Why keep playing if your opponent is more skilled? I should think that one would steer clear of that— if, that is, one was intelligent."

William Daniels grinned wider than he had in some time. But he had no retort, just admiration for her wit. And yet, there was something about her cheekiness that bordered on impolite. There was no hiding the fact that she supposed that Samson was unwise in playing, or losing that is, six matches; however, her comment was delivered with both sauce and kindness, almost as if she was simply seeking an answer to the previous question.

Samson tilted his head slightly, smirking. "Indeed, it may appear on the surface to be a disagreeable quantity of games. However, there is always something to gain from losing. A true hero is not the one who always wins, it is the one who gets knocked down repeatedly and gets back up."

She pursed her lips together in a smile, nodding, and said, "Honorable philosophy. What a delightful answer!"

Turning toward William, she continued speaking. "Now I shall answer your question, Mr. Daniels. My reasoning for quantifying your intelligence earlier held no more meaning than simply that you chose your company wisely. In short, you sat near me."

Daniels heard himself say in his head, *Yes, I did.* However, Samson was the one who made the statement audible. He could not help himself but feel a strange urge of displeasure arise towards his comrade as Miss Bennet thanked Samson with a smile.

That initial feeling of displeasure was quickly displaced by one of forgiveness, as Samson followed his statement with a question, a query that William himself had long desired to know. "I am afraid I do not know your Christian name, Miss. . . ."

"Miss Elizabeth Bennet. You are Mr. Samson, am I correct? I noticed that you worked along Mr. Daniels while clearing the canal. There were no two harder workers."

William was about to respond, as she had complimented him too; however, the blasted man next to him took the glory from him. Again.

"Thank you, Miss Elizabeth."

Daniels exhaled with a bit more exacerbation than he meant to show. He looked around the room while Miss Elizabeth and Samson conversed further.

He knew what he was feeling but did not wish to give it power by dwelling on it, let alone naming it. There were only a few people William remembered ever feeling such an intense desire to converse with.

Miss Elizabeth was one of them.

Miss Elizabeth.

How beautiful the name. So classic and regal; it was the name of queens.

William Daniels truly did not care what Elizabeth and Samson were talking about. His distress came more from the fact that she was talking to Samson rather than himself.

Daniels started to admire the kindness in her tones, but a short moment later, he realized those tones were directed at Samson. And when he found himself starting to smile at her humorous remarks, he wondered if she was trying to impress Samson. Was his friend the cause of her smile today?

What was the cause of the odd glances she sent William's way? She was a bit guarded and difficult to read. How would he ever know? Was there any hope at all? Or had Samson upstaged him?

There was no other officer to whom he could have respectfully resigned defeat. Samson was likely the closest friend he had had in the last five years. Most of the officers were disagreeable or not worthy of Daniels's notice. William, being a man who spoke but little, his decision to allow Samson into his circle of trust was not insignificant.

Samson was the second son of a modest landowner, one who did not have other estates to offer to the spare. There must have been little family money to offer when purchasing Samson's position in the militia, for any good, financially healthy estate could deliver two or three sons a position higher than that of lieutenant.

William's thoughts of Elizabeth were briefly derailed as he wondered how he knew that.

He found himself cycling down the old familiar rabbit hole of things that he shouldn't know but had great confidence about knowing. It was knowledge about estates, estate planning, managing tenants, and harvest amounts. He recalled strange customs, nay, traditions around the holidays that one could only dream up.

The rabbit hole began to deepen as he pondered other things of late that he had remembered, or simply had a sure knowledge about, and he frowned with concern for what it meant.

Surely he had not been of the first waters.

Yet, what did it mean that he knew what things should go into a supply box that is delivered on Boxing Day?

He remembered the last time he was in London and walked past a French bakery. Why would he have recognized the type of fine French pastries in the bakery window as he walked through London? He not only recognized them but had named every one: *mille feuille, tarte tatin, choux pastry, madeleines, brioche,* and *tartelettes amandine* . . . and he had heard himself say those names with a pure and perfect French accent.

Up until that moment, he hadn't known he could speak French, and realizing that he could speak it flawlessly was a bit unsettling. Considering he had no knowledge of his life prior to five years ago, let alone his country of origin, he could not help but fear he may have had a parent who was French. After all, now was not the time to be French, considering Napoleon was still fighting strong. It led him further down the rabbit hole as he wondered if he himself was escaping to France when the boat sank.

Who was he? Where was his family now?

Was his name actually William? Of course, he knew he had created the sir name of Daniels. He came up with the name Daniels for no reason in particular other than it started with the letter D, the letter on the ring around his neck.

The ring that had been on his finger when he woke after the accident. It had the letter D on it with a cross inside the D. A cross that, in the right light, appeared to be crossed swords. The detail was ornate and likely painstakingly etched by a master crafter. The decoration was a beautiful, elegantly scripted D, one that was likely worth a good deal of money.

But the ring was worth more than any amount of money to Daniels. It was the only possession of his previous life he had left.

His mind was quickly pulled from this pondering when he heard his name.

"Lieutenant Daniels, do you not agree?" Miss Elizabeth queried inquisitively, her brow arched, tempting him out of his somber mood.

Her question had its intended effect, and he felt a small upward turn in his lips.

"My mind had wondered, please accept my apologies. You must think I am disagreeable to not be attentive as you were speaking. Pray tell, Miss Bennet, whom should I agree with?"

"Oh, my, you should be left without any doubt with whom you should agree with. However, I believe the question that would be wise to ask is, what are you agreeing to?"

Her lips pursed together tightly to prevent herself from grinning widely. Her eyebrow arched temptingly, egging him to respond in kind.

The look on her face was adorable and entirely encouraging, a memory he hoped to always remember.

He relaxed, just enough to let his grin widen.

The magnificent vision before him settled his heart and mind.

There was no doubt; her charming impertinence was no match for Samson.

But himself? Yes, he could keep up with her cheekiness.

The ugly beast of jealousy seemed to dissipate in its entirety in that precious moment.

He understood now that Samson had not won Miss Elizabeth's affection in a single sitting. Nor would Samson ever win her.

Samson's heritage may not have been of the first waters with lucrative assets to spend frivolously, but neither had Samson ever had to go without. Knowing this, it explained why the militia had been so difficult for him. He had no true understanding of working for what you wanted nor the necessity of a long-term plan for the direction of his life.

Yes, in short, Samson was shortsighted. He only wanted to be gratified in the moment and was too impatient to understand what a lady such as Miss Elizabeth was ultimately looking for.

But Daniels knew this lesson well. It was unclear by half exactly how he'd learned this lesson prior to the shipwreck. However, now he had more than five years of making work his kind, yet constant companion.

There was no competition between Samson and Daniels.

There was nothing to be jealous of because Samson was playing "tea at the Bennets" just as he had their game of chess. Elizabeth was too smart for his narrow perspective.

Miss Elizabeth was never one to be taken from him, nor stolen either for that matter.

She was one to be cherished.

She was one to be earned.

*****

Elizabeth had not meant to widen her eyes. In fact, she had been determined to hide her grin too. But there, on Mr. Daniels' face, was the same intense smile that reached his eyes that she had witnessed in the meadow.

Daniels's words were delivered with precision. "One would think that, as a gentleman, I should immediately side with the lady. However, I sense a likeness in Miss Bennet, which I too possess, that resounds loudly of a love of debate. Am I far off, or have I hit the mark? Forgive me once again for sketching your character, Miss Bennet."

"Mr. Daniels, I have not corrected you thus far;

however, you may call me Miss Elizabeth. If my eldest sister Jane were here, she would be very confused indeed."

He paused, opened his mouth to speak, then said her name like a caress. "Miss Elizabeth."

She didn't dare respond verbally in case it came out in a croak, for she had never heard her name said so beautifully.

She folded her hands in her lap, raised her eyebrows, then looked up again, seeing that he was indeed still daftly smiling.

When he failed to finish his comment, she removed her gaze from his and scanned the room.

Mr. Wickham had been looking directly at Elizabeth, despite the fact that Lydia was leaning far too forward to be proper in her day dress.

Why was Wickham looking at her when Lydia was showing her wares so blatantly?

The proper thing to do would have been to smile and look away, acknowledging the eye contact; however, Elizabeth steadied her gaze on Wickham as Daniels spoke beside her.

"It is a rare thing for me to forget someone's name. I do make an effort to address them properly. But clearly, I am guilty of this infraction."

Elizabeth was only partially listening to Daniels because the irregularity of what was occurring between herself and Wickham was nearing complete rudeness. Wickham hadn't nodded, smiled, or dropped his gaze. He just kept staring at her, blinking normally, but his concentration was so focused that she wasn't certain he knew he was doing it.

Suddenly, his gaze shifted sharply to Daniels. It was such an intense and focused expression that Elizabeth couldn't help but continue watching Wickham.

What was occurring in Wickham's mind?

"Miss Elizabeth, are you unwell?" Samson asked quietly.

Wickham must have heard the question because he briefly glanced away from Daniels, then smiled at Elizabeth. At least it was intended to be a smile. It was forced, as if painted on in an instant. Wickham then turned back to Lydia, returning to the confident, arrogant, boisterous soldier with whom Elizabeth was more familiar, fully exploring Lydia and her cleavage.

"Miss Elizabeth, is there something amiss?"

She collected herself quickly, smiled at Samson, and said, "Of course not. I was distracted for a minute. Too many conversations in such a small room."

Daniels scooted forward in his seat and asked, "We could walk in the meadow or travel up Oakham Mount. The militia has been in Meryton for two weeks now, and I have yet to see it."

She smiled and nodded. "That would be delightful. I will have to change into my half boots." She then looked around the room and realized that the only escorts available would not likely leave their captive audience. "Oh, but I am afraid that there is no chaperone unless I ask a maid. AnnMarie will not be happy about this, but she owes me for a certain secret that I have held for her since last Saturday."

She stood, which forced both Daniels and Samson to stand and bow while she curtsied to leave then headed out the door. In her excitement to leave for a walk, she realized her curtsy had likely been poorly executed.

She stopped suddenly, turned around, and said, "Forgive the uncoordinated farewell, it was ill performed." She then bowed her head, tucked her foot, and carefully spread her skirts in a perfect curtsy.

When she finished and looked up, Daniels's eyes were bright with amusement. He didn't stutter, but his voice was shaky, and he cleared his throat a bit before he responded. "Think nothing of it. In fact, a phrase comes to mind that you may wish to adopt. 'Think nothing of the past as its remembrance gives you pleasure.' I believe you are a living testament to that statement. You appeared to have enjoyed yourself with that second attempt."

And if Elizabeth didn't know better, she saw a deep blush come to his cheeks.

As they looked at each other, she knew she should respond.

However, she knew, when she met his eyes, that she already had.

CHAPTER 4

Before the two were a hundred paces off the Bennet's estate, William Daniels had already opened the conversation with Miss Elizabeth. "I understand your father inherited the estate from his cousin? And that your cousin, rather than your sisters, will inherit next?"

"Indeed you are correct. How did you acquire this information?"

"From Mr. Bennet, of course. I am not the sort to listen to idle gossip."

They made a good amount of progress before Elizabeth responded.

"I had not known you had enough time to converse about such things as entailment of a new neighbor's estate. Granted, I suppose that topic would be far more likely to arise in a conversation amongst gentlemen than ladies. It is a sad bit of affairs for us, true, but what is to be done? Is it really so common knowledge?"

Daniels nodded. "It is a bit unusual to discuss it with those whom one is less acquainted; however, to further my blunder, it was I who inquired it of your father."

Miss Elizabeth looked briefly back at him then continued to attend to her footing. She was not only setting the pace but was leading too. William was in no way short of breath; however, their pace was not a casual stroll. He couldn't help but be impressed, for she showed no signs of distress either.

The well-worn, single-file path was not difficult, and he was intrigued with the scenery as he briskly walked to keep close enough to Miss Elizabeth to maintain a conversation.

He continued his explanation. "Mr. Bennet mentioned that he did not have a direct heir. And with five daughters, that meant the estate was entailed away, I believe to a cousin?"

Looking over her shoulder, she answered. "Indeed it is. To Mr. Collins, whom I have never met. When my father dies, we will no longer call Longbourn home, or as my mother says, we will starve in the hedge groves."

"That is a terrible thought, even for me, and yet I am not the one to have lived there. But I do know what it is like to be without a home. I said as much to your father, which is why he disclosed that the previous owner only had daughters as well."

This made Elizabeth giggle, and she replied with a smirk. "Indeed, for the last three owners, Longbourn has only bred for the weaker sex."

Daniels stopped abruptly.

Miss Elizabeth only took a step or two more before she stopped as well, turning back to him. No doubt his face was just as stern as ever.

He examined her for a minute. What had she meant by that? Surely she was smarter than to subscribe to such asinine notions.

But he wasn't sure. She had initially turned around with a smile. But now? Now she wasn't smiling. Rather she was almost glaring at him.

He was an opinionated man but knew when to hold his tongue. This, however, was not one of those times. Indeed, he was unable to hold his tongue.

Lieutenant Samson and the maid, AnnMarie, sent as companion, had caught up to them by now. They stepped off the path a bit to look at Daniels, and from his peripheral vision, Daniels could tell Samson was trying to assess the source of the tension.

But he held eye contact with Elizabeth.

When it looked as if he still held her attention, he said firmly, "A lady should never be called the weaker sex."

She cocked her head briefly one way, then the other.

Samson tried to diffuse the moment. "Daniels, she did not coin the phrase herself. You press your opinion too harshly."

Daniels almost spoke in rebuttal, but Elizabeth stood tall, both physically and intellectually.

"You are right to correct me, Mr. Daniels. And you also, Mr. Samson, for I hold little personal importance to the ill-favored phrase and should never have used it. However, I am beyond further words, at least any more than I already have spoken, until Mr. Daniels explains his intense reaction to a modern and often-used idiom."

She was accepting his opinion in full, not surrendering? Miss Elizabeth was not a simpering female, one who had no opinions of her own. Rather, it appeared that she was extending an allied arm on the topic.

He nodded, cleared his throat, and motioned to continue walking. After a pace or two, he began answering Elizabeth's question.

"Propriety dictates I should apologize. Samson has said as much. For my tone, or the manner of the delivery of my opinion, I do apologize, but not for the opinion itself. I believe that ladies are so much stronger than gentlemen."

He paused briefly, because it appeared that they were intending to pass over a few large, moss-covered rocks where the footing could be slick.

He offered her his hand as they stepped. She looked confused briefly but then took the offered hand.

Once at the top of the rock formation, she let go, then turned to him, reaching out her hand to help him up just as he had done for her.

He took it.

He didn't need her help, but she had offered. He knew in that instant that that was the exact reason she had taken his hand. She did not need his help, but she allowed him to assist her.

Their eyes locked again after both of them had traversed the slick rocks.

He was unsure how long they looked at each other before they were interrupted.

Samson said, "Do not you fret. I shall help AnnMarie up." It was said with heavy tones of humor, and they all casually laughed.

Daniels encouraged Elizabeth to continue to show the way as he continued to share his thoughts.

"Consider what one calls the 'underdog' in a fencing match. He is the least likely to succeed or win in a match, and is often underestimated. That is why the betting odds are so high. Yet, where there is brawn, which the world perceives as a benefit, one must sacrifice agility, for a large man moves far slower than one with less mass. Where a fighter has focused his attention is usually evident in the first few minutes. A man who has spent his time working his muscle rather than training with the foil will be slower in technique, and the saber will not benefit him in combat. On the other hand, a man who focuses his training using the foil will feel natural picking up the saber in combat."

"I think I am beginning to follow you. Please continue."

Samson chuckled and said, "I am afraid I might need a bit more from Daniels to follow where he is going."

"The foil is a lighter, safer-practice weapon," Daniels complied. "When one is ready, the student begins to practice with an épée, which is heavier and has a triangular cross section and fluting on the blade. But in true combat, the weapon is called a saber. It is used to slash and thrust, and is far heavier than a foil. Now the man who thinks strength, and not agility, is his ally may practice immediately with the saber. This does nothing for his agility or intellect. True masters will pull these students back, and they will resist. Strength is not the favored talent in fencing. It is the same for gentlemen. Intellect and understanding how your opponent thinks or works, or what drives their passion, is a far stronger talent to possess."

Samson nodded as he said, "And so you believe that, although ladies are not blessed with brute or brawn, they should not be underestimated due to their wit?"

Elizabeth answered before Daniels could. "No. I fully suspect there is more than what he has shared. But I must stop you both, for we have climbed a great distance. And it is now time for you to see where you have come and to visualize where we are going. Behind you, you will see all of Meryton. From the north to the south, I could map out where each of my associates resides, if you wish. Behold, Meryton."

William Daniels did as she bade and was struck with a breathtaking view, bathed in the late west sun, still several inches from the horizon. Each tree was painted with gold, as if each had already started to change colors, but he understood it was an illusion. The striking coloring was the power of the sun. Even the river, with its path bordering Meryton on the south, was touched with a warm glow. But he knew from experience—he had just bathed in the river that morning—that it was quite frigid.

The four of them stood in awe, their own faces touched by the same bronzing power that touched the tallest buildings in Meryton. He looked to Miss Elizabeth and realized that she was not looking at the town; rather she was looking up the trail, toward Oakham Mount.

It was then that he saw what she was looking at.

"Oh, good Lord, what a sight!" He muttered breathlessly, "Samson, look up there!" Daniels pointed at the rock formation ahead of them. "Have you ever seen such a pure quartz quarry? The stone glitters with such smooth and pure areas that could be mistaken for mirrors!"

Samson answered breathlessly. "Or windows into a mountain. I thought the view of the city was priceless, but Miss Elizabeth, show us the way!"

As they hurried up what was left of the mountain, Elizabeth explained that Oakham Mount was riddled with rose quartz. "Many men have tried to mine it, but the quartz is too pure, too solid to move or blast out. One would think that with this much quartz, one could build a rose quartz 'glass' castle. I imagine someone on the outside of the building could see a great deal of what was inside. Sadly, just like glass, it simply breaks when mined. Small pieces are worth a great deal, mostly because of the work required to obtain it. But the quartz is too brittle to obtain any pieces larger than a small gourd. For centuries men have tried to mine it, yet failed to bring this natural treasure down the mountain. With just the right sunlight in the evening, Meryton is a city that reflects the sun back boldly."

Samson moved closer to the edge of the trail and looked south, toward the curve of the river. "And since our militia is around the corner, none of us realized such beauty was just above us."

"The large oak forest covers the entire south side of the mountain, hiding this quarry from your view entirely, as well as from the main traveling road. Few know about this little secret, yet our town is on the road to London. Allow me to return to the previous conversations and add to your stated belief that ladies are in no way the weaker sex." Elizabeth had not paused a moment as she moved from discussing the splendor of the quartz to William's earlier observations.

Daniels nodded affirmatively, still caught in the grandeur of the sunset on the mountainside.

He was in awe of God's natural stone and crystal formations in front of him. As much as he wanted to look at Miss Elizabeth as she spoke, the powerful draw of the vision in front of him left him speechless as he looked up at the facets of the crystals.

"The value of a gentleman is often placed on his strength, or the power he possesses. This is not the same for a lady. In today's society, the value of a lady lies in her beauty, as well as her ability to produce more beauty. She is considered accomplished if she can paint or embroider, and has a thorough knowledge of the modern languages and can speak them with a perfect accent. The epitome of her ability to produce beauty is her posterity. A lady is required to hire governesses and tutors to help her offspring become icons for the public. However, in my eyes, her beauty and accomplishments do not make her a worthy opponent. Just like this quartz, beauty shatters with strain and pressure, or even simply with age. Please follow me around about a hundred meters more where the quartz is marbled with other elements. While it is not as impressive, the colored variety brings a unique value."

The group did as she bade, walking a few hundred meters until they came to a wide-mouthed cave. The entrance narrowed uniformly from all sides, shaped much like a perfect funnel.

As they entered, Elizabeth pointed up to the ceiling of the cave, which was highlighted by the descending sun. The bright, earthy colors included a variety of greens accompanied by a few golden stripes, but mostly the strong, low ceiling was a deep purple with tinges of orange.

The sun reflected off the facet of the uneven rocks just as it would dozens of mirrors. Even the darker areas of the cave were highlighted, bringing in a bit of the rose quartz. Intermixed throughout was other rock and sediment. Towards the entrance, sections of prairie grass and small groupings of weeds grew, complementing the overall affect and creating a strong smell of moss and earth.

"This is Rainbow Agate Cave."

"Aptly named," Samson replied in awe.

The four enjoyed a peaceful silence for a minute more before Elizabeth started to point out her favorite areas of the cave. Of course, the entire cavern was not made of crystals; there were just veins of it interlaced throughout the other rock and sand.

Elizabeth's voice trailed off then returned with a serene quality and a bit of sacred wistfulness. "Very few people venture past the beauty of the rose quartz seen at the top of Oakham Mount. They do not realize if they would just persist in their journey, they would enjoy this depth and natural beauty just beyond."

William Daniels had been looking at the crystal ceiling, but he thought he sensed meaning in her tone and wondered why such a statement would mean so much to her. He looked inquisitively at her.

William Daniels hadn't realized that he had entered farther than Elizabeth had into the cave, which meant he had to turn toward the evening sun in order to look at her.

His breath caught at the vision of her silhouette.

Her curves were entirely smooth, with proportions that his art master may have defined as less than ideal, yet they were intensely artistic.

Her features, when combined, far exceeded the parts individually

That is, her curves were more robust, accentuated even more than what was generally appreciated as the ideal feminine form. Each area had a distinct characteristic additive to the rest. At first glance, when dissected, one part of her body only minimally naturally flowed into the next curve, yet, it did in a very unconventional way.

For example, her shoulders should have looked broad, even muscular, considering the physical hobbies she entertained; however, with her long, elegant neck, her strong shoulders were clearly required to frame and mount her head and soft, curly brown locks.

At the moment, her head was tilted slightly down, with her gaze down to her right. The angle allowed him to see the curve of her chin and petite, slightly upturned nose, which only accented the high cheekbones and fleshy, enviable lips.

Enviable? What an odd adjective for a man to use when describing a woman's lips.

He stared at them a moment longer, steeling his self-control not to follow her curves lower to the chest and hips.

He fixed his gaze upon her face but hungrily drank in what was easily deciphered with his peripheral vision.

Today, focusing on Miss Elizabeth's lips would be a token reminder of what it meant to be a gentleman. She casually shifted her weight to the other hip, forcing him to recommit to this singular visual focus.

Her lips, focus on her lips, he told himself repeatedly.

As he gazed, her lips parted just long enough for her to begin nibbling on the lower one. It was not helpful by half to be concentrating so hard on that particular pair of lips.

He realized he had to comment in some way on the intensely sacred comment she had made a moment ago.

What exactly had she said?

What had she said with those lips. . . .

He cleared his throat and collected himself.

She had said something about seeing past the initial beauty, about how others failed to do so and therefore missed the depth and natural beauty inside the cave.

He felt it before he thought it. But as the words came out, he heard himself saying the words, not as a comment but as a suggestion.

"Beauty is always in the eye of the beholder. But if you do not behold her, you cannot partake of her beauty."

He held his breath. He hadn't even had time to think the words, so how had he dared to speak them?

He should be committed to the madhouse!

He opened his mouth to apologize, beg if necessary, but something about her made him hold his tongue.

She must think me a cad! His heart began racing faster than it had at the steepest climb of the journey up to Oakham Mount.

Her form stood upright, or perhaps it was just that she redirected her gaze to his face.

No, she had actually shifted the weight from one hip to both equally, standing with perfect posture. He knew this because the shadows of her legs were barely distinguishable with his peripheral vision.

But see them he could.

How he wished to pull the inflaming words back. He had never said such flirtatious and rakish things to a woman, at least not that he could remember. He reached his hand up to his trimmed beard and pulled on it nervously.

He no longer cared if she spoke or not, he just longed to make his farewells and depart immediately, but his feet were intensely heavy at the moment.

Finally, she broke the awkward silence. "Mr. Daniels, how eloquent. I am afraid that I did not recognize the author. Which poet can I attribute that to?"

His heart began to slow, and he exhaled.

If you loved it, attribute it to me was what he wished to say.

Instead he just smiled. "I am sure I can find the source of the inspiration."

And with one last glance, he took in her beautiful form.

CHAPTER 5

That night, as Elizabeth prepared to retire, she contemplated the events of the afternoon.

Or at least she tried.

So much had occurred.

So much was said.

Yet, not enough.

For example, Lieutenant William's watchful eyes on her that she couldn't understand. There were odd events and small evidences implying a significant mystery.

But not just one mystery, it was several.

She thought about how Lieutenant Daniels seemed to be eager to sit by her, which, of course, was flattering, but then he conversed so little! Why sit near her only to have no conversation?

There were also times that he had such displeasure on his face, contrary to their previous interactions. Her mind brought up one specific memory: when they conversed in Netherfield's meadow. She took a breath and sighed. Did he enjoy her company, or had he become disenchanted?

And there was the mystery of Lieutenant Samson. He was kind enough at tea, even conversed with ease, only to take a more significant conversational interest in her maid during the travel up Oakham Mount. In fact, looking back, she realized that he had said very little once they left on their excursion.

She pondered this particular mystery only momentarily for her curiosity about Samson felt inconsequential.

And then there was Mr. Wickham. Now there was a mystery. He had almost glared at her or, at minimum, stared at her with such fervor she felt both unsettled and slighted.

Of course, her courage always rose in circumstances such as those. But Elizabeth could not set aside Wickham's eerie, false smile and effusions as they departed, which brought unwilling shivers to her spine. The gooseflesh returned even at this very moment as she recalled them.

Wickham had definitely glared at William Daniels, and with such passion and intensity that she knew there must be some unwelcome history between the two gentlemen.

She perceived that William Daniels would never disclose why there was animosity between them. Or did he even know? Looking back, the glaring and intensity was indeed only coming from Wickham, for Daniels gaze was hardly removed from Elizabeth.

Why did Wickham appear to loath Daniels? She had to know!

No, Elizabeth, you do not. Not everything must be puzzled out.

As she checked herself and the ill-favored desire to know of the bad blood between the two men, she continued to review the facts in her mind.

Perhaps they weren't exactly facts, perhaps just observations to ponder.

And there seemed to be plenty to observe and ponder.

She couldn't hold herself back from the flood of thoughts.

When reading fiction, Elizabeth adored mysteries far more than romances or historical accounts, although the later usually held her attention longer than the honey-sweet romances.

Historical books fed her desire for debate, but romances? Romances fed a different beast, one which she dared not feed.

She was determined to be governess to her sister Jane's seven perfect children. Indeed she would be; what other options did she have?

She may not have been blessed with Jane's innate beauty, but Elizabeth fancied herself blessed with a bit more common sense, perhaps even considered herself intelligent.

And because of her intelligence, these mysteries fulfilled her need to debate for the time being.

But in this instance, the present mystery felt multidimensional. And she was eager to take on the challenge. She continued to muse upon the things she had noticed.

For example, William Daniels spoke with a proper, refined, and slightly Northern accent. His vocabulary was intriguing and refreshing because it was vastly extensive. As he talked about his book, it appeared he was well versed in many of the same great authors she also loved.

Yet, didn't he mention that he knew what it was like to not have a home? What had that meant? She had hoped he would have expounded on that comment, but he did not. This particular mystery lingered in her mind longer than many of the others.

Elizabeth Bennet had not met a single gentleman who held such unique and progressive convictions regarding the value of ladies. No other gentleman in her acquaintance would accept her offered hand, equal repayment for what he had done for her. Oh, she knew William Daniels had no true need of help. Neither could she pretend that it was a great mystery, for it had been a test of his conviction.

Many men can articulate ideals that appear desirable, but few stand by their convictions with the honor that Lieutenant William had shown.

For Elizabeth, this action indicated that he meant what he had said. She concluded that he had a good measure of integrity, and with a simple, single movement, he had earned her trust.

Kind words, even firmly given or well spoken, could sway many ladies to fall for a gentleman as handsome as William Daniels.

Handsome?

That was a thought she had not yet knowingly admitted to herself. There were definitely moments where he could be described as fine looking, perhaps even strikingly handsome.

Although he was not so handsome when he was glaring at Samson. No, not then.

But perhaps he was handsome when he had quoted the unknown poet in Rainbow Agate Cave. What had he said?

"Beauty is always in the eye of the beholder. But if you do not behold her, you cannot partake of her beauty."

And that was yet another mystery! Why hadn't he simply told her who the poet was?

She looked at herself in the mirror. Her reflection was hazy, not only because the candle had burned low but also because the mirror had been at Longbourn for at least a century. Spotted with chips and scratches, the glass was no longer true to reflection. The mirror's framework, however, was so exquisite that no one wanted to dispose of it. The shape of the mirror inside the frame was just like the curves of a woman, wide at the top, narrower in the middle, and even wider at the second curve near the base. It would take a master glasscutter to replace such a mirror, and frankly, she didn't dare ask her father for the outrageous expense.

But the ornate carvings, even the shape, made her think of Daniels again, although she couldn't fathom why.

His eyes always held a novel's worth of mystery and depth, yet he spoke so little. Occasionally he seemed to catch himself in saying something, which made him all the more mysterious. William Daniels said just enough to be polite. Well, perhaps he was polite most of the time. At least he was not a simpering mute. It took no true observation skills to determine that he seemed to be more relaxed and open with small parties.

Her mind rolled one way then another, but in the end, it returned to one question in particular. *Why does he understand what it is like to be without a home?*

She could only pray he had not suffered too much in his life. Logically, with the interesting conversation and intelligent, refined speech, he had to have been raised in wealth. Perhaps a second son? Heir to nothing, which must be why he was serving in the militia.

Her thoughts had circled around again to the original thoughts and, filtering through them all again, she was once again left without a single answer. She had to have answers!

*****

George Wickham glanced sideways at Fitzwilliam Darcy as he studied his precious books.

Oh, yes, he knew who the man actually was.

William Daniels was the heir of Pemberley, of Derbyshire. His wealth was unmatched in three counties.

His true name was Fitzwilliam Darcy.

But why did he now go by the name of William Daniels? Why would he disown such a valuable birthright? And what the hell was he doing in the militia? Had he been disowned?

It had been two months of training together and three weeks of being tentmates, yet Wickham still had no answers.

Why hadn't Mrs. Young answered his inquiries? He had sent her several letters, none of which had been answered with any degree of information, let alone anything useful.

From what Wickham could tell, Darcy was trying to disguise himself for some reason. A tastefully trimmed beard, although not in fashion, covered his face, but not the most recognizable part of his being.

The Darcy eyes were undeniable.

And his build, his speech, his very walk, revealed who he was: he was the heir to Pemberley, the home they had shared in their youth.

Wickham had to hold back audible sounds of disgust as he recalled, weightily, their imbalanced childhood relationship.

George Wickham was heir to nothing. He was only the son of Mr. Darcy's steward—Mr. Darcy Sr. that is. Until the age of twelve, George and William Darcy were pondmates, as they called themselves. They grew up together, made devious plans together, and fought together. Well, perhaps the later would be more appropriately described as fought *with* each other.

Wickham chuckled audibly, bringing temporary notice from the very man he was thinking about, his current tent companion, Lieutenant William Daniels.

His pondmate.

The Darcys owned several small rowing boats and had an expansive pond, which was well stocked with fish, ducks, geese, and even swans. And of course, all the creatures that two young boys would desire.

Almost daily, from the moment they broke their fast through dusk, the two boys were either on the pond, in the pond, or around the pond. The setting even served as their schoolroom when lessons had to start. Their parents and tutors knew where to find the boys as well as how to utilize the pond to their educational advantage.

Every bit of education was frosted with the tantalizing natural life of Pemberley's greatest pleasure, their pond.

Pondmates. He resisted the urge to scoff.

Now they were brothers in arms in the militia!

Equals at last.

Wickham had never had better memories than being pondmates with young master Darcy, which is what he was forced to call him. His true Christian name, Fitzwilliam, was what Wickham called him when they quarreled. Yes, William Daniels' full name was actually Fitzwilliam Darcy of Pemberley. By gads, how he loathed that name! Fitzwilliam was a family surname, one that men should have let die with the antique ancestors that allowed themselves to be known by that horrific moniker.

Wickham could not even say it until he was nearly ten years old, which is why he just called his companion Darcy, Will, or William.

He chuckled again, thinking that now he calls his childhoold friend William on purpose, so as not to call him Darcy!

He smiled to himself thinking, *I don't blame him for not going by Fitzwilliam in the militia!* If others found out his real name, there would be nothing to do but surrender to the mockery.

But knowing William Darcy and his family's vast influence among the *ton*, the name was tolerated and even admired. Few estates in England made greater than ten thousand a year, and Pemberley was one of them.

Darcy had a knack for being poised and stoic. Even if someone was mocking his given name, he would have nodded respectfully, as if complimented.

It was infuriating that William Darcy was always respectful and respectable.

For reasons he could not fathom, Darcy was likeable too. Wickham had to admit Darcy was more likable now that they were equals! Yes, people liked him, yet the poor man hardly had any true friends except Samson. Whereas Wickham had many friends and a vast influence among them.

George Wickham was the one envied now.

A new surge of anger filled him. Why must Darcy always be in control of himself, always self-righteous, poised, and so damn rich? To be refined at twelve was too much to ask of a boy, yet it was drilled into the Darcy males as soon as they began to crawl.

The tent flaps suddenly opened, letting in a breeze, and Wickham turned his attention in that direction. A soldier entered, holding an envelope. "Wickham, who do you know in London?" he asked incredulously.

Wickham stood up, attempting not to be too eager for the news, but he doubted it was completely concealed. "Just give it over." He reached his hand out purposefully, to no avail.

The soldier pulled it back quickly, saying, "It is written in a lady's script! Are you sweet on someone?"

Wickham steeled his facial expressions and broadened his shoulders, pushing out his well-developed chest.

It worked. The man handed the letter over and showed himself out.

As he turned around, he saw that Darcy had been watching with intrigue, but no questions emerged. Wickham had no desire to read the letter in front of him, just in case it held valuable information about Fitzwilliam Darcy from Mrs. Young.

It had been many years since he left the schooling that the senior Darcy had financed for him—it wasn't the finest school, not the one that the senior Darcy sent his own heir to; of course not.

Regardless of leaving for school at twelve, and then not completing the grades paid for by Darcy Sr., Wickham had learned some important lessons of life. George Wickham had a thorough understanding of many things, but none of them measured more importantly than this: there was nothing more valuable than information.

And in Wickham's hand was information. Finally! Mrs. Young's answer to his own inquiries, and from what he could sense, the envelope contained two or three pages of information.

The corner of his cheek pulled up sharply even though he attempted to keep his mouth closed.

The letter was a beautiful reward for Wickham, and as his mind churned on what the letter might contain, he felt a bit giddy. Will it contain information on how to destroy his tentmate and former pondmate?

*****

"Oh, dear, Mary, you cannot mean that!" Jane said.

Mary's face was tight with frustration. "But I shall!"

Elizabeth pondered what Mary had proposed but chose to clarify before responding, to ensure she heard her sister correctly. "Mary, I am shocked and do not think it is proper. May I clarify the stance you have taken? Because, sweet sister, it is not common for you to have opinions that are not distinctly classified as black or white or in opposition to what society believes."

"That is not true, I have my own moral platform. I always have. Although I tend to agree with most of what society deems appropriate, I see this circumstance as. . . well, shall I say, less rigid. I never have liked the rule that a widow must maintain a year of mourning if her husband dies. What if she was with child when it happened? How would the wife provide for herself and the babe if she were not given the opportunity to remarry!"

"Yes, however, it is custom—" Jane tried to finish her sentence and couldn't, her mouth held open with awe at the unique perspective Mary had voiced.

"Customs can be changed. We must be willing to question what centuries have done before us. If it is the right thing to do, we must allow for change."

Elizabeth tipped her chin up and reflected a bit. "What about paying your respects to your deceased spouse? Would it not be disrespectful to prance around town in bright colors? Or do you fail to see that by dancing with eligible men, it would dishonor your dead husband?"

Mary sat forward a bit more in her chair, almost eager to explain. "The way a lady lives while her husband is alive is much more important. It shows far greater respect to him while he can appreciate it than how she mourns for him when he has passed."

In her heart, Elizabeth wanted to agree, but society had never questioned the practice of mourning for a year, especially for women. "Widows who do not maintain black for a minimum of six months have been shunned from society. You have seen that here in Meryton with Mrs. Cogsworth."

Jane came to Mary's defense. "Mrs. Cogsworth was a Frenchwoman. She would have been shunned no matter what she had done."

Mary said, "You are correct, Jane. However, even if she was the elite in London and not the mistress to Lord...."

Both of her other sisters immediately shushed her.

Mary sighed. "Elizabeth, of all my sisters, I hoped would understand. Women, or ladies, should be revered, even honored, but not shackled or imprisoned for things not in their control. You are very aware of my opinions on choice and accountability. But why punish a lady for her husband's death. Has she not suffered enough simply by having her husband die? Let alone having to shoulder the household independently. Why must there be an arbitrary number of months—twelve in this situation—that society, not the widow, has determined reflects that she has sufficiently mourned her husband?"

"I do see your point, Mary. Jane and I both do. It is not necessarily fair. Ladies cannot have a profession, at least not respectably, and support ourselves in the same method or level of comfort as we do when we have husbands in our lives. But I would caution you from vocalizing your displeasure with a firmly held, perhaps even considered sacred, tradition. Society would mark you. Perhaps even the whole of us."

Mary nodded. "I understand. Perhaps I am a firm believer in what is right. And it simply is not right to force anyone to abide by what society considers appropriate. Let us not judge others on our own moral platform, for theirs were made with different materials, in a different time, in a different manner, and by different people. I pray someday that a widow will not be judged for reaching out with hope to love again, regardless of how recent her husband's death has been."

From downstairs they could easily hear that their mother was having one of her fits of her nerves, and from the vibrato of the wails, this one may be trying.

Elizabeth directed her sisters. "Jane, fetch her smelling salts. I shall attend to her. Mary, will you ask Cook to make the chamomile tea and perhaps add a bit of honey and lavender oil."

They each rose to do what they always did when their dear mother had an episode.

Usually, due to the hysterics, no one could tell what was wrong for many minutes, and this time was no different.

Upon reaching her mother, Elizabeth took her hand, rubbing cream onto the aged skin in slow, gentle motions.

Elizabeth nodded affirmatively when her mother screeched something that sounded like a question but was completely undecipherable.

Usually agreeing with her mother was the correct response, but this time, the nonsense apparently should have been deemed too terrible to agree with.

Understanding the true cause of this particular episode's distress was diverted until after Elizabeth heard a very mumbled and unstructured monologue of how terrible it was that Elizabeth agreed.

Agreed with what? Or whom? She still had no idea what was at the source of the hysteria. But she reached for more cream and rubbed just a little firmer until the furor subsided. Her sisters had brought the tea, as well as her mother's smelling salts, and Kitty had joined in the efforts by fanning their mother. Each, as they performed their functions, let out sighs of exasperation. It was difficult, indeed, but she was their mother.

As Mrs. Bennet began to breathe in a more regular pattern, her words came out more understandable.

"Hedge groves. He has decided to come after all. As if . . . do you hear me, girls? As if he were to inherit tomorrow! And we have no time at all. None. Mr. Collins will be coming tomorrow to Longbourn!"

Elizabeth looked to Jane, who shrugged momentarily then looked at Mary. Mary mouthed the name Mr. Collins soundlessly.

"Ah, I see. Is that what is so concerning, Mother? Mr. Collins, our cousin, is coming to Longbourn today?"

A new set of wails erupted, and Mary offered more tea to her nodding mother.

"No, Mary. I need something stronger. Fetch the apothecary!"

Jane put her hand on her mother's chin gently and turned her face towards her. "No, Mum, you must have your wits about you when he gets here. No laudanum this time. You can do this. We are here. We are your medicine."

Their mother filled her lungs deeply, nodded, then exhaled one enormous breath and reached up and patted Jane's cheek. "My sweet Jane, you are so handsome. And you are quite right, quite right."

She sat up and removed her hand from Elizabeth's, repositioning herself on the chaise. She cleared her throat. "Quite right. Yes, I must be smarter than he. Quicker, and wiser, and smarter. Did I just say that? Oh, dear."

She exhaled again multiple times in a row and was nearly in control when there was a loud knock on the door.

A look of pure panic darted across Mrs. Bennet's face; her eyes could not have widened further.

"I say! The nerve of him! He is a day early! Oh, dear. Oh, my! When he says he is coming, he does not have the decency to wait until we have broken our fast! Oh, dear! Ahhhhhhh, hedge groves . . . and Mr. Bennet is not dead yet!"

All of the Bennet sisters held their breath as they waited to be told who was at the door.

In a volume above their mother's wails, Mrs. Hill shared, "Lieutenant William Daniels, Madam. Shall I let him in? He states he has a letter from Miss Bingley for Miss Bennet. "

The wails halted, and Mrs. Bennet struggled to sit up, pushing away the hair by her cheeks. "For my Jane? From Netherfield? Oh, this can only be good news! Well, do not just stand there! Let him in!"

Mrs. Hill, fully aware that Mrs. Bennet had just had an episode of her fits, paused a moment before asking, "Shall I give you a minute?"

"No!" Mrs. Bennet screamed.

Quickly Jane stood and arranged things differently. "Elizabeth and I will receive him in Papa's study. Show him in, and we will follow shortly." She then looked down at her mother's confused face. "I wish to read the letter first, Mum, and will most definitely share what Mr. Bingley's sister has to say. You stay here and dab a cool cloth on those puffy eyes."

Mrs. Bennet just nodded and then put her hand out for the cloth, wiggling her hand impatiently, which, of course, Mary had only just left to fetch for her.

Even though Jane was poised, Elizabeth knew as they walked down the hall a few minutes later that she held a great deal of trepidation for what the letter might include.

"Miss Elizabeth, Miss Bennet, thank you for seeing me so early. Forgive me for coming unannounced, but I . . ." His words trailed off, leaving a silence in the room.

Elizabeth attempted to calm his nervousness with her words. "Good morning to you, Mr. Daniels. The weather must have allowed for good time. Did you walk or ride?"

"I rarely turn down an opportunity to test a good mount. Mr. Bingley is somewhat of a connoisseur of mares and racing stallions, an expensive hobby for sure. He showed me several of them this morning. That one there," motioning out the window, "is the finest piece of horseflesh I have seen for some time."

Elizabeth curtsied and asked with a bit of impertinence, "So you are a bit of a connoisseur of horses?"

He startled a bit then frowned.

"Forgive me, it just appeared that you knew how to decipher quality," Elizabeth continued. "I was just assuming that you enjoyed the same pastime or hobby since you appreciate it so much."

All Elizabeth wished to do was understand the mysterious Mr. Daniels.

William Daniels did not respond right away; instead he pursed his lips together, and his brows found a deeper mark than they had ever before done in Elizabeth's presence.

Daniels looked hard, even stern.

But then the hardness faded, and he looked down, then to the right. It was as if he had no idea where to look, either that or was thinking incredibly hard. He shifted his weight a bit, opened his mouth to speak, but instead closed it again.

He repeated the silent motions, indicating an internal war of thoughts happening. "I must take my leave," he finally said. He placed his trifold hat back on his head and gripped both hands behind his back.

And without so much of a nod or a bow, William Daniels marched toward them with fervor, forcing the sisters to step aside so he could pass through the threshold they had barely crossed.

Jane looked at Elizabeth then motioned with her eyes at the letter clasped behind Daniels' back.

"Lieutenant! Are you forgetting something?" Elizabeth said, trying to rescue her sister from panicking. "You came here for a reason, have you not?" She reached out her hand gently.

He paused but did not turn around. His hands relaxed a bit then finally released altogether. Elizabeth witnessed his shoulders rise in a calming breath, and then he turned. He took another breath, bowed a perfect bow to Jane, and handed her the letter wordlessly.

"Mr. Daniels, please, do not rush due to my insensitive assumptions. I have a tendency to speak the exact words I think, never truly understanding why someone may not wish to hear all my unadorned thoughts aloud. Truly, sit for a spell. Have some tea before you rush away on your borrowed stallion. Tell us of Mr. Bingley and his sister. We have not seen them for over a week, near a fortnight."

William Daniels eyes bore into hers, searching for something. Whatever he was searching for she tried to provide. Did he want to know of her sincerity, see her humility? Or was he seeking evidence to the contrary? She felt acute remorse that she had spoken out of turn. She had even interrupted him. "Please, I ask you to stay, if only to calm my mind that I have not injured you."

A subtle nod was all the communication immediately given.

CHAPTER 6

"Let me ease your mind then, Miss Elizabeth. You have not injured me in the slightest. It was ghosts of my past, which I cannot name, that came unbidden at an inopportune time. And yet, how I wish I could name the ghosts of my past."

William Daniels let out the rest of his breath before adding, "Truly, you have done me no harm. It would give me much pleasure to take tea with the eldest Bennet sisters." He attempted to smile, but even as he did so, William knew it likely appeared a bit awkward.

Miss Bennet smiled and turned straight away to ring the servant's bell, which was just over her shoulder.

Everyone waited until the instructions were given, then Miss Bennet said in a soft, kind voice, "We all have ghosts, Lieutenant. I almost wish I could forget mine, yet you seem to want to remember yours. I sense your unease. Would you like to talk about it? Elizabeth is the wisest of all my sisters, and her advice follows suit. I have excellent ears; they have an innate talent to listen." Jane winked ridiculously, so as not to have him miss the humor of what she said.

Elizabeth added to Jane's comments, "My sister has the right of it. I shall attempt to listen too, if you so desire to share." A small smile graced Miss Elizabeth's face as she said such genuine things.

"I do not even know where to begin, yet I do not know where I started," replied William. The contrast between the statements was distinctly ironic.

Elizabeth added one of her favorite thoughts, "As usual, you were in the middle, before it began. This is indeed quite common."

William nodded agreement then vocalized it. "Indeed, I was in the middle . . ." The truth was he was so preoccupied preparing to reveal his thoughts and memories that he didn't fully understand the phrase's meaning.

Was he actually going to discuss his lost memories with this fresh interest and her elder sister? He had shared the story with so few over the last five years. He had learned to master steering the topic away from anything personal.

But this time, as he watched the ladies of Longbourn find their seats, he saw their kind eyes watching him without a speck of judgment. He too took his seat. How much he would share depended on them.

"I cannot explain why I know so much about his stallion, or even why I can appreciate other equestrian beauty. For I do not know who taught me. Forgive me, perhaps I need to begin with what I do know, not what I do not."

He looked away from their faces, hoping it would help ease his inner tension. That attempt failed; his mind was filled with turmoil. He found it far easier to be looking at Miss Elizabeth. So he spoke directly to her, enjoying the blessed opportunity.

"I think my name is William, but I do not know for sure. Daniels was a name I chose for myself. I do not know my surname. I think I have a sister, much younger than I am, or at least she was some sort of relation to me. My only solid memory prior to waking up from a shipwreck five years ago was witnessing her die a painful death, with blood that stained her golden locks. It was my sister who called me William on her deathbed, so I have retained the name."

He paused to let the wave of emotion pass as the sharpness of the trauma riddled down his spine. "It has not been easy, even after five years, to recall that moment. She and I were sharing a room on a ship. Where we were going or returning from, I am still ignorant. However, what I do know with some degree of certainty was that I was rescued by an elderly couple from a small town located on the southern coast near Falmouth. Mr. and Mrs. Hemmingway were their names. I was injured, even unconscious for a few days, and then awoke with a start. Nothing was clear or made sense for a few days, although the Hemmingways state it was more than a fortnight until I became reasonable." He chuckled to himself as he added, "Some might say I have yet to become reasonable."

Miss Elizabeth giggled daintily while Jane smiled kindly but nodded encouragement at the same time.

So he continued. "I remember nothing of who I was, where I lived, or what family I have. I have no memories other than my sister's death. And even then I can only assume she was my sister. She was far too young to share chambers with me unless she had been."

There was a lull in the story for a brief time until Jane softly asked, "What things do you remember? Do you recall what the name of the ship was?"

He shook his head and said, "No, and the Hemmingways never heard word of a shipwreck, or they would have reported it. For months I had to eat delicate or soft foods, as my jaw had been broken. I grow the beard to cover a distinct unsightly scar from the injury. Mrs. Hemmingway had a good recipe for hearty fish soup. However, deep down, I knew that their generosity was easily given but painfully spent. I was using up their stores of food quickly. After two months, and with no memories to go on, I understood that I must take my leave and wished them farewell. I still write them from time to time, but Mrs. Hemmingway's health is failing.

"You asked what I remember. Facts? Places? Situations? People from my former life? None of it is clear, not even a fraction clearer than the day I understood I had been in a shipwreck. I may be short on memories, but knowledge? Now that I am well stocked in. For example, deciphering quality horseflesh. I seem to have retained an amazing amount through the ordeal. I know things, understand processes and other complicated things on topics you would not suspect, and that leads me to believe that I was very well educated.

"For example, I understand several languages and am proficient in speaking them. In fact, besides English, I am entirely fluent in French and Italian. I am not aware of what I know until . . . well, until I know it. But the knowledge is usually spot-on. Either I was well educated or had a great deal of experience in life during my previous life. What I recall is so accurate that I have begun to put a great deal of trust in this instinctual knowledge.

"I knew that if one were to join the army, or militia, one could obtain a salary. Where there was coin, there was food. I walked mile after mile and accepted offered transportation many times from strangers until I worked my way from Falmouth down to Hertfordshire. I had no other option but to join the militia and since then have moved from different sects and districts. I transferred to this militia approximately three months ago. Dear me, I have shared a great deal. Are you sure you want to hear more?"

"Oh, yes!" was Elizabeth's reply.

"If you would like to share, we will listen. Perhaps even help," Jane added.

He nodded his appreciation. The heaviness that had been his constant companion these last five years was lifting, and breathing and speaking came easier.

He leaned forward, putting both hands on his knees with straight arms. "I am very uncomfortable when others start to ask questions or probe about my history. As you can imagine, it is not a pleasant experience for either party when I repeatedly answer questions with 'I do not know.'" His voice shook, but he took a steady breath to gather his senses.

Elizabeth reached out her hand and touched his, ever so lightly. "Did we make you uncomfortable, Mr. Daniels, with our questions?"

Up to that point, he had been able to remain quite calm, perhaps calmer than he had ever remembered being. He had felt comfortable enough to disclose the little he did know, and they had openly received it.

He looked down at her hand, admiring the feminine narrow pink nail beds, but suddenly she removed her hand, as if his skin burned her.

He looked to her face, confused.

"Forgive my forwardness if it was unwelcome," she said stiffly.

He had become confused and uniquely discombobulated. She usually did that to him. Indeed, he was shocked when she touched him, but it was certainly not unwelcome. But what had caused her to withdraw her hand?

His heart pounded a bit harder, and the time it took his mind to process the sensation took more than it should have.

He formed the words he wanted to say in his headfirst. *No, it was a pleasant feeling to be touched with friendship, and not unwelcome at all.*

He opened his mouth to say it but saw that the moment had already passed. Jane was reassuring Elizabeth silently with compassionate eyes, and Elizabeth sat up straighter as if she had just been reprimanded.

The only thing he could do to repair the miscommunication was to continue offering trust. "You lovely ladies are the first I have discussed this with. And I thank you. Perhaps I have overstayed my welcome?" He looked toward Elizabeth as he said the last part, because Miss Bennet did not seemed as affronted as

Miss Elizabeth. He posed it as a question, hopeful that they would dissuade him and ask him to stay longer. When neither sister answered, he added, "It has been enjoyable for me."

Dare he hope? He had not ever felt such a powerful thing as hope. At least not that he could remember.

Jane assessed Elizabeth with her eyes and then returned to Daniels, nodding. "Please, go on."

The relationship between the two sisters appeared to be unique. Jane seemed to be the less dominant one, quieter, for sure. However, she had a motherly nature that seemed to calm Elizabeth. He had noticed much nonverbal communication between them as he had talked.

"How I wish I had what the two of you have."

Miss Elizabeth finally looked up at him, her brows furrowed slightly. "Mr. Daniels, I cannot claim to comprehend your generous compliment. However, we thank you."

He nodded his acceptance. "Your relationship is admirable."

Elizabeth's shoulders relaxed, and she smiled. "Have you ever searched London's news for such an accident? There could not be many shipwrecks in that area, and most are reported and the news spread through the *London Times*. Especially during times of war."

"The archives are open daily in London between a working man's hours," William responded. "I must provide for myself, and that means I must go where the militia takes me. I often get a day or two off at a time, but it has never coincided with a sufficient amount of time to travel the four hours to London. However, with Bingley's fine specimen of a horse, I could now make it in less than two!"

Both Bennet sisters laughed with him briefly.

He finished the rest of his tea and decided that he truly could not take more of their time.

He stood, placed his hat on his head, and said, "Farewell, ladies. It has been an honor and the deepest pleasure I have felt in some time. I shall let you read and respond to Miss Bingley's invitation. Perhaps I shall see you tomorrow at Netherfield?"

Miss Bennet's face lit up, and she clutched the letter tighter in her hands. Her smile was all the response he received.

Elizabeth stood too, and gracefully curtsied. She seemed to hesitate, but finally she added her own reply. "Indeed. I shall hope we do." She again curtsied, this time even lower, and glanced up at him as she straightened from the gesture.

Her forward glance was more than he could have hoped for.

He wanted to ask, "Miss Elizabeth, are you flirting with me?" Or perhaps he could have said something equally as flirtatious, such as, "Dare I ask who that 'come hither' glance was for?"

He could have said a hundred things, but instead, he said nothing.

She followed him to the door, where he bowed once more and departed.

Once on his horse, he said to himself quietly, "I hope so too, Miss Elizabeth."

*****

The next twenty-four hours felt more like a week. Perhaps it was because William Daniels was anxiously waiting to see Miss Elizabeth again at Netherfield. Thankfully, time, although slower, did pass.

Netherfield was a comfortable estate, approximately fifty percent larger than Longbourn, and significantly smaller than . . .

His mind paused . . . no—halted—in mid thought.

He almost had said a name, even had a mental picture of an ornate sitting room. No, he corrected himself, it was a music room, not a sitting room.

He pressed his mind to recall the name of the place that he had recalled in the last second. The words felt only a finger's reach away but, in truth, were actually an arm's length away. The memory was gone before he could recognize what he had.

The name of his home was now well beyond his grasp; however, the memory remained. He studied the fractionated image in his head. He massaged it and allowed his mind to be occupied with the tiny glimpse of a beautiful room with deep, sunflower-yellow floral wallpaper on the lower third of the room but a distinctly baroque, or earlier, mural on the upper two thirds. The ceiling height was exceptional and domed, with carved wooden walnut beams elegantly displayed against the white ceiling.

It was the Yellow Music Room. His sister's favorite room.

But where was it? What was the estate called? How could he find his home?

He felt frustrated, to be sure. However, he was grateful for the distraction at the moment, because the ladies from Longbourn had not yet arrived.

He may not know what his home was called, but he knew that he was terribly impatient that the Bennet sisters were late.

Poor Bingley. At least William had this new minute bit of information to occupy himself.

"I shall be driven mad if the eldest Bennets do not arrive soon!" Bingley complained.

Mr. Charles Bingley was a pleasant fellow, a man who was pleased beyond measure with everything. However, Daniels felt he was entirely correct because he mimicked Daniels own thoughts.

Daniels had barely met Bingley a week before but had taken a liking to him from the start. He was jovial and had pleasing manners, but did not cross the lines of inappropriate hilarity or uncouth loud laughter.

He was truthful, and his kindness held up behind closed doors as well, even after a brandy or two.

Bingley was humble but respectable. For example, he was willing to ask advice of him, a lieutenant, and even utilized the advice when it was offered. In fact, even when the advice was unsolicited, Bingley seemed to pay it a good degree of respect.

For example, yesterday morning, when Mr. Bingley asked if William Daniels fancied the Bennets, Lieutenant Daniels openly shared his concern that Mrs. Bennet was likely to pawn off her daughters to any gentleman who showed the slightest bit of interest, especially those who came from money.

Daniels had politely omitted the damning evidence of overhearing Mrs. Bennet instruct her daughters to "plump the ladypairs" in their corsets.

When Daniels carefully implied that the mother was a bit of a mercenary, Bingley nodded and said he would proceed with caution. Smiling, Bingley added, "But proceed I will in my pursuit to gain favor in the eldest Miss Bennet's angelic eyes."

William Daniels felt a kinship to him in that moment, specifically to that last sentence. Elizabeth once told him he had fine eyes, but it was she who tantalized his every thought.

He too planned to proceed in the pursuit of Miss Bennet. Miss Elizabeth Bennet, of course.

Bingley had kindly returned the gesture and warned Daniels about another woman. Bingley claimed his sister, Miss Bingley, was the icon of the "shallow elite." In jest, he insisted that in the dictionary, the very word *shallow* was said to display a portrait that had a likeness of Caroline Bingley which one could not dispute.

Bingley then corrected himself. "You need not worry though, you are just a lieutenant. She desires much more than you have to offer. It will not stop me from accepting and improving this new acquaintance with you, Lieutenant." Bingley's overt disregard of their exaggerated difference in station was refreshing yet unnerving at the same time. Daniels found it comforting that he was regarded as an equal in Bingley's mind. However, something told him that Bingley's portrait might be found next to the definition of *naïve* or *trusting*.

William had a deep desire to stay close to this gentleman, for Bingley likely needed a friend, as did William. More importantly, Bingley needed a friend who would look out for him and not abuse his kindness.

In another world, Daniels believed they would have been fast friends. But for now, it was a relief to be associated with someone who respected him and his opinions, as well as someone who wouldn't interfere with his pursuit of Miss Elizabeth Bennet.

Who was late today. Very late.

Where are they?

The Bennet sisters had sent a correspondence yesterday evening that they would be arriving shortly before eleven.

He heard the clock chime. Each stroke buried his hope further that the ladies would be attending Netherfield's noon luncheon. Truth be told, it appeared more certain that they would not have time to do much more than drink lukewarm tea and return home before the storm arrived.

In fact, it would be too late for even that, Williams realized. The storm had already arrived. From the look of the small puddles growing rapidly outside, the storm had been here for some time, and his latest memory of the Yellow Music Room had prevented him from noticing.

The twelfth chime rung, leaving an echo in the main hallway where the two bachelors were standing expectantly, with far too many glances at the door that had not been opened for hours.

The Bennet sisters were over an hour late.

Both Bingley and Daniels sighed.

The east clouds were growing darker, even ominous, and the trees indicated the wind had picked up from earlier in the day.

"Well, Bingley, I am afraid it is noon. Shall we wait longer, or shall we send notice to Longbourn that we are suggesting to reschedule?"

Bingley slowly pulled his disappointed gaze from the front door, looking at Daniels with concern. "What if . . ." He swallowed then rapidly said, "Excuse me, I am not usually so pessimistic, but what if something happened in their travels?"

William Daniels absorbed the thought that hadn't even occurred to him until Bingley had uttered the words. "Did they indicate how they planned to travel? Or perhaps we misunderstood the time they planned to arrive?"

"No, the letter did not detail their plans for travel." Bingley shook his head, looking more concerned, and hopelessly handed the letter he had already read several times to Daniels.

Daniels reached for it with a bit of dread.

To ensure there was clear reason to be worried, Daniels read the letter carefully. It had been written by Miss Jane Bennet and left no doubt that the two planned to arrive shortly before eleven.

Bingley had already turned back towards the silent front door.

Daniels folded the letter and placed it on the side table next to the vase. He took a step forward and pounded Bingley's on the back twice. "Let's put on our greatcoats," he suggested. "We should find the Bennet sisters. Knowing Miss Elizabeth as I do, they likely walked the three miles, even though it rained heavily last night."

Bingley looked up at Daniels, for he was a few inches shorter, and a small, grateful smile brightened his face a bit. The smile did not hold strength enough to alter the dominant emotion of angst.

Both gentleman nodded once to each other, the way men do, and the servant readily handed them their coats.

"Brilliant idea, Daniels, brilliant. They may have come into some trouble on their journey."

Daniel's guilt in assuming that their failure to come was by choice grew as Bingley recited the many tragedies that might have befallen the sisters.

It was highly uncommon for William Daniels not to worry, for it was his nature to worry. As they mounted the horses, Daniels pondered why he had not considered the women's safety earlier. It might have been that Daniels respected Elizabeth's physical constitution, for he had seen her march to Oakham Mount without a moment of distress. He attempted to comfort himself, hoping that to be the reason.

William certainly was not indifferent to their plight. But the guilt grew as they galloped across the field.

"There are only two main paths they could have safely walked," observed Bingley. "There is a horse trail that follows the river. However they would have been required to cross over the South Meryton highway bridge or the smaller bridge that is less often traveled and is said to barely be horse-worthy."

With his distant forward gaze, Bingley added, "It would have been safe for the sisters, though, if they came on foot." Bingley said the last sentence as if he was trying to convince himself.

"Precisely." Daniels wanted to encourage him as well as keep both their minds from worrying. "Most of the hills from the Bennet estate to those two bridges are open field. If we cannot make out their location between Netherfield to our side of the bridges then they likely made it back home. If not, we shall be able to spot them easily across the field."

"Splendid. We shall focus on the two miles between here and the bridges." Bingley's voice had an element of false bravery, but Daniels didn't comment on the vibrato in his voice.

The hastened pace was set, and the gentleman rode about fifty yards apart to cover as much ground as possible.

Bingley yelled out to Daniel, with a ridiculous intention of making small talk across the field. "Netherfield had not been occupied for three years until I leased it. I have not known where to start in taming the underbrush."

"Not to worry, Bingley. You have only occupied it for a few months. Most of the brush is short, and the horses are managing it without complaint."

When Bingley didn't respond, William looked over to him and saw that he had stopped his horse and had his head in his hands, rubbing his brow with such ferocity that Daniels heart dropped.

He spurred his horse hard and raced to Bingley. "What is it, man? Did you find them?"

Bingley looked up at the sound of the rapid hooves pounding on the dirt and shook his head. "I should have offered to collect and escort them, or at minimum sent a carriage! This is all my fault."

Daniels sighed and slowed his horse. "Bingley, collect yourself. I need you now, for it is far faster when two are searching than only one."

"Yes, yes, thank you for the reminder. Right you are. I shall refocus my energy and press on. But what if my angel . . ."

"She will be found, and she will be well. If you need to, repeat that as if it were a prayer to recite. Are you a God-loving man?"

Bingley looked shocked, pulling his chin back in affront. "Of course, man. What do you take me for? A heathen? Or worse, a man who has no morals?"

"I do not. It was intended to remind you from where to request strength. And for the record, I would not care if you believed in God or not, even worshiped eggplant in the moonlight or depended on the skin of tomatoes on your brow to fulfill your life. I have witnessed for myself of your goodness. Now press on."

Without a word, the two men proceeded in the direction of the highway bridge, naturally spreading and picking up the pace.

They called out a time or two, but there was still sufficient light and certainly the ladies of Longbourn would have heard the horses and called out if they needed help. Daniels wasn't the type to raise his voice, even in the open country, and Bingley likely didn't trust his to be steady.

Once they reached the bridge, the pair thoroughly searched the bank and scanned the field on the other side.

Nothing.

The waters were disturbingly angry and pounded at the banks as the quickened river flowed under the bridge. The former night's rainstorm had measurably influenced its usually peaceful quality.

Daniels turned his horse, heading upstream. "Let us press on. Keep an eye out for the ladies in the field across the river as well. I do not see anything now, but there is almost a kilometer of river before we reach the other bridge. Make haste, the clouds are darkening." He didn't have to add that the wind was picking up also because, at that moment, Bingley was dismounting to fetch his hat, which had blown off.

Daniels took the lead, choosing to call out every ten yards.

Bingley followed his example.

It wasn't long before Daniels was tightening his greatcoat around him from the chill in the wind.

Occasionally, Daniels felt what he thought was a raindrop or two, but the moisture turned out to be the spray of the river hitting the rocks as the curve of the river forced it to turn another direction.

Travel was slow for two reasons: the riverbank was unsteady, wet, and overgrown, and the horses were unsettled with the thunder and lightning that had begun around them.

The uneasy feeling in William's stomach was growing too, and he pressed the horses to pick up speed.

Several times, he had to redirect his horse further away from the riverbank to avoid floating debris and broken branches. The debris likely had been swept downstream in the river's current, the sodden material obstructing the path.

William caught a glimpse of the walkway that followed the path of the river when he had to skirt around the debris, and scanned it up and down thoroughly.

He looked back at Bingley who had a questioning look on his face, and Daniels shook his head.

He could not see any indication of the Bennet sisters.

He continued in his quest, looking for footprints—two sets of course—but found no evidence that the two young women had crossed the river.

Bingley cleared his throat and called from behind. "The walking bridge is likely where they crossed. We probably should have started there."

Daniels felt a tinge of regret in the decision as well, but he had made the choice in hopes that Mr. and Mrs. Bennet had been thoughtful enough to send their daughters in the carriage, especially as it had looked like rain. Alas, there had been no footprints, but neither had there been carriage tracks in the wet ground.

"Bingley, why do you not ride near the walking path? I shall ride a bit further out. We can cover more ground that way."

"Brilliant. Yes, I shall do that straight away."

William looked back and saw Bingley's horse was cooperative and very willing to leave the overgrown brush and blackberry bushes. Daniels too had to move around the thickest brambles out of kindness to his borrowed horse.

His tan knee-high trousers had faced a few thorns during the morning's quest and lost. There would be mending to do when he returned to camp.

They had made significant progress, and so they called out much more frequently than when they started their rescue attempts. William was not as familiar with the grounds as Bingley was, but he fully expected to come across the walking bridge at any time.

Daniels was about to call out again when he thought he heard something. He stopped the horse as he heard a branch breaking nearest to the river.

"Hello, there! Who goes there?" He hadn't meant to make his voice carry so loud and deep, but he had called out for some time with no response.

This noise was new. It wasn't the storm, or Bingley, or the horses.

He could hear Bingley's horse stop too and turned to take in his concerned expression.

Daniels put up a finger to his mouth, encouraging Bingley to stay where he was so he could listen closer.

Crack. There it was again! It sounded like a branch hitting a rock but not just because of the ripples of the river. The sound was as if done with intention.

William jumped down from the horse and wrapped the reigns haphazardly around a large branch of a felled tree.

He heard Bingley gallop closer and looked back to see his newfound friend dismount in mid trot, landing expertly on his feet.

Bingley had brought his horse whip with him and took the lead, pushing grass and brush aside, his urgency more than apparent.

"Miss Bennet? Miss Elizabeth? It is Charles Bingley and Lieutenant Daniels. Where are you?"

To their immediate left, they heard a moan then a fragile, weak voice. "Here. Over here. Jane is . . . not well. Help her."

Both gentlemen bolted through anything that attempted to stand between them and the ladies, and found Elizabeth sitting against a large boulder on a small, muddy, sandy outcropping. Her legs lay unmoving, in the water.

Cradled in Elizabeth's right arm was what William feared was a lifeless eldest Miss Bennet. The pallor of both their faces was sickening, not a bit of color in either of their cheeks. Miss Elizabeth's other hand held the branch with which she had been hitting the rock. She held tightly to her sister. However, with the relief in being rescued, her shaky, cold hand dropped the branch.

Bingley jumped down from the boulder and was about to sweep his angel up when Elizabeth said breathlessly, the concern and urgency evident in her command, "Be careful. I think she hit her head . . . and her left hand is broken."

Most of Miss Jane Bennet was still in the water, all but what Elizabeth was gripping to with all her might.

The muddy outcropping had no room to maneuver and had a very steep bank, one that Elizabeth would have never been able to climb out of or pull her sister up from. But the way it was hidden behind the boulder meant the angry water bypassed them for the most part, leaving the occasional wave of rapids that hadn't entirely died, hungrily lapping at their skirts.

Bingley was frantically assessing the situation, finally choosing to put his footing about half a meter into the current. He found it slightly deeper than expected when its natural strength challenged his balance briefly. But he readjusted and was able to secure his footing closer to the miniature outcropping of a riverbed.

He commanded Daniels in a way that left no room to argue. "Obtain my horse! Now! There is rope on the saddle. And we can use the horse blankets to protect them from this damnable wind."

Daniels obeyed, as the situation demanded a level head, and unbelievably, Bingley was quite clear in emergent situations. William's respect continued to grow for his new friend.

By the time William had returned, Bingley was holding Miss Bennet in his arms tenderly, one arm under her underarms and one under her knees. Her head had fallen back limply, but Bingley saw it as well and readjusted, pulling her closer to his core. The movement allowed Miss Bennet's head to shift toward him, landing safely against Bingley's chest.

The next necessary task was easy to decipher. Daniels wrapped one end of the rope around the tree at the top of the precipitous riverbank and threw the rope down between the bank and the large boulder.

"Wrap it around your waist and then hold onto the main lead. I will pull you up."

Bingley hesitated, looking down at the pale Miss Elizabeth. Deeming her secure enough to leave, he said, "We will be back, Miss Elizabeth. Stay there. Do not move."

He again readjusted Miss Bennet enough so she was propped onto a shoulder and, with one hand, lassoed the rope around himself, tossing the end of the rope repeatedly around the lead and the loop around himself.

"Daniels, I am depending on you."

Daniels removed his greatcoat, throwing it aside for now, and picked up the rope.

"My footing is excellent. The ground up here is more solid than anything we have traversed so far. On your mark."

Daniels pulled the rope tight, and Bingley held onto the lead at the knot he had made with one hand. Daniels recognized the knot as the bowline knot, also called the lifeline.

How ironic that he remembered that, especially at the moment. These memories, or knowledge, revealed themselves at the strangest times.

He tugged on the rope to test its securement and, in doing so, tightened the knot, ensuring confidence in both gentlemen.

Bingley looked up and instructed, "Ready. Go slow enough for me to walk up the boulder. I may have to adjust her weight as we go perpendicular to the ground."

Daniels walked backwards, allowing a bit more distance than before, and prepared to pull. He wrapped the rope around his back but did not tie it. Instead he wrapped the end of the rope a few times around his back arm. This would allow himself a chance to use the weight of his body to walk backwards instead of depending on forearms and shoulders to hold the strength of two grown adults.

The first steps were the hardest as Daniels pulled with all his might. He had exaggerated when he stated the ground was solid, but minimizing the truth seemed the lesser of two evils, and frankly, it was necessary to have Bingley trust him rather than panic.

It wasn't long before William was breathless, begging God to guarantee the strength he needed for the task he had to perform. Sure enough, Bingley's hatless red hair eventually emerged above the top of the boulder. William's strength doubled in that moment, and his relief was exceptionally enjoyable when Bingley dropped his hand that was on the lead rope, gently further securing Miss Bennet.

Daniels dropped the rope too and was about to untie Bingley, but Bingley protested. "No, take her. Leave the rope on me. We have to rescue Miss Elizabeth."

"Charles, you are spent. Anyone can see that." Daniels reached down for the horse blanket and unfolded it, laying it across Miss Bennet's back, then reached for her.

Bingley reluctantly agreed to switch the rope so he could remain in possession of his angel. Daniels did no more than gently place Miss Jane Bennet on her back on the grassy area farther away from the river, tucking in the blanket edges to cover her more securely. She was still unconscious but breathing easily.

He then turned to Bingley, reached his hand out for the rope. "Let me assist Miss Elizabeth."

Bingley simply nodded, removing the loop of rope that had been around his waist.

Daniels threw the rope on the ground, stepped into the circle of rope, and shimmied it up past his belt. Daniels watched as Bingley secured the rope in preparation for lowering Daniels down to the muddy bank.

"No need to have it tight yet. I can jump down. Save your strength for the journey up."

They both nodded to each other, and Bingley provided plenty of slack, while glancing over to the lady on the ground.

William Daniels landed in nearly the same spot in the river that Bingley had, but his footing and balance was, thankfully, stable immediately.

"Are you injured? Can you stand?" He asked.

He kneeled down to Miss Elizabeth, whose eyelids weakly lifted at the movement.

"I tried to save her." Her cold voice cracked unnaturally, her words breaking his heart.

Shushing her reassuringly, he prompted her to reach around his neck. "I am going to help you. Allow me to slide my arms under your legs."

She hesitated then nodded, grimacing with closed eyes. The movement clearly caused her pain.

A bright flash of lightning lit up the dark clouds directly above them. and the immediate clack of thunder that sounded afterward jolted Elizabeth into a more alert state.

Daniels did not hesitate a second longer. He reached his arm under her legs, and she was, thankfully, able to hold onto him around the neck. This allowed him to hold onto the lead with his other hand. He had one arm under her legs, and his outstretched arm supported her back even further.

"Ready! Pull!" he instructed.

The line went taut, and Daniels began the assent, placing each foot as securely as he could. The boulder was wet now with river water from when Bingley brought up Miss Bennet, and William was grateful that he had resoled the military boots he was wearing.

The ascent did not take long, for a surge of energy drove him up the boulder more rapidly than he would have normally been able to move.

Once on top of the bank, Bingley dropped the rope, moving to assist him, but Daniels shook his head. "Remove the rope. She is safe in my arms."

Elizabeth lifted her head, speaking unsteadily. "Please put me down. I can walk. I just did not have the strength to get her out of the water by myself."

William desperately wanted to maintain the proximity he had with Miss Elizabeth, yet the struggle to acknowledge her wishes weighed on him. But then she dropped her head back onto his shoulder.

With another attempt, she squirmed just enough to force his decision, and he gently placed her onto her feet. He held on for an extended amount of time, ensuring that she truly was strong enough to stand on her own.

Which she was not.

Her knees buckled under her, but there was no way Daniels would let her fall. In a single sweep, she was back into his strong arms. "Bingley, fetch my greatcoat and help me put it around Elizabeth. Let us get them to Netherfield before the storm drops its wickedness further."

*****

Elizabeth was weak and intensely cold.

She dared not rely on what she perceived was happening.

Was Jane going to survive? Of course, she was more worried about her sister than herself, but she questioned her own fate as well. She could not remember feeling half so cold and weak at any point in her entire life. As if Death himself was hovering, waiting to suck the last uneasy breath from her frigid lungs.

She was lifted up, jolted one way and then another, and every joint ached with the movement. Every time she opened her eyes, she grew more confused and dizzy.

She could smell a man, and he was delightfully warm. Propriety be damned, he was balm to these horrid chills that pulsed throughout her body. She reached her arms around his neck and embraced her rescuer.

At one point, she became aware enough to know that it was Lieutenant Daniels and Charles Bingley who had come. At the moment, she did not care which gentleman was carrying her, but she sensed it was Daniels. She might have just hoped it was.

That was until she had heard Daniels call her by her Christian name. Her confusion grew when she felt something warm lightly graze her brow. His whiskers tickled her forehead, but a soft heat spread further. Her inside warmed, as she heard him gently whisper, "You are safe now, my darling."

She had most definitely become delusional and no longer cared to make sense of the conscious world.

CHAPTER 7

Mrs. Reynolds stood her ground. "I am afraid not."

"I need Mrs. Darcy, if ye will alert her I am here." The currier stood stiff and unyielding.

The currier was clearly forcing the refined London accent he was using, and poorly too. He had begun his requests in polite tones, but now his voice had escalated to tones that bordered on demanding.

Mrs. Reynolds cleared her throat and stood as tall as her small Irish body would hold her. She clasped her hands in front of her, lifting her chin proudly and glaring right back at the man. The visitor was two heads taller than Mrs. Reynolds; his shoulders alone were twice as wide as hers.

But by Jove, no one had ever demanded anything of Pemberley's housekeeper and gotten away with it.

Her voice held more determination and a bit of ice this time. "Thank you kindly, but I shall not repeat what I told you before. Mrs. Anne Darcy is not up to taking visitors. On my honor, I shall deliver your missive directly to her."

He was getting frustrated with her, and the refined accent faltered. "Look Miss, I can't allow that. I got strict orders to deliver it in person. It is of the 'utmost importance.' I shan't get paid if I don't deliver it m'self."

"Why did you not say so? I am plenty willing to pay your expenses, but ye shall not be admitted to Mrs. Darcy."

With that offer, he relaxed a bit and held out his hand eagerly. "Five pounds, please."

"Aye, you are a weasel, a smart one at that too. Give me a moment." She turned momentarily to make him think she would actually pay that much then turned back. "May I at least inquire whom the missive is from?"

Mrs. Reynolds waited for a reply, and when there wasn't one readily supplied, she added, "Any good thief ought to know the worth of what he is carrying. If you cannot tell me who it is from, can you tell me what it is regarding?"

"I think ye be trying to change the stakes. Ye might try to say that what I got ain't worth five shillings, let alone five pounds."

She pursed her lips together impatiently.

He swiped his well-worn hat off, revealing filthy, oily hair. "Please, madam, I ain't trying to do nothing wrong or harm her. Me family needs the help. I must deliver it directly to Anne de Burgeses Darcy. I was told it is from a former childhood friend."

He had mispronounced the mistress of Pemberley's maiden name, but he clearly knew to whom he wished to deliver the letter.

Poor Mrs. Darcy. She was grieving for her husband harder than any widow Mrs. Reynolds knew.

She hoped this letter was not more bad news.

"I am willing to pay one pound, but you must surrender the letter first for my inspection."

She knew she had won the negotiation when he bowed his head in defeat, handing her the letter.

The script was educated, ornate, and masculine, from a G.W. at a London address. Childhood friend? No one immediately came to Mrs. Reynold's mind, but she paid the dues and sent the man around to the servant's quarters for soup and leftover bread prior to his journey home.

Mrs. Reynolds knocked on the mistress of Pemberley's door, gently at first, but when there was no call to enter, she knocked a little louder. Per their usual tradition, she entered the room.

Mrs. Darcy was seated at the window, her right fist clenched under her slightly parted lips, her left arm wrapped around her knees. Mrs. Reynolds' heart dropped as she noticed that the mistress was mindlessly rotating the sapphire wedding ring. Her black nightdress was the same one she had been wearing for nearly two weeks, ever since she was notified of Mr. Darcy's death.

The housekeeper examined the abandoned breakfast tray, which had not been touched. The bread was curled from drying on the edges where the butter had not melted. Touching the teapot, she felt it cold and uninviting.

"Would you like me to ring for fresh tea, Mrs. Darcy?"

Anne Darcy shook her head slightly. She continued to stare out the window.

Mrs. Reynolds examined the letter in her hand again from G. W. in London. Dare she present it? What if it held more devastating news for her mistress?

Many considered Mrs. Reynolds stubborn, perhaps even overbearing at times, but disobedient or deceitful? No one dared accuse her of such abuses. She would carry her integrity with her to her grave, no matter the consequence. The letter was not hers, nor was it her decision whether or not to deliver it.

"Pardon me, ma'am, a letter has arrived in a peculiar manner. The man who was hired to deliver it insisted that he deliver it directly into your hands. He was not of the trustworthy sort, mind you, and I gave him a talkin' to about demanding such an invasion of your privacy. But in the end, I paid for his services and promised to give it to you."

Her chest puffed out in pride when she saw that it had caught her mistress's attention, at least to some extent.

Lady Anne Darcy had turned her head and stared at the letter. She then looked up inquisitively.

Mrs. Reynolds asked, "Would you like me to read it to you?"

"Yes, please." Mrs. Darcy's voice was barely audible and coarse from nonuse.

Mrs. Reynolds unfolded the letter and scanned the first few lines. Whoever it was from had been aware of the senior Darcy's carriage accident in Falmouth and started with flattering condolences. "It is from G. W. in London." She looked up at Mrs. Darcy briefly then added, "I do not rightly know who that is."

Mrs. Reynolds was about to begin reading it aloud when Mrs. Anne Darcy spoke again. "George. George Wickham." Her mistresses voice was stronger, and she reached out her hand for the letter.

The elderly housekeeper felt chills run up and down her spine at the name she hadn't heard for almost fifteen years. There was little in her life that caused her spine to quiver with dread. "The boy? Young Master Darcy's old friend?"

Anne simply nodded and requested the letter again. "Thank you, Mrs. Reynolds. You may go now."

Mrs. Reynolds hesitated a fraction of a second. Her instinct was to throw the letter in the fire. She was tempted to betray her moral life code in a single instant, but she conceded.

"Certainly." She handed the letter to her mistress, curtsied, and exited.

Once outside the mistress's suite, she allowed herself to recall all she remembered about the boy who was now a grown man. The same age that Master Darcy would be right now if he had survived. The thought caused her to reach for the wall momentarily for support.

She knew things about the Wickham boy that no one would believe.

He was always hungry, not for nourishment but for more than life had given him: money, power, influence, and rights he did not earn.

Her heart sank as she pieced the timing of the correspondence together.

Currently there was no Master of Pemberley. The senior Darcy's remains had arrived home just two days ago from the Falmouth coast. Services were scheduled to be on the morrow.

Miss Reynolds recited aloud to herself what her mother had taught her in her youth. "There is a stubbornness about me that can never bear to be frightened at the will of others. My courage always rises at every attempt to intimidate me."

She stood tall, turning back toward the mistress's door. Without a second thought, she spit on her palm and wiped it on the top of the doorframe of the mistress's suite. "I may not believe in God, but I firmly believe in tradition! Harm shall not pass this threshold! Not on my watch."

She began to walk away but returned, using her apron to dab at the spot just enough to blend it. She vowed that the moment she knew danger had passed by Mrs. Darcy, she would scrub it clean until it needed a fresh coat of paint.

She took one more glance at the threshold that she had marked and then walked down the hall, murmuring to herself, "No good can come from that boy. A toad does not grow up to be a stallion. No, it does not. That letter will bring trouble."

*****

Daniels held Miss Elizabeth for as long as possible. He clung to her while Bingley did the same for Miss Bennet as they raced as safely and as fast as they could carrying two chilled, and nearly unconscious, ladies of Longbourn.

The storm fought them the whole way. Wind whipped at William's face, stinging the parts that were not protected by his beard. Visibility was poor, but he continued to follow Bingley, who was more familiar with Netherfield grounds.

Even with the weather's obstacles and the difficulties keeping the ladies safely seated on the mount, they made good time.

Bingley called out urgently in front of Netherfield as they halted to a stop. "Help us! We need immediate assistance!"

Daniels joined him in shouting for help, calling out loudly in his deep baritone voice. Surely the groundskeepers would not be on the grounds in this weather, but he prayed there was a maid near any of the front rooms.

Luckily the stableman heard their pleas and ran quickly to assist, waving to others behind him who had taken temporary shelter in the stable.

In no time, the ladies were carefully removed from the horses. Both men dismounted, and Bingley pushed through the front entrance and was about to shout orders when he turned back to Daniels with a blank stare. He put his palms up and shrugged his shoulders.

William Daniels stepped in and began instructing any servant who hurried to assist in the commotion. Somehow he knew how to help someone with exposure to increment weather.

"We need hot water for baths immediately. Instruct Miss Bingley's lady's maid to come at once! Prepare two guest rooms with fresh sheets and extra blankets, and stoke the fires in those rooms to the hottest level considered safe. These ladies have been in the river for at least a half an hour, maybe longer. They are chilled to the bone. We need blankets warmed by the fire and ready to use immediately after they are bathed. There is no time to lose."

Bingley nodded and instructed the two servants who were carrying the ladies. "Take Miss Bennet to the mistress's suite and her sister to the blue room. Send all available female servants to those rooms to assist. Make that bathwater immediately, and hot too!"

Daniels looked around as everyone worked furiously on all that was needed, then added to Bingley, "Someone needs to fetch the apothecary. And get your finest sherry; they will need it."

Motioning to the kitchen maid, Daniels continued, "You, miss. Forgive me, I do not know your name."

With a brief curtsy, she looked down and said, "Laura, sir."

"Please ask Miss Bingley to provide two of her nightdresses for the ladies."

Laura looked up with a confused look on her face then turned ninety degrees and looked at Miss Bingley, who had entered the entrance way and stood about two yards away, staring at them with a mortified look on her face.

Miss Bingley's grimace and disgust was apparent, but William waved the maid on and addressed Miss Caroline Bingley. "The ladies will need warm, dry clothes."

"Surely the dirty vagabonds will be returning to their home! Those chits cannot stay here. I do not care how sick they are! Mr. Bingley is an eligible bachelor!"

William Daniels stood as broad and tall as he could, stepping forward and glared at her.

His voice was firm and deep. "And you are a proper chaperone. Find your nightclothes, or I shall spread the inhumane comment you made just now to every gentleman in London."

Her mouth dropped open, and her eyes narrowed and grew hot, but she turned sharply and marched up the stairs. She called back to her brother, "Charles, if you allow your guest to speak to me that way, I shall depart this residence immediately. And someone had better clean this filthy mud off the stairs. I will fall and break my neck! We might as well take in street rats and vagabonds who live in the sewers of London!"

She continued to rant as she climbed, but her words were too disturbing to give heed to the contents.

The two gentlemen turned towards each other and exhaled simultaneously.

Charles Bingley was apologizing with his eyes, although it was uncertain whether it was for his sister's behavior or not knowing how to direct his staff. It mattered not, and Daniels accepted the apology with a nod.

"Right then, I shall fetch the sherry. Would you like a finger or two as well?"

Daniels shook his head. "As tempting as that sounds, I cannot. My nerves have a way of churning out the contents of my stomach when alcohol is added to the mix. I would rather not cast up my accounts while I am overseeing their care. How far away is the apothecary? I could summon the militia's surgeon."

"The more help, the merrier, but do you dare go back out into the storm? I say, write the request, and I shall send my man on the fastest horse."

"That will work splendidly."

William followed Bingley to the library.

The dispatches were sent out to request the apothecary and the surgeon, and Bingley collapsed into the large armchair in the library.

Bingley had already finished one glass of sherry and a few fingers of rum, and was nursing a second glass of port when he said, "Miss Bennet was so weak. Did you see her color? Sickening white." Then he added somewhat proudly, "But she knew it was me who rescued her." He rotated his head to look at Daniels and smiled weakly.

"She will likely see you as her hero."

The silence stretched longer than normal for a conversation; however, Daniels added his own thoughts about their ladies. "Elizabeth's voice vibrated a time or two on my shoulder as if to speak, but I could not make out what she said."

Bingley raised his head curiously and asked, "Elizabeth? Has she given you permission to call her by her Christian name? I had not known you were so well acquainted."

Daniels looked down then met Bingley's inquiring gaze. "Unfortunately, we are not. I made the same blunder twice on the rushed ride back to Netherfield. I pray she will not remember, for how would I explain it?"

Bingley sat up and leaned forward, his elbows propped on his knees. "Lieutenant Daniels, do you fancy Miss Elizabeth? Is that why you suggested she accompany Miss Bennet today to tea?"

The question was not met with an answer but rather silence.

Bingley paused, waiting a bit longer for an answer. He continued eyeing Daniels, then slapped his knee, "You do! Well, I will be damned! I did not take you for the sentimental type. You appear so level headed, so pragmatic, but you are a romantic. I suppose still waters run deep. Well, I hope the surgeon, or anyone, arrives soon, for both our ladies' sakes."

William Darcy sheepishly nodded. "Might you have a change of clothes? Besides my extra height, we appear to be about the same size in chest and possibly shoulders." He knew he was stretching the truth, but the wet clothes were giving him a chill.

Bingley looked him up and down, "Pantaloons will likely fit at the hips, but you are far too broad to fit in any vest or waistcoat I own. I have plenty of white shirtsleeves however."

"I will take the largest vest you can spare, and button what is possible. Thank you."

Bingley agreed with the plan and stood up, lifting his glass as he did so. "To our ladies of Longbourn!" He then drained the last of the port in a single gulp.

CHAPTER 8

Mr. Bennet safely watched from his study at the graveled front pathway. He was thoroughly diverted as he watched a man in trousers that clearly did not fit him attempt to dismount from his horse.

The man was saturated from head to toe from the storm. As he landed, one foot caught in the stirrup, and he had to hop twice before he was able to disengage the foot and stand with any measurable amount of stability.

Shame, thought Mr. Bennet. *It would have been amusing to see my cousin, and the heir to Longbourn, meet the estate for the first time in such an intimate way.*

Mr. Collins yanked on all sides of the waistband of the oversized trousers and then adjusted its ties in the back, securing it so the heavy, wet pants would not fall to his knees.

As Mr. Collins turned, Mr. Bennet could tell that his seat had a saggy droop from where another man would have filled it out. It appeared his cousin, Mr.

Collins, had no buttocks, but from the arrogant lift of his nose, he might just be a proud and stubborn . . .

No, I was going to clean up my language, Mr. Bennet thought. But the word came anyway.

No matter what word he used to describe his cousin, no one would deny that Mr. Collins was lacking meat on his bones. He struggled to unlatch the bags with which he had laden his horse. It required arching backwards to lift one medium-sized bag that could not have weighed more than eight kilograms.

The movement confirmed that the man was, at minimal, a weakling, and as Mr. Collins sneezed, Mr. Bennet murmured to himself privately in his study, "A sniveling weakling."

He was contemplating going out to help his cousin, but the glorious rain had worsened, and its beauty was far easier to enjoy from inside his study.

Helping Mr. Collins simply did not hold any true motivation.

Was it inhumane of Mr. Bennet to hold some ill feeling toward Mr. Collins? Any good Christian is asked to love his neighbor, but should he help this man? A man whom, upon Mr. Bennet's death, would take over the running of Longbourn and likely evict his wife and five daughters.

Collins would have the law on his side.

The animosity grew for a man he had never met.

Damn entailment! He paused. *Damn it! I was trying not to swear anymore!*

Everyone knew the estate was entailed away, through the male heir. The only legal way to break the entail would be to have the heir, prior to inheriting, relinquish his inheritance and sign the papers to change the entailment. What gentleman in his right mind would give up such a birthright? Only one who had the means to support himself without the estate, and clearly, the cousin who had just put down his bags into the mud in order to remove his comb and draw it through his windblown, drenched hair, was heavy on self-importance and weak in sanity. Add to those characters the borrowed or reused clothing, and there was evidence Collins did not have the means to support himself either.

There was a moment of familiar grief as he reflected again on the fact that his daughters would truly have nothing upon his death. But it was brief, as this was only confirmation of what was already known.

Grief is a beast, but it can be mastered with time.

As Mr. Bennet conceded to the reality of the entailment, he also reminded himself that his cousin was not at fault for this. Thus, he pushed his self-pity aside and chose to, instead, extend an offer of help to his cousin.

However, just as he turned to leave the study, he heard the thundering of a horse's hard and hurried hoofs galloping to the entrance.

This rider leapt from his horse, much more gracefully than Collins had, not pausing even momentarily as he bypassed the awestruck man to pound on Longbourn's front door.

"Mr. Bennet! Urgent message for Mr. Bennet!"

Mr. Bennet gently but quickly swept past Mrs. Hill, who was about to answer the door. "I will open it," he said.

Opening the door, Mr. Bennet instantly recognized the man. It was Mr. Bingley's manservant.

Breathlessly, the man exclaimed, "Miss Jane Bennet and Miss Elizabeth Bennet went into the river! They are recovering at Netherfield. I come to report their condition."

"Come in, Mr. Jefferson. But, hush now, it is vital that I hear of the details before my wife perceives there is a problem, or I shall not be able to hear you over her wails."

They heard a muffled sneeze a few yards away and glanced toward its source. Mr. Collins was looking at them with his mouth slightly agape. He had clearly overheard.

Mr. Bennet motioned Mr. Jefferson into his study and whispered to his housekeeper, who had followed closely behind. "Hill, heed the needs of my cousin who just arrived. Do not mention anything you might have overheard. Let me assess the situation first. I assure you, they will be fine." He said the latter part for his own comfort.

There was another sneeze, less distant this time, at the threshold of the front door, and Mr. Bennet hurriedly closed the study door behind him.

Mr. Bennet did not move farther into the room; rather he stood just by the door that had just closed. He turned and nodded, encouraging Mr. Jefferson to proceed.

"Yes, sir. The walking bridge gave way in the rush of rainwater coming downstream. The elder Miss

Bennet is in and out of coherent speech but stated that Miss Elizabeth Bennet saved her from the rapids by jumping into the river after her. The elder Miss Bennet has broken her left hand. Both are fevering, but Miss Elizabeth hasn't said a word for the last hour or opened her eyes.

"She was indeed more conscious than her sister at the time they were found by my master and Mr. Daniels, but now Miss Elizabeth cannot be wakened. They were awfully chilled by the water. The surgeon had just arrived when they sent me to inform you, sir, and the apothecary has not sent word yet of being able to come. He was delivering a babe and could not accurately predict how soon he would be free."

Thomas Bennet took in all that he had heard. His two eldest daughters, both so dear to him, had been out in this storm. Fury began to build in him as he recalled the conversation that morning.

"Mama, may we use the carriage?"
Jane had asked.

Mr. Bennet didn't even lift his eyes from the book, simply beginning to nod until his arm was grasped firmly by Mrs. Bennet.

"Absolutely not. Oh, by all means possible, you shall attend the tea with Mr. Bingley, but not by carriage. No, not by carriage."

Mr. Bennet looked up in time to see Jane appeal to him with her eyes. "Perhaps the horse then? We both could easily ride together."

Mrs. Bennet screeched, "Oh, no, not the horse. I am quite confident that it will be occupied. Needed, that is, around the farm, to . . . move the summer manure to the southwest lot to cure. No, you must not ride the horse."

Never, in all the years at Longbourn, had they ever moved manure to the southwest lot. The southwest lot was untamed and held too many boulders, the size of which would break a wheel with little effort. The field was no place to cure manure that would later be needed to transplant back into orchards and gardens.

Elizabeth pursed her lips together, sensing ulterior motives.

Mr. Bennet had the same look on his face, surprised and appalled at his wife's absurd reasoning.

"Why ever not?" Elizabeth's words were pointed and held a stubbornness that would not be stayed until it was answered.

Their mother's mouth opened part way, then she looked to Mr. Bennet for help, which he did not offer.

Instead he said, "This is your reasoning, not mine. Do not presume I will defend the logic of a lady's mind. And I most certainly would not attempt to understand yours, not unless I have a desire to sleep in the barn for a week. Go on, answer your daughter's question."

"When she is so quarrelsome, she is your *daughter." Mrs. Bennet pointedly turned her back to her husband with a glare. Smoothing her skirts, and without looking at her daughters, she said, "If you must know, I must use the horse and*

carriage to go into Meryton. You know I have not the constitution of walking as you two. Be ever so kind, and allow me the chance to obtain what is needed."

"But, what do you so desperately nee—" Elizabeth's words were halted by the single silencing shake of her father's head and Jane's words.

"Yes, Mama. Of course you can have the carriage," Jane said.

"Yes, Mama." Elizabeth then stood and excused herself, catching the appeal for forgiveness in her father's eyes.

He waited, barely breathing, for the last part of the information that Mr. Jefferson finally shared with trepidation.

"Mr. Bennet, the servants have warmed them, but they both have developed fevers and chills already. Mr. Bingley would like to know if they are permitted to stay until they are well. We welcome your visits and even, if you require, your residence at Netherfield as well. However,

Miss Bingley has agreed to postpone her travels to London to chaperone."

Bennet rubbed his chin with his left hand then looked up at Jefferson. "Has she indeed? This is something Miss Caroline Bingley offered?" Mr. Bennet huffed once. "Indeed not. Well, forgive me, but as soon as the weather clears, I will bring Mary over by way of carriage. If Bingley is willing, please allow Mary to stay as well. She will see to their needs, and I assure you she will be more willing than Miss Bingley."

"I will pass on the information." Mr. Jefferson bowed and turned to leave.

"Jefferson," Mr. Bennet turned away and looked out the window into the darkness. "Is it your opinion that they might be more fragile or less fragile than you report?"

"I speak the truth. I do not taint my words for persuasion."

*****

The entirety of November ended in a blur. Netherfield had been preparing for a ball, but of course, those efforts came to a halt the day the ladies of Longbourn were rescued.

Miss Jane Bennet required surgery to set the wrist, but her fever resolved within a few days. She was able to join the gentlemen shortly thereafter in the main level, but it was rare that she left Miss Mary alone to attend to Elizabeth by herself.

William was granted leave for a fortnight due to the valiant rescue. It might have been the first time Lieutenant Daniels had ever asked for leave from his duties.

William Daniels did not hesitate to accept the invitation from Bingley to stay on at Netherfield during his leave. There was no place he would rather stay than near Elizabeth. He had to hear news of her recovery, and being here meant he heard it more readily. He prayed for that moment when he could witness the recovery for himself.

The days were riddled with updates, as many as he dared ask for, but he struggled when nightfall came. It was hard enough not to ask about Elizabeth's condition, which he managed to do every once in a while, although he dearly wanted to make the request hourly.

He never gave up hope that his own assistance would be asked for, but the chance to physically see her progress was never granted.

William even maintained being dressed when he retired to sleep, as he had the first night, in case there were needs in the middle of the night.

Every night, William listened and waited for that moment of need. If he did drift off, he always startled awake with every squeaky footfall on the floorboards coming from the hall.

Within four days of giving high attention to the sounds at night from the hallway, he knew who was walking as well as whose chambers they entered or exited.

Miss Jane Bennet's footsteps were the easiest to detect, although she had only been up and walking for one night: soft, and distinctly padded, most likely trying to tiptoe down the hall to her sister's chamber. It soothed his anxiety to know Miss Jane was doing better and that Elizabeth had both her favorite sisters attending to her.

Bingley's tread had a hesitant, or perhaps indecisive, nature. He would take a few steps in the direction of the ladies' rooms, halt, then turn around and return to his chamber at least two or three times a night. From what he could tell, Bingley never entered another chamber. He simply went up and down the hall, changing his mind a time or two before retreating back to the master suite.

The servants were not quite as easy to determine, but William knew when the breakfast trays came, even without the clue that dawn had broken. This was because of the heaviness and the cautioned steps, intermixed with the occasional cling of metal trays and covers against the dishes.

It was the best part of the night, when breakfast came. That moment meant he could leave his sleepless bed and obtain the first report of how Elizabeth fared.

For nearly ten days now his mind had imagined the comings and goings of Netherfield's west wing through sound. And based on the night's activity, he knew if the morning report would be good or bad.

Tonight's activity had been nearly restful, or at least much less bustling than the previous ten nights. Earlier in the day, it had been reported that Miss Elizabeth was much more awake but only for short periods of time.

Up until now, there had been little movement through the hall. That is, until the hour struck four o'clock.

Something down the hall alerted his senses, and his eyes opened in the darkness and looked to the door. For no logical reason, he watched the handle of the door for movement.

Of course, the handle didn't move, and William forced himself to look the other way, glancing at the moon. The glowing orb was large and, in these wee morning hours, hung low in the western sky. In another day or two, it would be a full moon.

Even though the door handle didn't move, he still hoped for the visitor he imagined in his mind. He wondered why that was.

Why did he want Elizabeth to come to his room?

Because he wanted to go to hers. And it was maddening.

William Daniels lifted up his head to listen more acutely because he thought he heard a new set of footsteps. More correctly, he heard not just steps but someone moving their hands down the wall as they walked.

It wasn't Jane, nor Bingley, or any other known visitor or servant.

It had to be Elizabeth! Was she well enough to walk?

He listened and took in the sound. He heard soft, slow steps that were dragging slightly and . . . was she barefoot? She mustn't be out in the chill without slippers!

He threw back the covers, primping what had come discombobulated, and walked to the door. He tilted his ear close to the door and, at the same time, tilted his head up at the ceiling, his mind already adding stories to the new sounds he was hearing.

The volume of the steps as well as the hand brushing against the wall was increasing, clearly drawing nearer to his own room. He dearly desired to open the door. If anything, he just wished to place a face to the new footsteps, but the footsteps suddenly stopped.

He took a controlled breath and slowly opened the door.

"Good Lord, Elizabeth, you look dreadful! What can I do?"

*****

Elizabeth tried to smirk, but breathing took all her effort. "Mr. Daniels, I suggest you mind—," she took another breath, "your manners."

Awareness dawned, and William bowed his head in deep remorse. "Forgive me, what a terrible thing to say to a lady. In truth, you appear far better than I have imagined these last ten days."

Ten days? She had been ill and at Netherfield for ten days?

She smiled slightly and nodded. "You are forgiven, for you were likely . . . telling the truth. I appreciate the directness." She had to take a breath. "Disguise of every sort is my abhorrence." She shifted her weight a bit harder onto the supporting arm that was against the wall.

"Of course. Well, in that case, you look like Death who has imbibed until crapulousness."

The mental fog she was feeling was bewildering. She had never felt like she was half-witted, but she couldn't find understanding of what Lieutenant Daniels had just said. "I am afraid the meaning of your verbiage escapes me."

Elizabeth felt a bit lightheaded and worried that she shouldn't have gone searching for a book to read. She added, "Is that a common word?" Perhaps she should be searching for a dictionary.

For some reason, he furrowed his brows and then slowly moved toward her. "Perhaps it was a bit crass for a lady. It means imbibing until the state of drunkenness, including symptoms of headache and nausea." He reached for the arm that she was not leaning on. He assisted her to shift weight again onto his arm. The assistance was sorely appreciated.

She let out a weak giggle. "Thank you. Well, I doubt I have imbibed, but the headache and nausea qualifies me. I thank you again for the honesty."

"Are you hungry? Would you like some tea?"

"No, I am weary of my lodgings. I needed to move about. But I have to admit I am regretting it by the second. If it were possible, I think I feel more ill."

He looked to the door he had just exited then down at the floor. He cleared his throat before saying, "There is a chair just inside my ... er ... this room."

It wasn't a suggestion. She knew all too well that he had just directed her to sit down. It didn't cross her in any way because he had said it with gentleness, even tenderness, laced with fear.

She nodded and allowed him to assist her weary body into the room. As soon as she had done so, she exhaled, and her legs gave way to the welcomed relief of the chair.

He carefully placed the arm he had been supporting down on the curved and delicately carved hickory arm.

She continued to admire the striations of the light and dark pattern of the wood, when she felt her legs lifted and feet placed on an ottoman. She took a deep breath and leaned back into the back of the chair. It was a high-back chair, one that held more support in the low back than the head, so her head relaxed back, as if the weight of it was more than her neck could bear. Indeed, it seemed to be so.

She heard little movements around her, but they were sounding farther and farther away. Was a door closing? Or was it opening wider?

Elizabeth thought she heard the scrapping of metal on brick, which was most likely Mr. Daniels stoking the fire as she smelled wood burning a moment later. She felt a knitted throw placed on her legs, her toes secured with the end.

Something was wrong with the situation. She willed herself to open her eyes, but her will was weaker than her lids, and they stayed closed. How far down the hall had she gone? What room had she made it to?

It was disturbing to not fully understand, but she reached for enlightenment anyway. "What . . . are you . . . doing? Where are . . . we?" She didn't dare ask if they were alone; a third question would have cost too much in air. Her breathing was already so heavy, and her words were clipped as she sought for breath. She almost didn't recognize her own voice, it was so slurred.

"Shhh, my Elizabeth. Please do me a kindness and rest. I shall take no debate on this issue. Sleep now. Sleep."

Did he just say, "My Elizabeth. . ."?

CHAPTER 9

William stood in the doorway of his chambers with one hand rubbing his chin and beard and the other wrapped around his chest. He alternated pivoting onto the left foot, leaning to get a look down the hall for visitors, and then shifting to the right foot, the one in the room, to look at Elizabeth.

The decision must be made soon.

Even being so far from the window, he could see the sun was highlighting more than just the tops of the trees. He had no idea of the true amount of time he had watched, mesmerized by her gentle breathing. It hadn't been gentle at first, but now it was relaxed and easy.

Every time her chest rose and fell, he found his did too. He tried to change the pace of his own breathing, but to no avail. He couldn't help but feel anything but discordance when he tried.

The fact that she lived and breathed energized him.

Attempting to breath opposite of Elizabeth was like putting on another's shoes, ones in which the leather had stretched and formed to the exact form of the rightful owner. It felt wrong, unnatural, and even uncomfortable.

He wanted to breathe with Elizabeth. He wanted to be the breath she needed, and he wanted to breathe her in, always.

So why was he standing at the arch of his doorway, weighing options? One option: to leave and simply walk down the hall. The other: to take a step or two back into his room and close the door.

Of course, if he chose the latter, others would notice her absence from her sick bed, and soon. No amount of explaining would persuade anyone that, in her fatigued, delusional state she collapsed into the chair next to his bed.

She would be forced to marry him.

He was an eligible bachelor. He wasn't a bad match, was he? William Daniels may not be the heir to anything, but he had earned his position of lieutenant in Britain's militia. He could afford a wife, although a meager life it would be, but he was willing to continue to work up in rank.

If he chose to return her to her own chambers, he risked being caught in her room. His reputation would not be tarnished as much as hers. But there was still that chance he would never be seen.

He feared that the longer he waited to make the decision, the decision would be made for him.

Passively making her his wife by doing nothing was tempting, yes. But he could never force her to marry him. He dearly wished to earn her affection, and he was confident that they had made an excellent start.

When the clock struck at the top of the seven o'clock hour, he startled. It was now or never; he had to do what was right for her. He would never allow himself the indulgence of getting what he wanted with no effort.

"Miss Elizabeth, you must return to your bed."

Her breathing deepened, and a small, feminine sigh escaped.

Daniels! Get control of yourself! Now is the time to act, not react!

He consciously unclenched his fists, opened the door to the hall even wider, and moved to lift her from the chair.

With gentle but urgent arms, he moved to gather her into his arms. Not unexpectedly, he found his mind was besotted with all manner of inappropriate thoughts. He had an easy time standing erect, which was a bit surprising, as she was full figured. He had always adored her full feminine figure, and now he no longer had to imagine what her curves felt like.

Her fragrance was incredibly enticing, though not particularly distinguishable. Her usual vanilla and lavender scent was distant, barely noticeable. But this particular scent was far more natural and pure. It brought a smile to his face. This is what she smells like without her usual application of toilette water. He had no words to describe the musky scent and chose to inhale again to try to capture it in his memory.

It was a luxury he knew was risky. But with that breath, he smelled another scent altogether. When he had reached the arm around her back to lift her, her head had fallen to his neck. He realized that she had a sweet, fruity breath, as if she had just eaten strawberries, oranges, and plums.

It made him hungry, and not for the fruit of which her breath smelled, but to taste the very breath itself. He collected himself. He knew better, and knew she expected him to behave as a gentleman, regardless if anyone was watching.

He also knew he was running out of time, so he redirected his mind. This had been a very healthy young lady, and she was currently very ill.

He took a calming breath and whispered to her, "You must get better, my darling."

He finally pivoted towards the hall and took the first few steps into the hall.

The chill in the air was not what made him shiver.

Elizabeth had stirred in his arms and instinctively he paused his walking, holding his breath. She let out a heavy sigh, right into his neck, forcing him to close his eyes momentarily.

"Daniels! What the hell are you doing?" Bingley whispered as loudly as he dared, and William did not miss the heat and anger of his words, regardless of the actual volume.

"I did not— she— nothing has— it is not— oh, damnation!" Daniels pressed forward, forcing Bingley to step back into the doorway he had just exited.

"Bingley, please open her chamber door! We can talk about this later!"

"Bollocks!" Bingley hissed a bit.

He cleared his throat and looked hard at Bingley, whose eyes were wider than Caroline Bingley's were when she was forced to provide nightclothes for the Bennet sisters ten days ago. He indicated with his head that Elizabeth's door still needed to be opened, and Bingley reluctantly performed the requested action.

Grudgingly but thank goodness wordlessly, Bingley pulled the coverlet and sheets down further and adjusted the pillows, picking up one that had fallen to the wooden floor.

Daniels slowly lowered Elizabeth's legs, knees, and hips, and then began to lower her shoulders and head, paying careful attention to where he laid her soft figure. He removed the arm from under her knees, then used that hand to cradle her head and tilt it away from the crook of his neck. With his left hand holding her head, his right arm was able to slowly pull out as he lowered her torso.

She seemed to welcome the pillow, rolling further into the bed, trapping the hand that had been holding her head.

He was mindful of Bingley, who was staring at him, willing and ready to put a hole in the back of his head.

He was done for, if Bingley's heavy, angry breathing was an indicator.

"Elizabeth *will* recover from this," William said, partly for Bingley's benefit, giving him hope that William had not compromised her. But he had also said it to himself.

Bingley set his jaw and said, "It is more than I can say for others in this room."

*****

She strained her ears, but it seemed like minutes passed before she heard any sound. She attempted to open her eyes, or moan, or move, but fatigue engulfed every sense.

The bed was easy enough to recognize, and it was welcome, but her senses were on alert.

Was there someone in the room? Yes, possibly even some shifting of weight causing the floor boards to creak. For the time being, she held her breath to focus on the sounds she heard.

She needed information about Jane!

"Elizabeth will recover from this." She was sure it was William Daniels who said that, but it was said with a shaky voice.

"It is more than I can say for others in this room."

When she heard those words spoken by Mr. Bingley, it felt like everything stopped in a jerking motion: time, her breath, the world—it all halted.

Surely it meant nothing other than a status on Jane's poor recovery. Had she taken a turn for the worst?

She strained to hear more, but there was nothing else said. Nothing but heavy breathing to hear, but it might have well been silence with all the tension in the air.

Finally she heard movement, but it was simply two sets of boots walking out the door, and then . . . the door closed.

She strained further to hear Jane's breathing, a cough even, but there was nothing.

Where was Jane!? Oh, no! Is Jane doing poorly? Elizabeth had to do something. She found enough energy to roll over and look in the direction of the door.

She pled with all her might to have Jane walk in the room. As she focused unblinkingly on the door, rehearsing her pleas, her eyes began to dry again and get heavy. But then something even more disturbing woke her entire being.

Why did Bingley sound so angry? Was he already grieving?

My dearest sister, my best friend, cannot be dead.

*****

Bingley ushered Daniels into the study with a stiff arm, then closed the door loudly.

Before William could even turn to face Bingley and attempt to explain, the lecture began.

"Under my roof! You violate the trust I have placed in you. There will be nothing you can say that can alter what happens next. I cannot decide if I should defend her honor like a gentleman, here and now, or march you in handcuffs to her father. How could you? Of all the soldiers, you were the one I took a liking to. You were wise and refined, intelligent even. And at one point I was sure you would never do this. I was sure you were not some opportunist. But there is no mistaking what I just witnessed. She was in your room! Worse yet, she was in your arms, while you were in shirtsleeves!

Do you realize her face was against your neck and chest?

"Good God, Daniels!" the rant continued. "I would have never expected this of you. Never! I do not even want an explanation for what I just witnessed. You should have seen the guilt on your face. I will never forget that moment for the rest of my life. For the record, it is entirely inappropriate to call her by her Christian name, and 'my darling' is a term of endearment. Whoever raised you failed to teach you common decency. I just thought of a third option. I shall take you to your parents and make them watch you be hung, strung, and quartered! To take advantage of your heartthrob while she is so ill . . . where were you raised to have learned such despicable behavior?"

Bingley finally paused long enough to let Daniels respond. "To the last question—I do not know where I was raised, but I do know I was raised with manners. I learned the kind of manners that insist that the trembling, disoriented lady who independently alighted in the middle of the night sit in the nearest chair before she collapsed. I learned that one must not be alone in a room with a lady, certainly without a chaperone or protection. Unfortunately, all I could offer at four in the morning was protection. I stoked the fire, placed a blanket on her legs, and prayed that the rest was enough to assist her back into her own chambers. I watched , from the doorway, for two hours, debating on how to move her without compromising her. I came up with nothing."

"You are clearly an intelligent man, more intelligent than I gave you credit for. What a bale of lies! Were you so feebleminded that you could not think to wake a servant? Or her sister? Of course there were options! Oh, heavens, how will I explain this to Miss Bennet? This is all my fault! I allowed a filthy swine into my home, and he ruined Jane's favorite sister! How?"

"Bingley, please, she was disoriented and ready to fall. I hardly touched her."

"Hardly touched her? I know what I saw!"

"I mean . . . hogwash, this is exactly what I feared. Look, I am willing and ready to make things right. I swear I am a gentleman. You have my word that I will marry her. You know that I hold her in high regard; you deduced as much the night we rescued them. But let me propose another option for me to atone for this morning, perhaps less costly on her reputation and with a minimal ripple effect of her family."

Daniels paused to make sure the last part of the sentence sank in. "I would like to ask her for a courtship. She and I have found an affinity for each other. At least, I believe it is reciprocated. At least I am not viewed ill favorably and, if I interpret recent things correctly, I believe she is even partial to me."

Bingley nodded, permitting him to continue.

"If she agrees to a courtship, I will further our acquaintance and marry her, properly and respectfully in a church, as soon as she is agreeable."

Bingley was clearly contemplating the proposed option, but he turned his back to Daniels for an extended minute. Without turning around, he asked, "What if she does not agree to a courtship?"

William Daniels sighed. "Then you may name the place and time. For the record, I am quite good with my pistol."

Nodding, he turned around. "Was she really disoriented?"

"Yes, and her form was swaying dangerously. The safest thing was to find her a chair, which happened to be just inside my room. When I opened my door, I could have touched both the chair and her form. I assisted her to walk less than two yards."

This time it was Bingley's turn to sigh. "I do not know if I actually believe you, or desperately *wish* to believe you."

"But you believe me."

"Yes, I do, but I do have a tendency to believe the best in people. Your character is one that is dependable, predictable, and even soothing to my erratic and spontaneous one. You could not have done what it appeared to have looked like, not when you have been so attentive to Miss Elizabeth's daily—nay, hourly—condition. You are besotted, through and through. Even my sister has taken notice. May I ask if you actually fancy yourself in love? Or are you just drawn to her?"

William pressed his lips together. It was a very forward question, one that had tickled his conscious mind many times. However, until this moment, he had successfully dodged a concentrated effort to answer it. With Bingley so newly peaceable, he did not dare circumvent answering the question.

Daniels grasped his hands behind his back, lifted his chin, and attempted to be honest with himself as well as Bingley.

"I cannot think of her in any other way but Elizabeth, and furthermore, *my* Elizabeth. I find when I am especially feeling low, Elizabeth lifts me. When she debates with me, I am filled with wonder at her forward–thinking mind. I know that I would gladly be wrong a thousand times just to have her correct me.

"More than once recently, the thought of not having her in my life has crippled me. I no longer eat, or sleep, or comprehend what I read, unless the latest update in her condition had been a positive one. I know, Bingley, that regardless of what her answer is when I ask for a courtship, she has made me find the better man in myself. I also know that I will spend the rest of my life trying to be the kind of gentleman she can call her equal, but I will never reach that goal. She is precious and unique. I know her worth, and she deserves someone who does, because she cannot always see it. My deepest desire is to be allowed to help her see her worth for the rest of our days."

"But love? Do you love Elizabeth Bennet?"

"Indeed, Bingley, I dearly do. If that is not love, then I do not know what is."

CHAPTER 10

Bingley stood erect, but his hardness softened as he said, "Then, come, let us see to our ladies. I have often wished to allow you to visit her, with a chaperone, of course. But now I think I shall. It will be important for you to be there as much as possible during her recovery." The last few words had been said with a growing smile.

"I imagine so for my own reasons. But might I inquire as to your reasoning?"

With a forced cough into his fist, Bingley added, "Ah, shall we say that there will be a greater chance we all can escape your broody nature."

"Broody?"

"Or perhaps darkly intense."

"Darkly?"

"Intense. Yes, that is what I said."

"Pardon me, but . . ."

"You could also be described as intense with a tendency to intimidate."

"I do not..."

"Intimidate? My friend, you do. It took every ounce of strength I possess to confront you just now. You can thank my loyalty to Miss Bennet for adding what I lacked to finish the job."

"I am in no way your equal! You are a gentleman, and I..."

"You are a gentleman, sir, in every way. You present grace and strength of character to those around you. You radiate power, and wisdom pours from your mouth. It is why I was so astonished to see Miss Elizabeth in your arms. I do not know what or who you ran from to join the militia, but return and claim your inherent rank in society. The topic of your past is a tenuous one, and frankly, I have been troubled at why a gentleman of the first waters is hiding in a remote part of Hertfordshire pretending he has no family."

Daniels heart sped up, faster and faster, as Bingley rambled. He pondered what his friend was saying and claiming about him; was so easily seen by others.

Was he of the first waters? Did he have a rank in society? A family who might still be looking for him? Perhaps another sister, other than Georgiana?

"This is a tenuous topic, Bingley, indeed. But the way you said it just now has never been said to me. In fact, it sounded as if my training as a gentleman was formally received, or shall I assume you might even say that it was obvious?"

Bingley chuckled then took his time finding a seat, which allowed William Daniels to do the same.

"Of course it is." He narrowed his eyes with a look of incredulity. "Are you saying you do not already know that fact? Do you truly not remember where you came from? I shall be shocked indeed if you claim that to be true. It is more obvious to me, and likely others, that you simply do not *wish* to remember. For example, Daniels, you say your shipwreck was five years ago, and you were found on the Falmouth coast. Why have you not researched the shipwrecks from that area and time? Surely there could not be too many to filter through."

"The thought has occurred to me, more times than I can count. Daily, in fact."

Bingley's laughter interrupted him again. When it died down, Bingley gestured for him to continue.

"I certainly am not trying to make excuses."

Shaking his head dramatically then switching to nodding, Bingley replied, "Oh, no, you certainly are not."

"Sarcasm is not my friend and makes those who use it look deceitful, ignorant, and cowardly. If you have something to say, please express it now."

"I think I shall. After all, I was given a direct order by a lieutenant in Her Majesty's militia just now! Allow me to utilize the freedom just offered. It is not me who is cowardly. It is *you* who fears facing who he is. Ignorant? My friend, with all the kindness of my heart, you have indulged this trait long enough. And as you have presumed, with your crossed arms telling me your feathers are ruffled, I will indeed accuse you of being deceitful as well."

A response rose to William's lips. "Someone who once told me he 'abhorred deceit of any kind'. . . oh, dear." William stopped abruptly then looked away, shocked at what he had just experienced. Was that a memory? He mentally chased the moment, the fragment of a moment in his previous life.

"What is it, man?"

"I, ah, I believe . . . the person who taught me that, who said it to me, was my father. Just now, as I said it, I almost heard his voice saying it, and there was a moment, perhaps a memory, where I was much younger, and he used this single sentence to discipline me. I must have done something deceitful, or told a lie and was caught. He did not lecture or paddle me, or remove privileges. He simply stated that single sentence. 'I abhor deceit of any kind.' More was taught in that single moment than he could have if he attempted to press in any other method, or even say it twice."

Bingley sat forward. "Go on."

He shrugged. "That was it. That is all I remember."

"His voice . . . did he speak like you? Was his accent like yours?"

"How would I know? One does not know their own accent."

"It is northern but polished. You do not fully drop your h's, nor do you fully smash your soft oooh sound into a more oh sound. But you slip every once in a while. Last night, instead of asking for a *coop* of tea, like those from London, you hardened it slightly and said, *cope* of tea. I hear it more distinctly when you are fatigued. That tells me you lived in the North in your youth and were likely educated at Oxford, or perhaps Cambridge."

Williams scoffed slightly. "Certainly not Oxford. *Hinc lucem et pocula sacra.*" William's eyes widened. "Oh, dear Lord! I went to Cambridge!"

"That is their motto on the coat of arms! I would add you have some intense loyalty to the school as well, just as intense as their rival, Oxford."

"You may be right."

"William, be honest with yourself. You know I am right."

"Are we back to the topic of deceit?"

"Indeed, we are."

Daniels did not know if he felt shame in never truly putting forth the effort to search or elation at finding several important clues to his past. Either way, the motivation to search was lit like an oil-soaked wicker basket.

"Til this moment, I never knew myself."

*****

As revealing as his conversation with Bingley had been, William realized that Miss Elizabeth was still at the forefront of his mind.

He quickly found an excuse to ponder what he had just learned about himself and was overjoyed that he no longer needed an excuse to check on Miss Elizabeth. The owner of Netherfield himself escorted him to Elizabeth's bedchambers where, with little or no persuasion, Miss Jane Bennet acquiesced.

Bingley closed the door behind him as he left, but not before smiling at William as he left William, Jane, and the maid alone in Elizabeth's chambers. The maid glanced up briefly at him, clearly showing her disapproval of what had just been permitted. When he caught her eye, though, she glanced away, busying herself with primping the linens and, after that, the curtains that had just been opened.

His first instinct, or perhaps desire, was to look at Elizabeth, but Jane was watching him intently. Perhaps she didn't approve? Or perhaps she felt uncomfortable herself?

"Do not make yourself uneasy," Daniels said.

When Jane nodded encouragingly without faltering, he began anew to wonder what she might be thinking. Perhaps she wanted more of an explanation?

He tried to answer that possibility. "I have a genuine respect for your sister. To have fought so hard through this illness, not to mention that she became ill by selflessly rescuing you, secures my admiration even more."

Her smile softened briefly and then returned brightly, as she blinked back newly glossed-over eyes. He waited, worried he had made her uneasy.

"My sister is so dear to me."

Daniels nodded. *Me too.*

He shook himself out of the thought, for this was not helpful by half to her care. He put his arms behind his back, grasping his hands together nervously where their trembling would not be observed. "How can I be of assistance? I have had minimal training with the medic in the militia. However, I was raised with . . ." His speech halted, but then he finished the statement confidently. "With an amazing housekeeper. She was attentive, and I believe she taught me things."

Oh, how that last statement was the raw truth.

He *believed* she taught him things. He couldn't be sure. In fact, he doubted he could recall a single directive or fact. However, he vaguely remembered a short, stubborn woman. She was strong on the outside and easily set to temper. But she was also affectionate, deeply affectionate.

Suddenly he recalled her name. "Mrs. Reynolds," he whispered to himself.

Jane tipped her head inquisitively and asked, "I thought you possessed but few memories of your upbringing."

He half smiled, looked down for a moment as he massaged this newly found memory, then met Miss Bennet's gaze. "I do not. I had not, until this moment. In fact, today has been highly unusual. May I?" He motioned to the other chair next to Elizabeth's bedside.

"Of course, Lieutenant."

William sat down and finally chanced glancing at Elizabeth's sleeping form. It had been the only proper timing, and he was not disappointed.

Her hair, which had been in disarray when attempting to walk in the hall, had been replaited to the side farthest from him, allowing him to take in her delicate long neck. He watched it move ever so slowly with her breathing, now noticeably easier than when she was walking earlier. And since she had her head turned away from him, the lean muscles and tendons were clearly defined along her long neck. But he made another observation that was enormously exhilarating; the blood vessel in her neck pulsed in a mesmerizing pattern. How he wished to feel the life it emanated. It was neither fast nor slow, and it was barely noticeable, but it captured him heart and soul.

"Mr. Daniels? Are you well?"

He snapped his attention to her sister, stating firmly, "Yes, why do you ask?"

"I asked a question of you. Twice, in fact."

"Oh dear, my apologies. Please, propose it again to me."

"It was quite unimportant, I assure you." She paused briefly, looking slightly away from him to her sister and then back at him. "I might be forward in this, but Elizabeth is definitely the strong one in our family. My mother has good intentions, but she improperly eludes that I am the fair one. Watching her angelic state right now, I am convinced that Elizabeth is far fairer than I am. In fact, it has been some time now that I have concluded her to be the handsomest woman of my acquaintance."

"Indeed, she is." William glanced away from Elizabeth to observe Miss Bennet and realized his impropriety. "Oh, Miss Bennet, I had not meant to slight you. You are both very fine, with admiral qualities. My intention was simply to agree with you in Miss Elizabeth's beauty." He cleared his throat and made to stand.

Miss Bennet reached out a staying hand and softly said, "Stay, please. I was not slighted in any way. In fact, you are officially the first one to have agreed with me on that statement. I attempted to share it with Mr. Bingley. However . . ." her cheeks flashed scarlet instantly, severing her sentence at the same time.

Bingley would have said Miss Bennet was his *angel*. He relaxed a bit and leaned back into the chair. "Miss Bennet, I think we are in agreement. Perhaps we shall save us both further embarrassment by pursuing other topics."

"I thank you. That was very considerate."

*****

Elizabeth felt awake, but her body was so fatigued. Never in her whole life had she wanted to stay in bed and sleep like this. Mornings were usually crippling for many in her family, but not for Elizabeth.

But today, on the one occasion that she *wanted* to stay in bed, her mind was alert and processing things far faster than she wanted. If her mind was a music box, she wished there was a way to close the lid and silence the noise for a few more hours while her body was screaming so loudly that it wanted more rest.

It was strange to have her mind and body at such odds. To comprehend and mentally move at a typical pace, yet her body alerting her of its refusal to cooperate. At the moment, her heart, or desire, sided with her body. It was hard to ignore such aches and weakness.

She attempted to slow her breathing and push the disruptive thoughts from her mind, seeking solitude in the blackness of sleep once again.

At least in sleep, she was less aware of the emotional pain of losing her sister Jane. Sleep seemed to push time away, but in reality, sleep just allowed it to slip through unnoticed. But when the morning came, that mountain of grief crashed in on her.

With her eyes closed, she tried with all her might to force the grief from her heart. But she realized that all her attempts caused her to hold her breath.

She exhaled dramatically and then demanded every ounce of will power she had to remove the covers. "This will not do! Mama will need help with the funeral. There is no time to sleep. I can sleep when I am dead."

With exertion, she lifted her legs from under the covers and rolled to her side, preparing to sit up. "Mr. Daniels, why . . . ?"

His face was contorted, even pained, but he did not look away.

She was in her nightclothes! "What are you doing here?"

"Please, Miss Elizabeth, let me fetch the maid. She just barely stepped out to retrieve hot tea as we could see you were stirring." He began to rise but then thought differently. Instead he scooted his chair forward just enough to reach a hand to her head and ask, "How are you feeling?"

His words were spoken so softly, almost tenderly, but that was not what made her shiver. He was looking at her with a sense of reverence, as if . . . as if he was desperate to hear her answer.

His eyes held hers like a caress, and as much as she wanted to, she couldn't look away. It felt familiar. Comfortable. It probably was not much more than an immeasurably short moment, but she sensed something different in his manner.

She answered him with caution. "I am extremely tired, my person that is. But I could not stay my mind or thoughts from the recent events."

"It has been greater than two weeks now."

She cringed and closed her eyes. That must mean the funeral had already been held. She sighed again. "I understand. I hope you will tell me about it sometime."

There was a flicker of the pained expression again, but he nodded. "Certainly. I will tell you anything you would like."

She was still laying on her side, in her nightshift, and she began again with the question she had attempted earlier. "Why are you in my room?"

His lips rolled together briefly, and then he nodded. He was partly answering her but also in part speaking to himself.

"Indeed. That is an interesting and fair question. Why am I in your chambers? That is one of the best and easiest questions to ask. Obvious, and predictable, in fact. Yes, I should have predicted the inquiry. I am afraid, though, it is much more difficult to answer. "

Now it was her turn to purse her lips. It wasn't as much out of distress as it had been for Daniels, but more because she wanted to allow him more time to provide the answer. She was stubborn but not impatient.

"I have Bingley's permission. I know that is not an adequate answer, but perhaps you could allow a postponement of this conversation to another time?"

The door creaked open, and the maid walked in, carrying a tray of tea. She looked at Elizabeth and smiled brightly. "Miss Elizabeth! Alas, you are awake! Oh, how thrilled I am that I'll be have'n good news to report! Such as the last few weeks have been, this might'n be the only good news! Look how bright and shiny your eyes are, Miss! For over two weeks, we nursed you back to strength from the very claws of the devil's mistress! I say mistress 'cause everybody knows that a woman is the real dangerous one. Am I right?" She made an exaggerated wink then repeated the gesture for good measure.

Then the maid did something strange. She looked to the lieutenant and nodded with only minimal acceptable politeness. "I am sure you agree with me, sir.

A woman has a pull, a power, over the strongest of men." Her tone simmered dramatically when she spoke to Daniels.

His reaction was to look at the maid, nod, and then briefly look at his lap. He then crossed one knee over the other and sat back, pulling in an exaggerated breath. "Indeed, Elaine."

He spoke to Elizabeth next. "Netherfield tea is of the highest quality. The cook steeps it a few minutes longer than what is typical, and it has a hint of boldness. As refreshing as it is, the flavor lingers and continues to satisfy for a healthy while longer. May I?" He asked while he gestured to pour her a cup.

She nodded.

Why was he here? And why had Bingley given permission for him to be alone in her chambers?

The maid, whom he had called Elaine, added to his comment. "Oh, the cook does more than that! But I shan't betray the confidence. Mr. Hankmin shared it with me when he was too ill to rise, but the master was needin' it. I brewed this'n myself! He trusts me. He went and gone to Meryton for the Cornish hens he wants to be servin'."

Elizabeth propped herself up and adjusted the sheets to cover her front. She felt a bit more modest with her exerted effort. When she finally deemed herself presentable, she looked up and saw that William Daniels had stood and was patiently waiting to hand her the tea and saucer.

"Thank you. I cannot tell you how desperate I am for something to drink."

"I have no doubt you are thirsty. Are you hungry?"

Sheepishly, she answered. "Famished."

Daniels nodded towards Elaine, and she bolted proudly to accomplish the task.

And they were suddenly alone again.

They each sipped their tea, and the moment it was cool enough to drink less femininely, she let her reservations go and asked for more.

He chuckled and said, "Gladly. Anything you need, it is yours." His words were spoken while looking in the direction of the tea as he poured, but when he turned to hand it to her, his voice lowered into a deep baritone as he distinctly added, "Your needs are my first priority."

She smirked at him. Humor was the only dependable method of coping with the words that had just sent chills down her back. "You have left me no choice, Mr. Daniels. I believe I shall abuse you with requests. Would you like to amend that last statement?"

Although her tone had successfully delivered sauce and impertinence, her excited heart rate would have betrayed her. At least for now, that was her little secret, and she looked away briefly, only to find strength again to glance back at him.

He was looking at her neckline. As he shifted positions, she could tell he hoped she hadn't noticed. But she had.

She casually touched her nightclothes to assure the sheets had not shifted. They had not.

"So, good sir, would you like to amend that statement? Or shall you be my private servant for all time?"

A slow smile started on his lips, lifting at a constant rate until he showed his perfectly white teeth and chuckled unrestrained. "Oh, how I would love to amend my previous statement, but I cannot, for the life of me, make it any better than you just did!"

She was in the process of taking a sip of the tea, but she paused by his bold statement. Had he realized what he had just said? She was dumbfounded at the truth in his eyes. He was not teasing her. There was no mirth in his gaze.

His look was pure.

It was rugged.

It was unpolished.

It was vulnerable.

It was hungry for her response.

It was . . . love.

Love? Yes, it was a pure, rugged, unpolished, vulnerable, and hungry sort of love.

"I have much to atone for," he said. "But allow me the chance to show you that I mean what I say. Elizabeth, I have struggled for weeks, painfully watching you wax and wane in health. I will not lose this opportunity, not when the risk of losing you has been such an unfriendly, but frequent, visitor of late. My chest is pounding, watching your every reaction as I share what I feel."

He paused suddenly, and she assessed her reaction to his continued boldness. Elizabeth did not feel shock nor disgust, and it was certainly not apathy.

She admired William Daniels' work ethic, as well as his consistent strength of character. She appreciated that he had a sense of humor. Many of the books he read were her favorites too, and he always offered perspectives that she had not seen previously.

If she had to qualify what she was feeling, how did she feel towards the man in front of her? If it was not shock, disgust, or apathy, dare she define it as hope?

He continued to wait patiently.

And remembering that the rest of the conversation was based on her reaction, she subtly nodded.

An enormous smile brightened his face once more. He fidgeted one way and then the other, responding excitedly. "Elizabeth, allow me to court you, to prove my devotion and adoration. I do not, in any measure, suppose you feel for me what has grown in me for you. I beg of you to give it time. I will prove my character and my ability to hungrily meet each and every one of your personal needs and serve you for all time."

As shocked as she was, she pondered why he only asked for a courtship. Of course he would ask for a courtship, as she was in mourning for Jane.

They could not enter into engagement or marriage, not when her favorite sister was hardly cold in her grave.

She remembered Jane, and how happy she would want Elizabeth to be. Her mind began warming with the thought that courting William would likely make Jane very happy that Elizabeth had found such devotion. It stirred a memory from not too long ago. Too many conversations about love and marriage had occurred over the years between the Bennet sisters—usually between just Jane and Elizabeth—but occasionally Mary joined in as well, each with different sensibilities or philosophies.

Mary was practical, insisting that marriage was a task, a requirement, and a necessary step to claiming the ultimate title of "mother." Marriage was not necessarily desired, but she did have preferences for her future spouse. He must have a deep respect for their betters, and be decisive and direct in his communication. She felt they could depend on her own intelligence to manage the finances and other household needs. But above all else, Mary insisted that he must put God first. For Mary, the ever-changing rules of propriety set by the ton *were constantly being assessed—and usually found wanting, for the most part. So her intended must be willing to cross those social boundaries when he feels a moral obligation to contest.*

It was Jane whose inner desires leaned far more towards the heart. She recognized this about herself, and even shared once that she would be willing to marry beneath her if it meant being married to someone who was entirely devoted and responded well to her carefully hidden emotions. She rarely shared her feelings; however, if she risked doing so, her husband must be attentive and responsive to those needs. It did come as a surprise, however, when the eldest Bennet sister sheepishly shared, "I do hope he is handsome too."

Rarely did Elizabeth fail to offer her opinions, for most who knew her loved her well because of her impertinent, outspoken mind.

But it took a great deal of prodding, even pressing her with guilt, to have Elizabeth share her views on marriage this time.

"We were willing to share with you. Do not fear us, we will not judge." Of course Jane would lead with gentleness and safety.

"You must match our openness. You cannot humor your way out of this topic." Logical Mary was dependable, that was for sure.

"My dear Lizzy, you are being so careful not to share your intimate thoughts, perhaps you might confide in us a sisters' worth of your thoughts." There was the guilt.

Jane's last comment was what finally made Elizabeth timidly disclose what she had known about herself for some time.

They had all been sitting on the bed Jane and Elizabeth shared, with their eyes on her expectantly. Elizabeth suddenly felt the bed was too small, even confining.

"It is true," she began. "I love to tease opinions and debates out of my associates. However, I pray as I divulge my stance on marriage that you not act surprised." She paused until her two sisters silently agreed.

Elizabeth drew a deep breath and pulled her knees up to her chest, wrapping her arms tight around them. "I only wish to marry for the deepest of love. That is it. I feel that if he truly loves me, and I him, then any hurdle or conflict we have between us will work itself out. I have no other requirements."

As she recalled saying those words to her sisters, Elizabeth spoke them aloud to Mr. Daniels. "I only wish to marry for the deepest of love. I have no other requirements."

"Truly? It does not disturb you that I am just a lieutenant? That I do not remember my family or where I came from?"

Her attempts not to smirk failed miserably, so she gave into the impulse and giggled. Elizabeth raised her eyebrow and cocked her head for a moment.

"You . . . you love me too?" he asked hesitantly.

"I am afraid, Mr. Daniels, that I failed to include how ardently I love and admire you. I believe I failed to say that for a very important reason. Forgive me, I see from your shock, even the hope in your eyes, that I must be more direct and filter my sarcasm, for both our sakes. I do not ardently love and admire you yet. However, I am willing to enter into a courtship. I will admit I am drawn to you when you speak. I am intrigued as I watch you interact among your peers. And if all we ever talk about is books, I think we shall never run out of conversation!"

She paused, swallowing the lump in her throat that had formed, then added, "That is an excellent foundation for the kind of love and respect that I desire. Of course, with the situation as it is, the courtship must last for a year." Her eyes glossed over with speaking of

Jane's death aloud, and with the last words, her voice cracked with emotion.

"Of course, I shall endeavor to patiently earn your love. May I say one more thing? You will not be disappointed. For reasons that are unknown to me, I am well trained in etiquette with ladies. I assure you that, at the end of one year, I shall be the only gentleman in the world whom you could ever be prevailed upon to marry."

Daniels stood, bowed deeply, and excused himself from the room, closing the door behind him.

She giggled again.

Perhaps he needs a refresher. I believe he has crossed the boundaries of etiquette already by being alone with me in my chambers. I am a compromised woman!

Instead of fearing what that meant, she turned over in bed and hugged her pillow, hiding the smile that had appeared with that thought. Another giggle escaped, muffled somewhat from the pillow, but she felt it deep in her chest.

CHAPTER 10

"Mr. Collins! I am just as surprised as you are, but I am afraid that my Lizzy—she is attached as well. Not officially, but he is an officer, and he has been at her sickbed nonstop. We expect that if she recovers an official announcement will be made."

Each of the Bennet sisters' necks lengthened in alert for what their mother might say. Their cousin, Mr. William Collins, had indeed arrived three weeks ago, the same night that they had been told of the accident. It had been quite miserable and, at times, intolerable for all of them.

Mr. Bennet was grateful that his wife had denied his cousin the chance to claim his favorite daughter. He knew that his Elizabeth would never find happiness with this fool.

Mr. Bennet took off his reading glasses and cleared his throat, hoping to gain the attention of his wife and his cousin, who likely had intended to have a private conversation across the room.

Mrs. Bennet started to comment again to Mr. Collins, offering, "But my Lydia . . ."

He cleared his throat again, louder this time, but it wasn't until his youngest, Lydia, whined to her mother, interrupting, "Mama! Perhaps we should hear Papa's thoughts on the subject! He surely would have grave objections to *Mr. Collins.*" She spoke his name as if it was sour milk, or unpalatable to even say his name.

She hadn't been wrong.

He was about to speak, but he noticed Mary stand abruptly. "Mr. Collins, would you accompany me on a walk through our gardens? You have not seen the west gardens. They are less tamed and a sight of the most natural beauty that God intended. I would like to hear more about the parish you govern. It must be ominous at times to be parson."

Mr. Bennet was not the only one shocked. By the look on Mr. Collins' face, and the stutter that accompanied his next statement, he was calculating and measuring the option of Mary as his wife as quickly as his fragile mind could.

"Ah, yes, yes. I have much to say about that. Miss Mary, am I correct?"

Mary nodded, looking down demurely in an overly feminine way that was more like his Jane than Mary.

Mr. Collins' confidence grew in an instant, "At times my effusions have filled my bosom, and the weight of the responsibility alone, of being prepared to administer at a moment's notice to Lady Catherine de Bourgh, my esteemed benefactor, is a task I do not take lightly. No, I do not. Not in any way. I have been invited to dine, and when I say dine, it is a far better spread than anything you could dream of being served at Longbourn, but nevertheless, I have been invited to dine three times . . ."

His cousin's ridiculous words trailed off as they exited the sitting room. Mr. Collins motioned for Mary to lead the way as he continued to speak. How did he manage to have breath for such long and ludicrous sentences?

From his position, Mr. Bennet curiously observed this strange situation while the pair put on their outerwear. Mr. Bennet could still hear Collins' overtly pretentious depiction of the esteemed Lady

Catherine de Bourgh. There was the occasional murmur of agreement from Mary, but eventually, the front door closed behind them ,and silence was finally upon those left behind.

The rest of his family had mouths agog to different extremes, but not a one of them dared speak. Mr. Bennet delivered a well-practiced look of sternness and, uncommonly obediently, all acknowledged his unspoken command.

In this he held firm. It was not the time to discuss what just occurred between Mr. Collins and Mary.

At last he would have the peace that he desperately needed, and hadn't had, for three weeks.

He placed his reading glasses back on, shaking his head in wonder. *Mary is one of my sensible ones!* That meant she understood what she had done, or offered, to his cousin. Mr. Bennet concluded that he would puzzle it out eventually, but for now, he would let the cards land where they may.

He cleared his mind with a rehearsed thought he had become accustomed to over the years, and it did not fail to bring him comfort, as it always had. *I shall never understand the silliness of my wife and daughters. It is an impossible feat to understand the workings of the mind of a woman.*

*****

Miss Elizabeth had just enjoyed the warmest bath that she could remember. Miss Bingley had kindly offered her fragrant salts that smelled delightful but were far too feminine for her taste. Of course she used them, but Elizabeth had asked for her own vanilla and caramel salts to be added as well. She did not want to disappoint her hostess.

She could not remember most of her illness. However, Miss Bingley had been at her bedside constantly, ever since she heard that she had nearly made a full recovery. She was excessively encouraging to Elizabeth, as she suggested being out of bed and eating frequently to gain back her strength. Elizabeth was grateful for the support; however, she couldn't ignore the suspicion about her underlying motive in getting her well.

Elizabeth was not naïve, but neither was she ungrateful, so she made sure to use the proffered bath salts. What Miss Bingley suggested was wise advice, and therefore Elizabeth always felt some shame in the fact that she accepted her kindness with unease.

With the exception of that first time, Daniels had no longer been allowed to stay in her chambers without a proper chaperone. Even at that, he seemed to come and go, anxious to see her, but once he did so, he was satisfied.

Miss Bingley, on the other hand, stayed for hours at a time. Conversations were unending, and rather shallow or held a spirit of meanness. However, Elizabeth had no other audience or source of entertainment.

Tonight was going to be different. Tonight she planned to dine with the master of Netherfield and his sister—and, of course, Mr. Daniels. It would just be the four of them. It would be the first time she would be downstairs for three weeks, which meant a thorough hot bath and some time spent taming her curls.

As the lady's maid began to put her hair into a simple braided bun, leaving plenty of locks around her face and at her neckline to naturally curl as they dried, Elizabeth pondered her new status.

Is this how a lady should look as she went to the first formal event with the gentleman she had entered into a courtship with? Her hair was worn in her favorite style. Simplicity was all she desired, but at the last minute, she asked Elaine to take a bit more time, perhaps two sets of braids leading to the bun. That lead to requesting a pearl or two at the bun, and Elaine smiled knowingly, which silenced any other requests from Elizabeth to improve her look.

With the hair completed, she adjusted her chemise, which was a bit too loose due to the weight she had lost. She saw through the mirror that the maid was bringing her pale yellow gown out of the wardrobe.

She turned around, "Elaine, no. Not yellow. I am in mourning. Have you not dyed any of my dresses black yet?"

Elaine had begun to approach her but halted. "Miss?"

Elizabeth smiled with her lips closed then softly comforted her. "Elaine, you have been very kind not to bring it up directly, but I am aware that Jane's outcome was not as favorable as mine. I will always be grateful for the efforts you made on her behalf. I promise to ask my father to compensate you as best we can."

"Pardon me, but Miss Elizabeth, I am afraid you are . . ."

"I know. Please, I cannot speak of it. Even now, my heart is too tender."

"But, miss!"

"I said not now. I have just pressed my face with powder, you would not want streaks now from tears, would you?" She sighed and apologized, "Forgive me, my nerves are shot. I have never heard myself sound l any more like my mother!"

"No, Miss Elizabeth, you are far from your mother's nature. I hope that was not too forward of me." She watched Elizabeth shake her head forgivingly and then added, "Perhaps the lilac dress?"

Elizabeth nodded. She would have preferred all black, out of respect, but there was nothing to be done this late in the hour.

Her unease grew further as she witnessed as well as felt the energy in the maid brighten. The change in Elaine's countenance, which was in no way flat before, rose to disturbingly cheerful levels. It was disturbing because it changed from pleasantly supportive and attentive to her needs to the energy levels of a child on Christmas morn.

Not another word was uttered between them while Elizabeth was helped into the dress. Elaine tugged and tucked, tied the ribbon, and then walked around to face Elizabeth, examining her from head to toe.

"There! I have never been more pleased with my work. I have no doubt that tonight you will be the happiest lady in Hertfordshire!"

Elizabeth's efforts to push her confusion away were in vain. The moment became more and more awkward. How could she be deemed the happiest lady in Hertfordshire and be grieving as well? She curtsied and said, "That would be a blessing from on high. Thank you, though, for your kind attempts. But I will moderate my happiness, as is appropriate for the situation."

If it was possible for Elaine to smile wider, she did.

Elizabeth brows furrowed, belaying the words she spoke. "Thank you again." Elizabeth turned to leave, glancing back at the maid over her shoulder.

The smile was almost wicked.

She hadn't walked three meters into the hallway when she was hailed from behind. "Miss Elizabeth, may I escort you to dinner?"

She turned and smiled, tilted her head, and curtsied. "That would be much appreciated. I am afraid it has been some time since I tried to find my way around Netherfield unescorted. When I was a child, the young master was fond of me. He demonstrated that in the typical eight-year-old manner, hiding from me in these rooms, only to scare me as I searched for him. Of course, he was supposed to be hiding, and I was to seek him out, but he never failed to find me himself. Usually with a tweak of my nose or a tap to the left shoulder, then moving to the right so I saw no one behind me."

Daniels smiled widely as he took her arm and proceeded forward. He had trimmed his beard and mustache much shorter than she had seen him in the last two days she had been awake, or ever, for that manner. He had even left the sides of his beard descending from his ears longer, in a well-defined exaggerated angle, as was customary these days.

He was very attractive, in a rugged sort of way. *Honestly, Elizabeth, he is handsome in any way!*

She continued examining him. There was evidence of an old, large irregular scar along the jaw and lower lip, which explained why he wore the beard in the first place. The more she looked at him, the warmer her cheeks felt.

There is only one thing to do! *You must look away,* she told herself. If she was successful, her cheeks should return to a natural shade by the time the main floor was reached.

Reluctantly, she followed her own advice.

The pair descended the stairs far more gracefully than she had ever felt. He had placed his left hand over her hand, which was wrapped around his right arm, making her feel secure in her footing going down the stairs. She smiled up at him. "Thank you. This is very helpful. I am afraid I am not at my usual strength."

He nodded, closing his eyes momentarily, and then his chest rose and his shoulders broadened. Was he proud to have her on his arm? She had never considered that a gentleman would desire her approval, let alone be effected so significantly.

They were six stairs from the main floor when she heard the voice of an angel. She stopped, searching frantically for the voice. It couldn't be! Had she lost her sanity?

But then she saw her!

"Jane!" Elizabeth detangled herself from the lieutenant in an instant. Her feet could not move fast enough! She picked up her skirts and ran to her sister.

Her arms wrapped around her, and the confirmation that her sister was alive and not some ethereal representation—or even worse, a mirage created in her sorrow to comfort herself. She did not want to let go, but she also wanted to see Jane's beautiful face again.

She mumbled her affection for her dear sweet Jane through choking sobs that were just as surprising to her as they were to Jane and everyone else around them who politely observed the reunion.

Although she hadn't noticed the tears, her heart and mind confirmed that she had not gone mad. She could touch her dear sister, smell her, and now she desperately wanted to see her again, just to reassure herself.

She grasped her sister's shoulders and pulled away just enough to gaze upon her sister, who was looking confused and entertained at the same time. "How? How are you alive? I thought . . . I thought I had lost you forever."

"Lizzy, I am very much alive and, apart from the broken hand, am extremely well."

"But where were you these last two days? No one updated me. No one corrected me when I said I was in mourning . . . except perhaps Elaine. Now I see she was attempting to correct me. Oh, I was awful to her!"

"The maid?" Bingley asked.

Elizabeth started laughing with what became a combination of unattractive sobs and sniffles. Someone touched her left shoulder, and she turned her head to see that Mr. Daniels was offering a handkerchief. She released her grip on her sister and took the offering.

While Elizabeth dabbed at her nose, Jane put a loving arm around her shoulder and guided her to the dining room. "Forgive me, I was . . . oh, Lizzy! I have so much to share! Mr. Bingley has asked for my hand in marriage. I was in London picking out fabric for my wedding."

Elizabeth's sobbing began again in earnest, this time in delight.

"My sweet Jane! I am so happy for you! You are, each of you, so complying, that nothing will ever be resolved on; so easy, that every servant will cheat you; and so generous, that you will always exceed your income."

Her favorite, healthy, and alive sister blushed so brightly that Bingley came to rescue her.

"Miss Bennet? I suggest we not delay Cook from delivering her finest. She has hung on the ready for Miss Elizabeth's recovery status to change sufficiently so she could make her specialty. I am told that no one can match the white soup or the truffle-seasoned potatoes. But, my friend, she intends to spoil us with crab-stuffed mushrooms and a lobster roll."

Bingley stood taller with well-deserved pride, especially when the crowd let out polite moans when the food was described.

Mr. Daniels then took Elizabeth's left arm at the same moment that Bingley took Jane's, and they sat for dinner.

The entire dinner was exquisite, and impossible to improve on the food served.

However, Miss Bingley never joined them. It must have been a misunderstanding that the fourth person was to be Jane!

The four of them made the night so magical, so memorable, that Elizabeth found herself in a deeply contented but contemplative mood when dessert was served. She felt such joy. As they delved into their strawberry ice with mint leaves, she observed how happy the intended couple were. Jane was perhaps the most happy that Elizabeth had ever seen her.

The hair on her neck moved, alerting her of Daniels' closer presence. In fact, the gooseflesh on her neck felt his presence before she heard him speak.

His breath was low and a bit breathy. "I am afraid, Miss Elizabeth, that my friend and your sister have set the bar vastly high when it comes to marital felicity."

She hadn't missed the mirth in Mr. Daniels' voice and turned her head in his direction to witness his charming smile, confirming the humor he intended. She teased him back. "Oh? Is that so? Do I sense trepidation that you can 'hungrily meet each and every one of my personal needs'? Are you hoping to rephrase your promise from two days ago?"

"Certainly not. Not only will I stand firm in what I said, but I shall up the ante." He paused, and his face became sincere and genuine.

She waited, not realizing she was holding her breath.

The jest in his tones had entirely dissipated. "You will never, never envy the amount of happiness in the future for Mrs. Bingley, for ours will not be measurable."

CHAPTER 11

The following week, Elizabeth and William held the equivalent of a month's worth of conversation. Many times it was over tea; in fact, Daniels was sure he had never drank as much tea before. But what more could they do? She had been in bed for over a month, and he was repeatedly reminded of how close to death she had come. She would try to hide it, but her eyelids would grow heavy, or he would watch her rub her thoughtful eyes, stating they were dryer than usual. But he knew when she had reached her limit.

When her endurance lasted longer than mid-morning, they began to take their tea outside and tour the closest gardens. She had always said that it does no one good to sit in one attitude for so long. He admired her desire to return to full strength and to push herself beyond what was simply easy, or what her current abilities were.

He saw a beauty of the spirit that drove her constantly. If she was too fatigued, she would inquire

244

what he had seen in the theatre. He knew all the dramas and tragedies, but he was less a fan of the superficial comedies. Not surprisingly, she enjoyed the wit of the comedies as well as the subtle sparing in them.

Of course, books were a constant topic of discussion, one that she could usually maintain, even when her energy was less animated.

All of it—the conversations, the quiet times ambulating in the house or assisting the gardener to finalize the grounds for winter, or the moment she fell asleep next to him in the library—none of it truly matched what he had expected to share with Elizabeth now that they were courting.

It had, in fact, far exceeded his grandest expectations.

And it had all been worth it as he watched her transition from stiff and working hard at maintaining conversation to a more comfortable, natural state of being.

She laid aside the rapid-fire questioning and began to appear comfortable in the silence they shared. He constantly reminded himself not to push her physically, or emotionally, and that they had all the time in the world for her to fall in love with him.

He doubted she loved him, certainly not like he cherished her, but she began to tease him instead of prattling nervously. When he suggested that they read a book together, intending to each read their own copy, she was energetic about doing so. However, he was surprised her intention was to sit together, occupying the same sofa, and reading out of the same bound copy! When he read to her, sometimes she would follow along on the page; other times she would relax against him, gazing around the room.

But when she read to him, it was his chance to gaze unabashedly upon her, taking in her beauty without it becoming awkward.

Tonight, however, the library had become chilly. It wasn't the first time she had become drowsy or drifted off to sleep, but this time—oh, dear Lord—this time she hadn't just drifted off to sleep. He knew already that this would become one of his favorite moments in all memory.

What started with him having his arm around the back of the sofa and her moving closer to follow along in the book slowly, inch by inch, had turned into the position in which they were now in. He doubted she realized what she had done in her sleepiness.

First, she relaxed against his arm and shoulder, and then, as she shifted while he read, she had taken off her slippers and tucked them under her skirts; eventually she leaned her neck and head onto his chest. She must not have been entirely comfortable, at least until now. Because eventually, as she squirmed, one of her arms had reached around his waist and, every now and then, she would squeeze and sigh.

But he kept reading, afraid she might notice the silence and waken. She would waken to find her arms draped around him and her bosom against his lower chest. Of course, her head prevented any inappropriate glances in that direction, but vision is overrated. He could feel her breathing, in and out, and her chest pressing with varying levels of pressure against him.

So he focused intently on the reading.

It was not only a distraction from the intense sensations that wracked his entire being, but when he did stop momentarily here or there to sip his cold tea, he realized that the vibration in his chest while he read seemed to keep her sleeping. And without the diverting vibrations, his mind could make out each curve, even playing out in his mind what he should not yet do.

He knew he must give her time. He had already crossed too many boundaries by being at her side in her sickbed, so he must maintain propriety. Her questions about why Bingley would let him do so had become more subtle, less direct, and recently they had stopped altogether. He wondered if she had come to accept what was and move forward. But he knew better. She was not naïve, nor was she unrespectable.

Eventually he would have to tell her about how she had collapsed into his arms in the hall that night, and he had brought her to his chambers. What had he been thinking? He could have returned her to her room that very moment. Or any moment in the following three hours he spent watching her sleep in the armchair from the doorway, debating on how or when to remove her from his chambers. Eventually she would be told that Bingley witnessed him carrying her, him in a nightshirt and open vest and her in her nightclothes, her bosom minimally modest.

Eventually he would have to admit that he had compromised her already and that being by her side in the sickbed meant little compared to that.

*****

Wickham was pleased. He was escorting Lady Anne through the Pemberley grounds, just as he had done for the last several days. It had taken him about a week of fawning and enduring wet shoulders as she cried before she was persuaded to leave the roof of the estate.

He continued to grieve with Anne De Bourgh, who was no longer just Darcy's cousin; somehow, she had also married Fitzwilliam Darcy's father! His old school chum, presumed missing or dead for the past five years, now had a cousin who was also his stepmother! Of course, it was on the opposite side of the family.

But even with the admitted lowness of Wickham's moral platform, he found room enough to let chills run up and down his spine when he thought of that.

Who else knew that young Darcy was still alive? Over the last two weeks, as he infiltrated the staff and occupants of Pemberley, he had become confident that he was the only one who knew that Fitzwilliam Darcy was alive and well, serving in the militia in a small town in Hertfordshire.

I believe it needs to stay that way.

Wickham had been raised on Pemberley grounds through the age of twelve while his father served as steward of Pemberley. Because young master Darcy was his same age, George Wickham was allowed to accompany his father to work each day. George and the young master had the same nursery maids, tutors, and masters.

With his father as steward, William had been raised with all the benefits of a true Darcy.

His father was well respected. The estate was run pristinely, with regular, healthy profits and yields from the tenants. The last time George Wickham had been at Pemberley was more than seven years ago. He had been invited back when his own father had died suddenly. Not only was that enough time to secure admittance and financial support to attend university from Darcy's father, but Wickham was proud at how well he used his grief for his father to secure a living after he graduated. Sadly, the living that was granted was for the parish, and Wickham knew that was no life for him.

Apparently, there had not been a steward since his father had died who could handle the estate more than nine months. Now another new steward was on the premises, and Mr. Brew was young, inexperienced, and hungry for advice.

Being steward was a daunting position, but if his father could do it then George Wickham could too.

He had plans to be the true heir to Pemberley. . . well, heir to the position of steward. He was qualified, after all; he had been through a few years of university before being asked to leave. Not to mention, he was his father's son! He was qualified and eager too, perhaps heavy on the eagerness.

Over the last two weeks, William worked in two directions, massaging them both equally.

Wickham had helped Mrs. Anne de Bourgh Darcy overcome grief, offering a friendly shoulder to cry on.

But he was perhaps the most proud of his excellent advice to the overwhelmed Mr. Brew, advice given both solicited and unsolicited.

William didn't quite know how it would pan out, but he was working to ensure that he had options which did not include being arrested for desertion or having to follow orders. Wickham had been granted a month's leave and was already in the process of requesting more; however, the militia would not be forgiving if he never returned. So he must have a living before he quit.

Lord help him, he never wished to dig trenches or carry diseased bodies again.

He was destined for the life of leisure. He felt most at ease with a bottle of port, a cigar, and rolls of money in his hands with which to drown him and his friends.

Pemberley's steward was the most likely of positions; however, Lady Anne had shown a great deal of neediness recently. She had a desperate need for companionship, and a need for affection from those who loved her, and Wickham was willing to help the widow in any way possible—just as he was doing right now.

She had been rambling on about several topics, and he nodded, offering shocked expressions when it seemed appropriate, but he didn't care to truly listen. That is, until the next words fell from her mouth.

"This is terribly forward of me, but I find solace in your presence here. Do you think I could write to your commanding officer and request more leave? Perhaps through the winter? I cannot part with you next week. I have never lived alone before. I simply panic when I think of it!"

Her voice cracked, and she released his arm to cover her face with her gloved hands. Her shoulders shook, and he moved in.

Grasping her, he made the slightest of motions to bring her in, and wouldn't you know it? The sobbing woman rushed into his arms with her staining tears again!

He had just had this greatcoat cleaned! He sighed as he patted her back.

Wickham may have been an opportunist, but he also had another talent. Knowing how to fish.

He knew that the line had been cast, and her nibbling had begun; he also knew it would only become stronger if Wickham pulled her in then pointedly pushed her away.

She must question his affection. And he must only offer that affection on his terms, in his timing. It was vital that he gratify her need to know if her love was returned but not when she asked for it to be gratified.

His favorite time to do so was when a woman was the most emotional and in the most doubt of her own worth or ability to deserve his love. Then, and only then, would he shower her with excessive affection.

Saturate her with the respect one would give a queen. He would exceed her expectations and validate every ounce of her insecurities.

You could call it a game of cat and mouse. Or a fox hunt. Or call it what it was: an arrogant philanthropist's game to secure an heiress. Being raised with the Darcys, he was fully aware how distasteful that game was, so instead of being that brutally honest, he usually thought of his actions as "ensuring a relationship of convenience."

Don't feel sorry for her, he thought to himself. Any wild game that is being hunted knows it is being hunted. They have every chance to run or escape, but they never do.

The reasoning for that always eluded him.

Why didn't they run? Why didn't Anne see his falsified affection or notice the irregularities in what he said compared to what he did?

As he held Anne close, allowing more closeness than a widow should be held, he leaned down and kissed her exposed neck, then felt her melt into him.

The timing was perfect.

He stepped away.

Only *he* would be allowed to define their relationship. But it had to sound genuine. So he apologized profusely.

He then turned his back to her, and even though they had walked out over a mile from Pemberley, he abandoned the confused woman.

Wickham smiled to himself as he heard Anne Darcy calling out to him to wait for her.

Why don't the hunted animals run?

His larger strides had obtained a measurable lead on her.

His smile transitioned to chuckles, and he answered his own question. "They do not run because I run first, making them chase me."

There is nothing worse for a woman who has been abandoned than being abandoned again.

He chuckled to himself and said to himself, "I most certainly can release my sights on steward! I shall run Pemberley in no time, but as master of Pemberley!"

Oh, how he enjoyed the hunt.

Patience, George, game meat is more tender as it ages. No need to go for it while savage and raw.

But even that sounded enticing, enough to require dabbing his handkerchief to the side of his lips.

*****

Elaine was practically dancing around Elizabeth this morning. She would hum one tune and then, in mid-song, change to another. The lady's maid was eccentric, but she was transparent too.

"Pray tell, what is the cause for such elation?" Elizabeth asked.

"Hmmm? Oh, me? Would you like me to stop humming? Is it bothering you?"

"Certainly not. If it were songs I was familiar with, I would hum along with you. But you are smiling today."

"Oh, miss, I always smile. It is how I tell the day who is in charge."

"It is a different smile today, perhaps one that is cheeky. Or maybe one that shows you have news that you are desperately wanting to reveal?"

"Perhaps it is not my secret to share!"

Elizabeth felt her mouth drop in surprise. "You do! You have a secret!"

The lady's maid started to hum again in earnest, then picked up the hairbrush.

Elizabeth caught the brush in midair and threatened, just as cheekily. "Disclose a morsel, or I shall not let you attend to my hair."

"You wouldn't dare go down the stairs so disgracefully, with your curls all around your face. I know you better than that."

Elizabeth giggled but then resumed her threatening face. "Oh, you presume too much! You are correct. I would not go down so unpresentable. No, I am not that presumptuous or desperate. I would do something far worse! I would tousle the work you are doing with that hairbrush, and give you all the credit for my distressed look!"

This time it was Elaine's turn to drop her jaw. She exhaled in a huff, revealing just how young she was, and said, "There are interesting rumors from the kitchen staff, that is all."

"About..." Elizabeth prodded.

"About you and Mr. Daniels. Good rumors too."

Elaine had held a significant amount of distrust towards Mr. Daniels but as the days passed, she seemed to warm to him. But today, it was much more than acceptance, it was excitement and unabashed approval!

Elaine waited for a short moment, smiled widely, then the news spilled out like a milk bucket that had been kicked. "Mr. Daniels was drinking in his study last night with Mr. Bingley. They were discussing Mr. Bingley's wedding plans. Jeffery, the night footman, was gathering the last of the port glasses when he heard Mr. Daniels tell Bingley that he loved you. No, it was that he 'dearly loved you.'

"I hope I get this next part right," she continued, the words now tumbling out. "Mr. Bingley asked him when he knew he was in love. You know, when did his feelings for you all start? Can you believe he would be so unswerving? One cannot back out of answering such a direct question as that. No, ma'am. Jeffery heard him say, 'I was in the middle before I knew it had begun.'"

Elaine placed the hairbrush to her heart with both hands then collapsed into the chair by the window.

Elizabeth felt her cheeks warm but not out of embarrassment; this feeling was something new altogether. "Fate has been kind to me. It has brought me Mr. Daniels."

*****

"Good morning, Miss Elizabeth. Do you feel strong enough to walk in the gardens? There are benches along the way, if needed."

Elizabeth did not even need to check how the weather looked outside, for her impulses and natural longing for the outdoors spoke for her. "Yes! A resounding yes!"

Elizabeth did not quite have her physical impulses at par yet, but she stood as quickly as she dared and followed Daniels to the front. Her steps were strong but slower than before the accident.

While Daniels spoke with the butler, requesting that two of the strongest footmen follow them from ten or more yards back, Jane protested as Elizabeth donned her pelisse and scarf. "Do you really feel you can do it? What if you get a certain distance and then lack the strength to return?"

Elizabeth nodded her head to the conversation behind her, just as Daniels amended his earlier request. "Perhaps three footmen would be better," he said. "But make them strong. Perhaps they could pull the handcart, just in case."

Jane smiled as Elizabeth winked. "If he could, I believe the lieutenant would ask eagles to scout the perimeter for predators in a two-mile radius."

Jane giggled in to her hand. "Or perhaps he could request Netherfield to give up its stock of magic beans, just in case you needed an immediate escape."

Elizabeth joined in Jane's giggling, then forced her face to become somber. "Magic beans? But that would simply encourage the giants to come!"

They both looked to Daniels, who glanced their way. A flicker of confusion flashed across his eyes when he noticed that both ladies wore exaggerated smiles on their faces.

Of course, that only made Elizabeth laugh harder.

His look transitioned from confusion to pleasure when he saw her delight.

He offered his arm. "Shall we?"

Jane took the opportunity to tug on Elizabeth's bonnet one more time to ensure no wind would hit her ears. She looked Elizabeth straight in the eye and smiled impishly. With Jane's back to Daniels, Jane winked at her sister. "Do not do anything I would not approve of."

Elizabeth gave her an exaggerated look, not quite rolling her eyes but definitely along that nature. "Thank you, Jane," she said dryly. "I will not ask you to be more specific."

Daniels wouldn't try to kiss her, would he? Would she allow it if he did? Her mind went blank with that thought.

It was not easy keeping her blush hidden from her walking companion, but she found solace in the fact that he was comfortable without conversation.

They walked for some time. The air was brisk, and each was actively looking around, deliberately not looking at each other.

This was the first time that they had been alone besides those short minutes the day she awoke from her illness. There was a new energy this morning that pushed their individual thoughts.

Elizabeth knew where her thoughts were. At the beginning, she was successful in pushing her mind away from the private nature of this walk and what might happen. But each time she glanced in his direction, her mind returned to the possibility of her first kiss like a stray dog that has finally been fed.

She had never wanted to kiss a gentleman before.

It was becoming more and more clear that, in the current situation, there was a growing amount of both desire and opportunity to kiss him.

However, neither the desire nor opportunity, even combined, was of greater magnitude than the trepidation she felt for the kiss.

Elizabeth understood that she was in a courtship with Lieutenant Daniels. She knew she respected him. She knew their conversations were highly entertaining and challenging. However, was she ready to allow the relationship to progress?

A kiss from William Daniels would likely be well performed and masterly delivered. Would he kiss more than once? A series of kisses, perhaps, stacked onto the one just delivered?

As she redirected her thoughts again, she was grateful for the silent companionship, for the silence was comforting to her.

Unfortunately the silence did not last. "The weather has been temperate. You have not had the chance to see and experience the early winter this year. It was a pleasure to watch the last of the leaves fall or be blown away. The autumn colors have been moderated to the neutral, hibernating greys and browns of winter."

Elizabeth looked toward her companion, but he was looking straight ahead. Perhaps he was doing so with concentration, his own efforts to hide his unease.

She murmured her agreement but then fell silent again.

Her hand that was on his arm was less covered and felt more chilled than the other, even though she felt the warmth of his arm on the palm through her glove.

After a few more minutes of walking, he spoke again. "It is your turn now, Miss Elizabeth. I talked about the trees, and you ought to make some sort of remark on the size of Mother Nature's trickery or the amount of birds that are still around."

"Whatever you wish me to say, I will. She has definitely tricked the birds into thinking winter is not yet upon us."

"That reply will do for the present." Mr. Daniels turned his head slightly and tipped his hat at her with a gentle smile. Then he sighed heavily.

They continued in this manner, with their steps slow and steady, only interrupted by the occasional deep intake of a breath by Daniels, as if he was about to speak. Yet he didn't say a word, not another word for nearly ten minutes.

Elizabeth had plenty of time to assess the reason for his timidity in conversation. She acknowledged it wasn't far from his natural tendency to brood, but he seemed more contemplative than usual. She feared that the last week and a half may have overwhelmed him. She admitted that to be courted was overwhelming. She couldn't imagine the pressure he felt to woo her, especially since his attachment to her seemed greater than hers was in return.

It was Elizabeth this time who took the courageous breath. "Is there something on your mind besides the weather?"

"The weather?"

"Well, yes. That is the only topic of conversation we have shared."

"Ah, yes, I recall now . . . the number of trees and the trickery of winter . . ." His words trailed off then started again. This time his words did not seem to correlate to the topic they had discussed earlier. "The moment you think you have what you always wanted, it changes. Trickery. Splendid, is it not? Perhaps, but deceitful to the core."

He reached his free hand out in front of him, palm up, then pulled it in toward his body briskly, his fingers clawing and attempting to grasp at an unseen item. "It is right there, within my grasp." His hand relaxed then lifted, as if he was releasing a butterfly. "And yet, snatched away. I wonder if I simply dreamt all of it."

William paused and took a steady breath before saying, "I should never have allowed myself to hope. No, no, no. Hope has never served this master, but it likely knows I am entirely its slave."

Elizabeth desperately wanted to ask him to clarify, but somehow she knew to be patient.

They walked a bit further, and he replaced his hand, the one that had just been demonstrating his point dramatically, back onto her hand.

And once again, it was a wordless amble.

Worry engulfed her. The weight of the dread she felt instantly replaced all the anticipation for her first kiss she had previously had.

Suddenly he stopped walking and turned to her. His eyes were darker than usual and intensely penetrating. There was a new level of pain in them. A pain that was directed at her!

"My sweet Elizabeth, how I wish things were different..."

"No. Please, do not say it." She did not want to hear he had changed his mind. How could she give her heart and word so quickly? By now all of Meryton had heard of their courtship. And now he was rethinking his choice? Was there something lacking in her countenance? Her looks? She knew she was not ideal, but she kept herself presentable and had admirable attributes.

She was about to look away from him in shame, but confusion flashed briefly across his face, pausing her to question her theory of what he had been about to share.

She looked down instead and murmured, "Forgive me. I tend to speak too hastily." Then, looking back up at him, she caught the softness in his eyes that she was becoming accustomed to.

He took both her hands and softly smiled. "It might be easier for me to speak plainly instead of in metaphors. The militia have been called north."

"North? But, so far ... north? Where?" Her words were trying to catch the breath that was stolen from her. Anywhere but Meryton was too far.

"We can write. We can arrange for travel a few times, with a chaperone, of course. You had said you wanted a yearlong courtship, and I am afraid that it is what this will be."

"But where?"

"They have not shared the details of the exact location yet."

He gazed at her tenderly, apologetically.

"But I will be here." She looked away as she said it, almost afraid to have it confirmed. But she already knew he would be leaving.

"Yes, my sweet."

He looked again at her, tilting his head to the side, trying to catch her line of vision.

She had found great comfort in their conversations, even from their first confrontation the day the militia cleaned the trench. Now that she had someone to impress, Elizabeth even allowed the lady's maid to adorn and dress her with greater care. Elaine did not mind one thread's worth that Elizabeth was allowing her to use her skills.

It had all been for Lieutenant Daniels, a man she had become quite fond of. Elizabeth had even admitted to Elaine that very morning how kind fate had been to her.

She reluctantly caught his eyes again. They were probing her for something.

"Elizabeth, my sweet, you must ask the next question. The where I am going is not nearly as devastating as the when."

Her heart dropped from her chest. "No, no. . . please, no."

"I leave in two days' time."

Suddenly she knew Jane had been right. She no longer had the strength to make it back.

Her heart may have dropped earlier, but the rest of her followed.

*****

As he entered Netherfield, William heard the breathlessness in his voice as he said, "She is well. Truly, she is well. Do not fret."

Daniels' feet moved quickly through the Netherfield mob, all whom were attempting to help in some way.

Questions came from all sides, but he only cared to ensure Elizabeth's safety.

"Did she take a spill?"

"Is it a fever again?"

"Let me take her from you."

"Cook! Make fresh tea! Extra hot!"

William continued determinedly through the entryway. "Make way. She simply got fatigued." He had caught her when she fainted, and it had been a brisk walk carrying her back to Netherfield. But there was no chance he was going to pass her onto someone less careful than himself.

As he hurriedly approached the nearest chaise, he slowed his feet and cautiously lowered her limp body to its red-velvet cushions.

The Netherfield staff immediately surrounded her. One brought blankets, another worked at untying her ankle-high boots, while yet another was wiping the stray hair from her beautiful face.

When he heard Jane's frightened gasp from behind him, he turned and answered what he knew she needed to hear. "She is well, just fatigued." He gave her a reassuring look, but she returned it with a look that doubted him.

"You told her." Jane did not ask it, she knew.

As did he.

It had been too early to shock her with his departing regiment.

He nodded. "I had hoped . . ."

"Mr. Daniels, thank you for all you have done. I need to attend to my sister."

Jane Bennet was usually cheerful and excruciating polite, but as she determinedly walked forward to Elizabeth, he knew he must step out of the way.

Bingley put his arm on his shoulder. "Come, she appears to have her color back. Let us make arrangements for the next several days. Elizabeth can be in no finer hands than my angel."

CHAPTER 12

It took several minutes to absorb her surroundings, but when Elizabeth recalled the walk with Daniels, all consciousness rushed back upon her.

Elizabeth must have been brought to her chambers, or at least the ones she had occupied for the last month.

She quickly sat up, searching for her slippers or boots. She could hear someone in the adjacent room, where Elaine usually helped her bathe.

She could see she had been placed in bed with her gown in place, yet the ties in the back felt loose. Reaching to her hair, she felt it in disarray, not completely down, but much of it was.

A new energy flooded her veins, and she called out while making quick work of the distance into the washroom. "Elaine! Help me become presentable. I must see William. . ." Her words trailed off in seeing that William himself was testing the bath water with Jane and Elaine observing him.

"Mr. Daniels!" was all that came out of her mouth, and for the life of her, she could not close her jaw all the way.

"Elizabeth, are you well?"

"Quite! Well, I suppose I was." Her need to see him froze as she realized the intimacy of where they were. The time it took to process the absurdity and rather unorthodox—*no . . . it was worse than that! It was highly irregular and improper!*

"Hello, sir, but please exit my washroom." Her instinctual words whirled from her mouth. She was clearly more worried now about her reputation than about seeing Mr. Daniels.

She held her gaze with determination. She wanted to look away from the pain and confusion she saw on his face. She wasn't quite sure where the emotion in her words came from, but she had said them nonetheless.

His confusion bruised her heart a bit. After all, he had been allowed in her very bedchambers, at her side even, while she was sick. She knew they had shared short periods of privacy; she had woken to him and him alone on occasion. He had earned Bingley's trust in some way, but to risk Elizabeth's reputation?

A mental framing began, almost from the beginning, as she casually inquired about the oddness of Bingley's permission. It could not have been any small thing. But her initial framing for understanding was simply this: the more she had learned, the more she did not want to know.

His confusion was only a reflection of her own lack of understanding.

He blinked a moment or two more, then bowed stiffly, walked passed her, and exited her bathroom, with full intentions to abandon her.

She heard Elaine mutter under her breath. "Obstinate, headstrong girl—" the last word had been sharply cut off. Jane likely had given the lady's maid subtle, and physical, encouragement to hold her tongue.

Elizabeth looked down as William passed her, and she knew having him leave was not what she wanted. At least not what she wanted *most*.

Moments ago, she had woken up frantically, with a singular purpose. She wanted to see William. And with her elder sister and maid in the washroom, they were well chaperoned.

She turned around. "Wait!"

He paused but did not turn.

"Mr. Daniels, perhaps I spoke too hastily. I am not accustomed to having gentlemen in my washroom. It is highly unusual, even for a couple with an agreement as we have. Do you not agree?"

She had not noticed that his shoulders had been hanging, but when he turned around, pleased to see that both of them were wearing apologetic smiles, she welcomed his urgent footsteps, and they embraced.

He held her head to his chest for a moment, his lips whispering something unintelligible to her, and she embraced him back cautiously. Well, perhaps it was cautiously at first.

When soft tears clouded her vision, she hugged him even tighter.

They were not tears of sadness, for how could they be? They were tears of understanding. The two felt a similar union, perhaps not in equal proportion as her feelings were just becoming known to herself. But there was no denying that they were of the same accord.

Her tears were also tears of gratitude. How could one not be thankful to have a person as selfless as William in their life?

And finally, the tears were of farewell. Or perhaps better said, longing. They had but two short days left to be in each other's company.

She pulled away slightly, and he gave way reluctantly.

"We have time, William. But I stand firm in our agreement. This does not change anything between you and I but that of the method of communication."

A subtle smile crossed his face, and he nodded. "Are you well? I could never forgive myself if anything I said had endangered you."

She stepped away and looked for the first time to her sister, nodding her head subtly to the door, silently asking for privacy.

Jane hesitated before finally saying, "Elaine, please attend to the bed linen. It appears my sister has recovered in an instant. She has color in her cheeks to spare."

"Yes, Miss Bennet. Of course, Miss Bennet. Right away." Elaine paused in her walking and turned to Jane, asking, "Perhaps you wish to inspect my work?"

Jane looked to Daniels as she answered the maid. "I am confident in your honor and reputation. You have been well recommended by my associates. But, yes, I will observe from afar." Jane followed Elaine into the bedroom, making no attempt to close the adjoining door.

Elizabeth had watched her sister with a smile, for she was a dear and loyal sister; however, Jane's trust was hard to earn among new acquaintances. Jane's words were the harshest direction she had ever heard her sister give. And there was no doubt the direction was not aimed at Elaine.

Smiling reassuringly, she received a final look from Jane before she exited.

Elizabeth and William were alone. There were so many things they needed to talk about. She had so many questions, so many fears.

Suddenly, her hands were being gently lifted from where they had hung casually by her sides. William had softly grasped them, rubbing his thumbs along the back of them, his gaze fixated on them. His concentration was that of an artist admiring another's work.

She too was watching their hands casually dance in each other's fingers. Eventually her eyes followed when her right hand was lifted up.

He placed a simple kiss on it. However, the kiss could not be described as simple; no, not in the slightest. His lips had brushed the top of her knuckles just a bit, from side to side, dragging the softer bristles of his beard so lightly that it tickled the soft skin.

She felt such wonder at what had just occurred. Not at the act of the kiss itself; rather, she was in awe at the reaction she had had.

William paused momentarily and looked up, still slightly bowed over her hand, and caught her wondrous eyes.

As Elizabeth smiled back at him encouragingly, he stood upright slowly.

As he did so, she studied his face more thoroughly. His eyes had softened, even deepened, since she had first become acquainted with him. His beard was groomed with exquisite care, following his memorable jawline with precision.

But it was not the beard or the jaw she was unknowingly searching for.

Her cheeks flushed a bit when she realized she was staring at his lips. Before she could look away, he brought her chin back to the forward position and then gently tilted her face upwards.

"I love your chin, Miss Elizabeth Bennet." The back of his fingers brushed the jaw from chin to ear, where he repeatedly tucked a stray curl behind her ear in a methodical manner. Each time he brushed the hair behind her ear, he returned to do it again.

She closed her eyes and admitted to herself that she did not wish him to stop. At the very moment she had that thought, he began following the curl down her neck just a bit, pausing halfway down.

She never imagined feeling the sensations William created by caressing her neck.

William's slow-moving fingers altered their course from touching her with the back of his fingers to caressing her with the very tips of them. He seemed to focus on that area of her neck just above where it connected to her shoulders. He would pause in one area, then dance a feather-light touch to another spot until he moved again.

He had been trying to find her pulse.

Heat flooded her as she realized what he was searching for, and she knew that very pulse would prove the anticipation she had been attempting to conceal.

He leaned toward her neck, which somehow had become slightly tilted to the side, exposing more silky skin. Had she tilted her neck welcoming his touch?

She needed another steadying breath, and there was enough time to take two or three at the pace he was leaning in. Then again, perhaps her breath had quickened a bit.

William moved even closer, then paused just inches from her skin, which was now likely riddled with gooseflesh from feeling his warm breath on her bare skin. He hesitated no more than four or five seconds, with his fingertips lingering lightly on her neck, when she heard him take a slow inhalation.

"May I?" he asked in an extremely deep, husky voice. It was also breathy, which sent the gooseflesh again into high attention.

She was unable to make a sound, at least not one that would amount to anything more than a squeak, so she simply tilted her head even further to the side, allowing him access.

He was still holding her right hand, so he squeezed it, pulling it to his chest. He reluctantly released it, but only to rotate the palm, placing it right where his heart was. As he pressed her palm to his chest, his penetrating eyes looked further than anyone had looked into her. William released her hand, letting it continue to rest on his chest. His hand moved upward to cup the weight of her head while his other hand and arm wrapped around her waist, pulling her hips towards him.

Like a hummingbird to a flower, he placed numerous small kisses to her neck, up and down, repeating the process until her head began to spin. With each kiss, he only parted from her skin long enough to return for another, just at the exact moment when she missed it and desired it the most. Her heart sped up as his kisses trailed back towards her neck to her jaw.

His lips parted from her skin long enough to search her eyes for permission.

She wanted more than anything to feel that miraculous sensation on her lips, for she had become exceedingly envious of, first, her hand, and now her neck.

But she need not have been jealous. He was extremely charitable to her lips as well.

Each time William placed his lips on hers, Elizabeth was overcome with energy, her heart pounding in her chest with such intensity and longing, her conscience screaming that it was not Christian of her. The magnetic pull of her heart launching from the safe and protected home it had known for so long was dizzying.

What was she doing?

Was it Christian? Perhaps not.

Natural? Perhaps it was more instinctual.

Disciplined? Definitely not.

Pleasurable? Good Lord Almighty, yes.

Necessary? At the moment, quite necessary.

Righteous? Her mind went blank, paralyzed with the answer that beckoned to be acknowledged. As he kissed her, he pulled her to him, simultaneously tilting her head back further and embracing her unrestrained with the arm around her waist and hips.

She knew the answer now.

Was it righteous?

Her devious mind, trained over years of cheekiness, whispered back the answer. *"It is right, but as Grandma Melanie always said, 'If you cannot be righteous, then you must be wicked.'"*

The thought was in no way a chastisement; rather, she was giving herself permission to enjoy the moment for what it was.

Her participation was received warmly, and likely a bit more than he was prepared to receive. He did not complain though, at least not for another minute.

After that precious minute, however, he pulled away, gazing tenderly at her. His breathing was rapid, and he attempted to steady it before he said huskily, "Thank you. But I must live up to the rumors of my gentlemanly reputation, which Bingley shared with your sister. I must alight."

He increased the volume of his voice, clearly for those in the adjoining room. "I can see now that you are in perfect health." He lowered his voice one more time. "I had thought that was all I needed, or wanted, to know. But your sweet lips told me so much more. I am to return to Netherfield tomorrow afternoon."

He stepped away and, with perfect form, bowed deeply to her.

*****

Mary arrived the next day at Netherfield to help Elizabeth pack her things for her return to Longbourn., But also to give her this wretched news!

"You jest, Mary!" Elizabeth cried. Her usually very practical sister had gone mad with the decision she had just declared.

Mary continued to place Elizabeth's belongings that had been brought over to Netherfield over the last month into the trunk. "I have my reasons, Elizabeth. The reasons are sound, and so am I in thinking so."

Elizabeth sat down into a nearby chair slowly, allowing her posture to sink as her heart had. "Truly?"

"Indeed. I have accepted our cousin, Mr. Collins. And why should I not? I shall remove myself from Longbourn for hopefully several more years, depending on our dear papa's health. But as you know, Mr. Collins is the heir, and when that dreadful day happens, Mama will not have to live in the hedge groves. And even if you do not understand my reasoning, I will become Mrs. Mary Collins in eighteen days. I do not ask for your understanding, but I had hoped for your support."

"Oh, Mary! You have it. Of course you have it. I shall miss you and your peculiar perspectives on trivial things, things I am not disciplined enough to examine. You stretch my consciousness. I shall have to visit Rosings many times over to get my fill of our unique debates."

Elizabeth stood up and hugged her sister. "Oh, dear, this shall sound so dull and vain. Whom shall I have left if both you and Jane marry? With Lieutenant Daniels' company being reassigned to the north, I shall only be left with my daily hiding-the-boots fight with Mrs. Hill. That is the single, lonely, and most absurd and wretched thing I will have left to divert me from boredom or loneliness! I suppose I can continue to explore Rainbow Agate Cave, but that was simply a daily ritual. I do miss it so much, but the hike is likely to be more than I can handle."

"There is nothing my sister cannot handle," Mary responded. "You are a gladiator, with armor of distrust and a helmet filled with decades of incessant knowledge from your books, along with shin guards, well molded to your lifestyle of kicking against things stubbornly. But most importantly, you have a sword of the finest wit, one that many have counseled you to restrain a bit more. But I say, yield to the sword. Do not sheath it because someone else wants to shape your behavior to be different than your nature."

Elizabeth didn't know if she should be in awe or laugh or cry at her sister's metaphorical tribute. She raised an eyebrow as high as possible. "Slay my dragons with my suspicious nature, using stubbornness and wit?"

Elizabeth caught a glimpse of concern on Mary's face, as if she realized she might have accidentally insulted her. But Elizabeth was not insulted. She was flattered as well as proud that her sister knew and appreciated her so well.

"Mary, I shall never, ever—even if I live to be one hundred—receive a more beautiful and heartfelt compliment. I feel so empowered, so confident in my strong nature. Thank you. This is something that I shall embrace and adopt in my own speech, both to myself and others."

The conversation ended there, and the two sisters stayed on task in their packing.

But Elizabeth rehearsed Mary's counsel in her head repeatedly. It was like a music box, and she wound it over and over again. And when it died down, Elizabeth wound it back up, only to hear it yet again.

Protect yourself with a distrusting nature.

*****

Longbourn was not as prepared as Elizabeth thought it would be for her return from Netherfield. In her absence, Mr. Collins' back had become aggravated with the guest room lodgings, and he had been offered her bedroom while she recovered from the river accident and the resulting fever. When she returned, she found she was to sleep with her sister Jane for the time being, as Mr. Collins had inferred that he must notify Lady Catherine, his "esteemed patronage," of his choice in bride. Mrs. Bennet assumed that meant he would leave shortly.

Elizabeth was grateful to have the extra time with Jane. With Jane and Mr. Bingley marrying soon, she wanted to help Jane in any way possible. Knowing Jane, Elizabeth suspected she already had elegant ideas for the wedding; however, they constantly heard their mother squeal with another idea to add or another person to invite, which occurred multiple times an hour. If she wasn't careful, Mrs. Bennet would be walking down the aisle instead of Jane, for their mother was planning every last detail, without inquiring of Jane what she preferred or whether Jane had other thoughts. Jane needed an advocate to ensure the wedding become what Jane always wanted rather than what their mother never got.

But no word had been spoken all afternoon with regards to Mr. Collins' plan to depart to Kent.

When she began to query about the situation, Elizabeth had been shushed by not only her mother but also Mary. Mary's attempt was better received than the uncouth methods of their mother. The day had been one of the longest in her life. Not only because of the dreadful conversation levied almost entirely by Mr. Collins but also because she had no desire to rest on Jane's bed, and certainly not her own, at least not until the sheets had been laundered.

The image of Mr. Collins half-clothed body on her pale-lavender sheets crippled her response when Mary asked her a question.

She looked up when her name was called again.

"Lizzy, I asked you a question. Do you feel ill? You shivered as if you were chilled."

She hadn't realized she was cold, and indeed she was, but the shiver was more accurately described as a shudder from the unpleasant image of her cousin drooling on her silk pillowcase that had come to her mind.

She sighed, smiling gently, and replied, "My mind wandered, and I was not paying attention. I am a bit chilled. Yes, perhaps I will put another log on the fire."

"I shall do it!" Mr. William Collins alighted from his chair so quickly that his antique chair screeched on the polished floor. The noise must have scared him, as he jumped, his arms parading around humorously, while everyone in the room pursed their lips and looked away from the theatrics. Elizabeth watched the longest, almost hoping to witness his awareness of his unrestrained reaction. At no point was he at risk to fall, but he flailed and spun to see the source of the noise, as his girlish screams and gasps were slowly replaced with deep-chested throat clearing and coughs.

Finally, he glanced around to see who witnessed the great performance. He was indeed pleased that no one was directly looking at him, which made him look a bit relieved. It was then that he glanced at Elizabeth, who could not, for the life of her, remove the grin from her face.

She nodded and tipped her chin. "Thank you, Mr. Collins. Another log on the fire will be much appreciated."

"Splendid, splendid. I am often accused of insight and selflessness. As I always say, one must simply observe those around him to know how to be of service to his fellow beings. I am a parson, after all. But that should not stop any of you from trying to follow my example. Thoughtful too. I've been accused of being thoughtful. I have so many thoughts. Most of them are in behalf of my neighbors and all that my body can offer them, which is a great deal. My body can do so many things, for I pride myself in being limber. That is, I have no hesitation in offering all of my body in service for their enjoyment and benefit."

Elizabeth's two youngest sisters snickered, causing Mr. Collins to first look confused at the humor, for he clearly did not see any humor himself. But then he appreciated their laughter, assuming it was for him rather than *because* of him.

Elizabeth had to hold back laughter herself, for he seemed to want to offer his body for the sake of others' enjoyment.

"Yes, Mr. Collins," Lydia said. "But if we all followed your example and put another log on the fire, your inheritance will burn down. Now finish with that rubbish topic, and tell us when you will leave!"

Jane sat up stiffly and said, "Yes, tell us of your plans to share with Lady Catherine how you won our Mary's hand."

As he started to profuse the strictest of loves for Mary, Elizabeth knew that was her moment to escape.

Now, where did Mrs. Hill hide my half boots?

CHAPTER 13

As Elizabeth left the room, she muttered under her breath. "Could they be upstairs in my room?" she wondered aloud. That was the only other place she could think of. She looked at the daunting climb ahead of her and sighed, preparing for the exertion.

"Miss Elizabeth, I believe you will be wanting these." Mrs. Hill smiled warmly as she handed the young Miss Elizabeth the half boots. "Always escaping. Or is there a someone special you might be anxious to find outside? You must learn to be settled, my dear. Be comfortable with where you are, and stop pressing yourself to achieve more than what comes naturally."

Elizabeth smiled back, taking the proffered half boots. "It is only natural that I return to my previous activities like walking. And I am settled, just not with the present company. Pray now, do not fret. I will stay in the gardens."

"May I suggest the pretty-ish kind of a little wilderness on the side of the lawn?" Mrs. Hill's eyes twinkled more than usual.

Trying to decipher what Hill meant, Elizabeth held her gaze a little longer. Sure enough, Mrs. Hill winked and calked her head to the west. They never called the west gardens "pretty-ish," but it indeed could be called a wilderness.

She trusted Mrs. Hill. "Indeed, that will be the closest I can come to the brush and wild flowers on my usual walk to Rainbow Agate Cave."

She took the nearest chair and laced her half boots. When she looked up, she saw Mrs. Hill still there.

The older woman stepped forward when she was acknowledged, large tears rolling gently down her face. "My child, you are so very blessed. Thank you for coming back to us whole. Go on, go to the west gardens. I doubt you will be disappointed at its. . . hmm, how shall I put this? Its coziness. I shan't send for anyone to disturb you for thirty minutes, but my integrity only stretches, it does not break entirely. So go quickly. Tell Mr. Daniels . . . horse scrap! I wasn't intendin' to tell you he was there!"

Elizabeth grinned widely, quickly standing and kissing her housekeeper on both sides of the face. "'Pretty-ish little wilderness?'"

"It weren't my words. He is the one that said it. I only used it because he did. Go now, he has been waiting for some time. Thirty minutes."

"Yes, ma'am." Elizabeth practically danced toward the exit, then turned and winked back, mouthing the words, *Thank you.*

Elizabeth wasn't expecting to see Daniels for several hours, seeing as he was breaking camp for their travels to the northern part of England. Their militia had been reassigned at the worst possible moment.

One side of the cast-iron gate stood ajar, for which she was grateful, because it was heavy and creaked horribly when moved. She doubted she could have moved it herself in her weakened state.

The west gardens were not expansive, but they were far too overgrown to see over the old shrubs that had never been cut back for the winter. The rock path was covered in patches of grass that grew through the pebbles, turning what should be a flat walkway into a bit of an obstacle course. The ground felt much like a cobblestone street that was missing stones or had just flooded, losing the stabilizing sand between them. As much as she deeply desired to look around for Daniels, she could only take a few careful steps before she had to unhook her skirt, which regularly caught on the wild rosebushes that lined the walkway. Only then could she look around.

She was nearly to the end of the gated garden when she heard a soft male voice whisper just ahead of her. "Shhhhhh."

There could be no doubt about who the voice belonged to. Elizabeth looked in William Daniels' direction. He had one finger to his lips as the other hand pointed to the top of a nearby tree. Her eyes followed to where he was pointing, and there at the crook of the branches near the top were two brilliant blue-headed birds with orange chests. They were larger than robins, with much bolder orange and red breasts. The blue head was brighter than she could recall ever seeing before.

Carefully and quietly, she took the last few steps and sat down next to Daniels, who was sitting on a rundown bench. He had clearly attempted to brush it clean from the dirt and decaying leaves.

"What kind of bird is that?"

"It is a rare breed where the female is just as spectacularly colored as the male. They have been preening each other. I think it is part of a mating ritual." He reached for her hand and put it into both of his.

They watched for many minutes as the beautiful birds caressed each other, over and over again. There was intention with each movement, and it truly was a dance. The female would look up, only for the male to swish his head into the crevice of her neck.

Then the male would shorten his body, squatting almost, and the female would slide her head from the top of his down his back. The male knew to stand at just the right time to allow the caress to reach further down his spine.

Elizabeth's heart rate was speeding up, and she had no idea why. It was likely the fact that every movement made by the birds was being re-enacted by William as he held her hand in both of his.

Wrapping, smoothing, caressing, and patting. She felt the need to take a larger breath, and she did. But then she had to remind herself not to hold it.

This was a moment she did not want to end. She felt William was sharing his heart in a physical way by holding onto her hand. And the heat of his hands only intensified as he moved with finesse around her left hand. The moment was ideal for a kiss, and she desperately wanted one. However, watching these birds making relations at the start of winter irritated her.

It was as if the birds were confused, or lost. Like they had forgotten who they were and that this was not the place they should be.

She broke the silence with a tearful cry. "But it is December! Surely nature knows it is a most inconvenient time."

"Being together is all that matters."

"I dare say that is not all that matters. And will they truly be together?"

"True, if the female is not ready, the union will not occur."

"But the timing! He cannot just encourage her and then leave!" She realized what she had said and bit her bottom lip. She looked down at her lap, then slowly turned her gaze to the hand he was still making love to.

Daniels' gaze was pulling hers to his face, as if they were tethered, and he was tightening the string.

She knew he was looking at her, pleading with her through his eyes to look at him. So she swallowed her embarrassment and looked at him. "Forgive me, that was uncalled for."

"No, it is I who seek your forgiveness. I have encouraged you, even pleaded with you, to accept my suit. But I am not my own man. I must do as the militia asks of me. They have already been far too generous with my time away while you were recovering. But we must make use of the time we have."

She nodded and soaked in the brown of his eyes. They were the perfect color of brown. Slightly golden but only in the right light. The tenderness in them softened her heart, and she smiled back at him. "I shall miss you terribly."

"No one can deny that we spent every possible moment in each other's presence while you were recovering. And I cannot deny that I am crushed with the timing as well."

"William, how long will you be gone? How long must I wait for us to wed?"

"It has only been a short while that I have earned an income worthy of sustaining a wife. Shall we say May?"

"May! Oh, dear, I had not considered we would be apart for five months! William, please, tell me what to do, and I shall do it. What can we do to not go crazy during this blasted season! And five months is practically two seasons!"

"Timing is not ideal, but we can still have moments when we are together. Did you not say your aunt and uncle live in London?"

"Yes, they do, on Churchill Street. They have an exceptional home, even grander than Longbourn. Of course, they have refurbished the entire two floors of their house. It has a more modern look to it than Longbourn. We have not updated much in the nearly one and twenty years I have lived here."

"Watch." Their attention turned back to the birds. The beautiful birds seemed almost to be dancing as together as they created their unique sound.

The birds both sang in unison, ca-ca-coo-coohoo, over and over again. And while they sang, they hopped, first farther apart, then each jumped higher into the tree, creating a distance of about two feet between them. One called out a melody to the other, and the other repeated it, adding to the end. They repeated the song more than ten times, then suddenly both started flapping their wings wildly and jumping up and down.

"What is the matter?" she asked quietly.

"Just watch and listen." He brought his hand up, cupping his mouth and mimicking the ca-ca-coo-coohoo sound that the birds had been making. It was nearly exactly the same sound. While his gaze was fixed on the birds, his arm reached around her shoulders, pulling her into a side-by-side embrace.

The birds both stopped flapping and began stretching their wings out, wider and wider. The feathered birds had been high enough that Elizabeth had not truly obtained an accurate assessment of their mass or size. With their wings stretched out, she could see they were much larger birds than she first thought; they were about the size of ravens.

William called out to them again. "Ca-ca-coo-coohoo!"

She giggled at him.

"You should try it. The sound is not hard to mimic."

"Perhaps when I am alone or while you are deployed."

He chuckled. "Very well."

The birds' wings looked as if their feathers were tipped with white lace. At first only one wing touched, then they turned toward each other and, with wings arching above their heads, they created an arch with their touching wings. It was a magnificent thing to observe.

William began rubbing her shoulder along the exposed area that had been revealed as the shawl had slipped down. His fingers were warm, comforting, and promising. They instinctively knew how she liked to be touched. His hands felt inviting, even enticing.

She looked away from the birds briefly and down at her shoulder. Sure enough, he had caused gooseflesh to appear, and there was plenty of heat racing through her veins.

She turned toward him, looking directly in his eyes. Their noses were mere centimeters away. She could smell the breath he had just exhaled, and it was delightful. She hungrily waited for him to breathe again, but it was not to be.

He was holding his breath and stealing hers at the same time.

She knew what she wanted. And just like the birds, it did not need to be communicated through words. Instead, she closed her eyes and tilted her lips to his.

And that was how the dance began.

Their hands reached first for the other's hands, then moved up to arms. Soon lips found earlobes, and eventually, when his lips traveled to her neck, she learned that the neck was a powerful motivator. It drove her to heights for which she was not prepared. Nor was she sorry she reached them.

It was just the two of them, two lovers who had found each other in the direst of circumstances. She was a country miss and he was a military man, only in Meryton for a season. The season may not have been ideal, but still a current of affection ran through her veins, coloring her neck and chest brightly, just like the birds.

William parted from her earlobe long enough to whisper, "I could do this for hours, and I will, my love, when the season is right. Watching these blue-laced triggers will be a memory I will always associate with you."

"Is that what the beautiful birds are called? Blue-laced trigger?"

He pulled farther away, looked at the birds, and said, "Yes, I believe so."

"How do you know that? I have never seen them around here before."

He paused for what seemed an extraordinary amount of time.

She almost apologized, assuming she might have touched on a raw topic, but then he spoke.

With a thoughtful expression on his face, William confidently said, "I know it as well as I know the back of my own hand. It is knowledge that is innate in me, or at least knowledge that I have known all my life. I am quite confident that those blue-laced triggers are a bird from my original childhood home, the home I do not remember."

"Do you truly not remember anything?"

He returned to gaze at her face, raising one eyebrow before saying, "Perhaps only the brilliant memories remain. I vaguely remember your lips pressed to mine a minute ago, but the memory is fading fast. Might I ask you to refresh that memory one last time?"

She closed the gap and tried to kiss him through her smile. Who would have imagined that the broody and aloof William Daniels would have such a fine sense of humor?

But his question must be answered with equal parts impertinence from her. "You need not ask for my kisses. However, I must ask something in return, and you must swear it upon your honor."

Elizabeth paused for effect, which produced a faint look of concern in his eyes. "Promise me that kiss will not be the last time. Do I have your word on that?"

She smiled saucily and winked, although the playful gesture did not represent how serious she was in her request.

He answered by hungrily claiming her back into his arms.

CHAPTER 14

William Daniels had said his farewells to Elizabeth a hundred times in his head over the last six weeks, each time playing them over and over again. He had only received one letter from her since his departure, but he had sent many, two letters a week in fact. Winter weather had settled in its fullness for the last four weeks, and mail delivery was not up to his standards, for he had not received any other letters from Elizabeth.

He had news from Netherfield though. Bingley should be forced to retake his writing classes. All William could ascertain between the crossed out words and the excessive use of adjectives, which were more plentiful than the ink blots, was that Bingley had decided to throw a masked ball at Netherfield. Knowing Bingley, he was likely planning to announce the date he and Miss Bennet had chosen to marry.

The masked ball should have been held last Saturday. William remembered that night vividly. He had laid awake as long as Elizabeth likely had, and in his mind's eye, he had asked repeatedly for her hand, first to the opening dance, then the next and the next and so on. In his mind, she never danced with another man that night. It was the warmest winter night he had ever experienced while in the militia.

In reality, however, it had been a cold, harsh month, one that he wished he could forget. There had been little to assure him of Elizabeth's safety. Why wouldn't Bingley at least mention it?

He studied each new rider who entered camp, but none of them brought him any news.

Brighton had seen constant rain and wind, and ample times when Mother Nature combined the two together. He hesitated investing in another pair of boots, for these had served him well for so long. He had already resoled them once. And William Daniels felt his money could be used for more important purposes, such as a wedding trip.

William had asked around for location recommendations, with everyone suggesting the Lake District. He had always felt a draw there; however, it was not a place he felt inspired or pressed to go with Elizabeth. It felt too casual, too normal.

Why would the Lake District feel normal?

This thought perplexed him greatly.

Weeks ago, in a letter, he had asked Elizabeth her preference for the wedding trip. However, with the delayed mail, he had not yet received an answer.

Where were his letters? Had she received them? Had she fallen ill again? Was she struggling? What if she had again fallen unconscious?

After six weeks, the militia left Brighton. Just as they departed the city, about a kilometer out, a rider carrying mail reached them. Daniels was delighted to receive not just one but four letters from his intended! With such a last-minute appearance, and with the men just starting their march farther north, William tucked the letters inside his front right pocket. As he pulled out his hand, the buckle on his uniform snagged the D-crested ring around his neck.

He felt it before he heard it fall, and heard it fall before he visually located it. The chain around his neck clearly had broken, as he felt the chill slither down his chest to the left.

He could not lose that ring!

Panic settled in his gut for three or four seconds until he saw it. He picked it up from the mud and tried to shake off the mud. He would have to clean the scripted D and crest around it later with a fine brush, but he slid it onto his right ring finger as it was for now.

He hadn't worn it on his hand for years; instead, for the last five years it had hung around his neck. Why hadn't he worn it? Wickham had hungrily examined it while William was in his shirtsleeves.

As William looked up, the captain's horse stopped directly in front of him. He observed the filthy ring on William's hand and then raised his eyes to stare directly into Lieutenant William Daniel's eyes.

William stood up, expecting to be scolded for the muddy knees, a consequence of looking for the precious ring.

"Lieutenant Daniels? Do you fancy a walk? I need to stretch my legs. Come," Captain Echols commanded. Without any doubt that Daniels would follow his orders, the captain dismounted and briskly walked away from the resting group of soldiers, all reading their letters from home. But not Daniels. He wanted to relish what was written, and he doubted his ability to refrain from letting the emotion show on his face.

Darcy readjusted the treasured letters from Elizabeth that were next to his chest and buttoned his vest. With more dignity than he had shown when ravaging the muddy footpath in search of his dropped ring, William marched quickly forward. He made a few adjustments to his greatcoat, but no one behind him would have suspected he was mortified at his behavior and dirty uniform. He had never received any disciplinary action, at least not before now. All for what? A ring that he might never understand its origin? And if it meant so much to him, why did he wear it around his neck rather than display it proudly on his hand?

The excuse William gave himself was that it felt odd to openly wear a crest of a name that he could not recall, a family that he did not remember, or possibly a birthright he no longer could claim.

More significantly, it felt wrong to wear the crest of a heritage, perhaps generations old, knowing that he did not honor that heritage.

Nevertheless, the ring felt good on his finger. It felt strong, and just having it there was more than just relaxing—it felt right. He caught himself playing with the ring. It was a new sensation to be on his finger. He would twist it with his thumb on the underside of his hand, first counterclockwise, which was the most natural, but then clockwise the same number of times.

Ten times to the left, ten times to the right, twisting at the same pace of his marching.

William caught up to the captain, matching his stride easily.

The two walked for less than 100 meters, but they were out of earshot, which was an unusual choice if the captain planned to deliver discipline. Usually, discipline is best when witnessed, a powerful way of teaching other soldiers what is expected or not tolerated.

With the ring securely on his finger and four letters from Elizabeth in his breast pocket, William's marching was invigorating and spry; he was not afraid of what the captain would decide.

"Lieutenant, how long have I been your captain?"

"On and off for over four years, sir. I was sent to several regiments, but the ones you led were by far the best. The first year I spent under the command of Captain Charrol, sir."

"Aye, and have you any doubt of my respect for you?"

Daniels only hesitated a moment, long enough to put words to his surprise. "I doubt there is a right answer to that. If I say yes, then I am presuming you respect me. If I say no, I appear to be seeking validation."

The captain's response—a loud chuckle—took William by surprise. "Neither, good man. But have you any idea why I hesitated and delayed your rank to lieutenant so long? Most men climb the ranks quickly, at least those with your loyalty and commanding presence."

William unintentionally found himself inhaling and broadening his shoulders, then he clicked his heels and saluted. "Thank you, sir."

Captain Echols looked away and said, "Put that arm down." He returned his gaze to glare straight into Daniels. The intensity of his stare was mildly disturbing, but this was a man that Williams had pledged to devote his life and obedience to. Until he was directed to, Daniels held the eye contact.

"Daniels, you lead the pack, pressing onward to our destination with energy. You are the first to start the work and the most devoted to the task of protecting Mother England. However, I fear you have been running too long. You exert far more energy into the regiment. You have never asked for any time off in four years until the accident on the bridge with the Bennet sisters."

"Forgive me, sir. It was extenuating circumstances."

"Good Lord, Lieutenant! Shut it!"

William took a step back and stood at attention.

"At ease, soldier. I am talking as a friend, or at least I consider you a friend. I resisted advancing you for so long not because you did not deserve it but because you do not belong here. I know it, my officers know it, and every savage who meets you knows it. For God's sake! Every savage can dance, but you command the dance floor. Your upbringing exceeds any in the company."

Lieutenant Daniels relaxed his posture and folded his arms behind him. Where was the captain going with this? This was quite near flattery, and usually he detested flattery, but this seemed different than idle compliments. These were confessions with a purpose. William listened more intently to hear the purpose of such a conversation with his superior officer.

The captain sighed briefly but continued. "You truly do not belong here. You are a born leader but not of soldiers. Of men. I know you do not know where you came from, and I've gathered enough from the rumors that you were in a shipwreck."

The pause was long enough that the captain said, "You may speak."

"I presume you wish to hear the story of what I cannot remember and, ultimately, why I cannot remember it."

"Damn right! But more importantly, I wonder why the hell *you* do not want to know who you are and where you came from yourself! You've never taken leave, so I am confident you never even looked. You do know there is a book of family crests at the London Tower Historical Library, do you not?"

Daniels opened his mouth to answer but stopped when Captain Echols held his hand out firmly to stop him. "I wonder if you have considered an important aspect of your future. I hear I am to wish you joy, as I just learned that you have an understanding with the second eldest Miss Bennet."

"Yes, sir."

"Do you love her?"

"Most definitely. With every breath, my heart calls her name. She is my reason for living."

"And those letters you protected savagely from the mud, they were from her?"

"Sir, I was searching in the mud for my ring. I usually wear it around my neck. But when I put the letters away, the chain broke. It is the only connection I have to my unknown name." He held his arm and hand out, then brought it back in and rubbed the dirt off a bit better. The mud had become dried and crusted.

"I see. A ring. Wait, let me look at that better." Daniels stepped forward, and the captain grasped his hand.

"No, no, no. I do not see. I do not have half a measure of understanding for you! You are a brilliant man, but you have been so irresponsible. You have a family-crested ring, and you have worn it for five years? Good Lord, son! That is all you need!"

"All I need for what? Do you know this family crest? Who I am? Where I am from? Do I have family still alive?" Hope flooded William faster than any other time he could remember, but that hope faded with the captain's unusual response.

Captain chuckled repeatedly, pausing only to rub his brow, and then chuckled again. It went on for a minute more.

To say it was disturbing was only partly true. It was maddening! Did Captain Echols know who he was?

"Sir?"

"Forgive me, but I have been debating how to approach this new information you have shared with me. You clearly do not see the significance of that ring. Suppose I ask you a very specific question. But I want you to pause and truly think before you answer. Do I have your word that you will pause and think?"

"Of course, Captain."

Captain's jovial nature tamed significantly, and his face became concentrated. "What name will Miss Bennet be taking when you two get married?" he asked.

"She has not accepted my hand yet, only a court. . . " The sentence caught in his throat, choking him. No, it was not the sentence choking him, it was the captain's question.

He turned away and reached for something to steady himself.

Elizabeth will not be a Bennet much longer, had been his thought.

But if not Bennet, what will her name be?

She cannot take the name he made up for himself. No, Elizabeth Daniels . . . it felt so wrong. Was he ready for his wife to be called Mrs. Daniels?

What a horrible thought!

He realized that he had tolerated calling himself Daniels for this long, but his beloved deserved to have a real name, a name that carried the heritage of the crest and everything it represented.

He had no right to take her as a wife then ask her to take on a fictitious name.

Suddenly, William needed to know.

He needed to know who he was, or had been, and possibly could be.

How had he not needed this before? In an instant, it had become vital to know who he was.

He immediately stood at attention and saluted again. "Sir, I am requesting two weeks leave."

"Denied. You may have a month."

With that, Captain Echols walked back to his horse and remounted. He immediately galloped down to the right of all the soldiers, calling out to the men. "Regiment 49, fall in!" There was a pause while the men scrambled to their feet and hurried into a rough formation of four rows on the road.

"Attention!"

The men, who were still somewhat scattered, immediately moved into four exact rows and stood at attention.

"Left face. Forward. March."

Captain turned his horse around, leading the soldiers as they marched on to Derbyshire.

Lieutenant William Daniels secured the bayonet that was across his shoulder and double-timed it twenty paces in the opposite direction.

He was off to London.

He suddenly stopped, paused, then ran back toward the captain.

Daniels was in excellent shape, but he was also carrying most of his belongings on his back. However, more energy was flowing through his veins than ever before. He knew his body would not fail him.

As he passed the marching soldiers, he heard his friend, Samson, hissed at him. "Daniels, what has gotten into you?"

Others heckled him for setting an inhuman pace and not falling into formation.

If he could not explain his urgency to himself, there would be no way to explain it to them.

He reached the front of the soldiers and pressed on even farther until he caught up with the captain, who was about ten meters ahead.

"Sir, may I inquire if Samson could accompany me?"

Captain Echols looked down at him, quietly assessing what he could without asking for an explanation. He paused a minute more, looked ahead, and then replied, "Granted."

Daniels nodded and turned back to the militia. He paused, however, when Captain Echols called out. "Company, halt. Samson, step forward!"

Two soldiers stepped forward, and he glared at the one he had not meant. "Lieutenant Samson," the captain clarified.

The soldier whose first name was Samson awkwardly step back in line.

Edward Samson, William's closest friend, hurriedly continued onward and then saluted when approximately three meters away. "Yes, sir!"

"I need you and Daniels to take a letter to London."

"Yes, sir!"

Captain addressed the militia. "Forward, march!"

Daniels could feel the questions emanating from his friend, but he just ticked his head west, and Samson followed along wordlessly. They backtracked about two miles before heading south again.

Samson had, of course, kept up with him and silently walked next to him. He tried not to catch the glances Samson tossed his direction, which, at the beginning, were many, but after three hours of marching at a hurried pace, were now few.

William felt the ache in his feet, and the chill in the air made their rapid breathing visible. It had been many hours since they had changed directions, but Samson had followed obediently.

The march had been trying, but finally, the time had come. Samson cleared his throat to speak, and Daniels felt some shame as his voice sounded raspy and a bit haggard from the exertion.

"I, ah, thought we might have a pint to warm up in the next city?"

They kept marching.

"Did you hear what I said?"

"Indeed," huffed Daniels.

"'Indeed meaning we can stop for a pint, or indeed, you heard me?"

"The latter."

"Lieutenant, is that supposed to be humorous?"

"You have your orders."

Samson came to a dead stop. "Yes, but those orders were not from *you*." Samson had purchased his rank, but that didn't weaken his commitment to do as he was told by an outranking officer. Samson was asking him to stop because the order came from the captain and not from Daniels, a fellow lieutenant, equal in rank.

Sampson wouldn't dare question the authority directly, not when Daniels had been given the charge, or billet, for this particular mission.

Daniels weighed the amount of land they must pass before they reached London, and he estimated that only about four kilometers remained before farms and houses on the outskirts of London would begin to emerge. Already, he could see the roads were smoother and wider, and travel had been easier.

He had waited for five years to begin the search, and his procrastination of the moment ahead of him was not his friend's fault.

William slowed and nodded his agreement; they should rest.

They searched for a place to prop their packs out off the mud and standing water. The sun had come out momentarily throughout their long journey but had never shone longer than ten minutes at a time.

Samson walked over to a clearing less than five meters off the road where there were a few felled trees. They set their packs on the logs and sat down next to them. Samson let out an enormous sigh of relief.

"Daniels, I usually adore rejuvenating silence, but in this case, this is just tortuous silence," Samson said. He wiped his brow with the crook of his arm and then rested his elbows on his knees.

Daniels chuckled. "Anyone else would have complained two hours ago."

"Complaining? Whom do you imply is complaining?"

He chuckled at his friend's humor. "Splendid! Then I would say your method of encouragement is a unique one. Let us depart then!" Daniels made a false start to stand and earned two things simultaneously from Samson: a cocked pistol and a look of disdain.

He let out a deep laugh and choked out the words. "I, for one, want no more encouragement. We will rest for a while longer."

"We will."

If Daniels were to write to Elizabeth what Samson had just said, he would have documented those two words as a command, not to be questioned.

Both pulled out the dried, flavorless crumpets that were their ration for the day. They ate it with less enthusiasm than Miss Caroline Bingley had displayed when she was asked to provide dry nightclothes for the two Miss Bennets.

After eating, they continued to sit for a quarter of an hour, staring at the menacing road ahead of them. They had caught their breath for some time, yet Samson was not making any moves to resume the grueling pace they had just completed.

After several minutes, William could hear Samson start to shift his person just enough so that he could prop his back against the boulder.

He watched as his friend removed his hat and placed it over his face to hide the late afternoon sun. Just as Daniels was about to look away, Samson murmured from under the hat, "I will be ready in ten minutes." After relaxing into the trunk, Samson said, "Make that twenty."

Within a minute, the breathing was deep and slow, indicating his friend had found sleep quickly.

Finally, William thought.

He slowly reached into the right chest pocket and pulled out the four letters from Elizabeth. He rifled through them, trying to decide which to read first. Did he want the first letter, meaning the one that she had composed first? Or did he want to read the most recent one to hear the latest news first? Did she get his letters? And why had her letters arrived all at once?

None of that mattered more than finding out how she was faring.

27 January 1813

Dear William,

My, how the month of January has flown by! Did you receive my first letter? By now you know that Mr. and Mrs. Mary Collins are wed, and truly, they had a splendid wedding. Mr. Collins managed to knock the flowers over only once! Of course, he stepped on Mary's dress and ripped the hem, but that is par for him. I do not enjoy admitting when I am wrong, but

Mary seems to be happy, or at least truly content, with this decision. I fear that I may have been too harsh on her when she initially shared the news. However, neither she nor I withhold our opinions often enough, so I can safely assume that she was as honest with her feelings as I was with mine.

Lady Catherine, or shall I say, "the great esteemed Lady Catherine," granted us the privilege of hosting her and her four servants when she attended the wedding! Longbourn was bursting at the seams! She even thought to bring a chaperone for Mary, but for what purpose? I shall not venture to guess, because now there is no need for one! For some people, reason is in short supply.

Lady Catherine seems officious as well as intent on imposing her opinions with fervor, so the chaperone was handed into the carriage with the newly married couple.

It has only been but a fortnight since I heard from you.

William, do not scold me for not addressing your concerns first; I will update you on my condition. I am improving every day, by measurable amounts. Each time that I think I have sufficiently recovered, my body is riddled with nocturnal coughing, and I pay the price of the exertion from the day. But other than that, I would suppose that my constitution is about halfway back to normal. I do wish to provide a better report, but you need not worry. Every morning, I look at myself in the mirror and set firm, reasonable boundaries for not taxing my lungs or body. Indeed, I do! You might doubt me, but I firmly set rules for myself then, without fail, I cross them. And the cycle repeats the next day.

I realized we have never discussed a time or place for the wedding. Jane and Bingley have decided not to wed immediately, as Mary did, so as not to pull any light or joy from their union. However, it was indirectly implied that they delayed their nuptials until you respond with your preference for our union.

Mr. Bingley is a daily visitor as Miss Caroline Bingley departed on her northern tour with her aunt, so until I am well enough to chaperone, Bingley must visit Longbourn.

Oh, dear, unless I wish to make this three pages, I must conclude. But one more piece of news! Mr. Bingley has decided to throw a ball in Jane's and my honor! A masquerade! I have never been to a real masquerade! How I wish you could be here, even to just sit with me while I watch.

My dearest wishes of safety and peace,

Yours sincerely,

Elizabeth Bennet

Lieutenant Daniels quickly opened the next letter.

9 February 1813

Dear William,

I still have not had any letters from you but the first. Jane is getting a bit antsy to set a date, but she hopes that we both might stand in for them. Mr. Bingley said he would write himself, but I do not think that has happened yet. He does not much like writing.

But I have news! Please take a moment to read the news article I included with this letter. The masquerade has been postponed for unnecessary reasons. Bingley can be extraordinarily stubborn sometimes!

I am well and gaining strength each day. I count every improvement as a mini-miracle.

I shall write again next to answer any questions you have for me. Other than that, Longbourn still receives Bingley on a daily basis, from before tea to dinner. No one complains in the slightest. He is besotted and follows Jane all day as she walks like a loyal hound.

Yours,

Elizabeth Bennet

NETHERFIELD MASKED BALL POSTPONED!

BUT NOW, ALL ARE INVITED!

MR. CHARLES BINGLEY WOULD LIKE TO BEG THE PARDON OF THOSE WHO RECEIVED AN INVITATION TO

THE MASQUERADE BALL
THURSDAY NEXT. HE HAD
THE SPLENDID, AND VERY
GENEROUS OFFER, TO
EXTEND THE INVITATION TO
THE ENTIRE TOWN OF
MERYTON!

THE NEW PROPOSED DATE IS
THE THIRTIETH OF MARCH.

MR. BINGLEY STATES HE
FELT IMPRESSED TO MOVE
THE DATE OF THE BALL TO
ALLOW FOR MORE
PREPARATIONS AND
SUPPLIES TO BE DELIVERED.
RUMORS ARE THAT THERE
WILL BE FIREWORKS AS THE
GUESTS TAKE THEIR LEAVE!

HOWEVER, THE BUZZ IS
DEEPER THAN SIMPLE
PREPARATIONS! HIS
INTENDED, MISS JANE
BENNET, HAS MADE THIS

REQUEST IN BEHALF OF HER SISTER, MISS ELIZABETH BENNET, WHO MET WITH MISFORTUNE MANY WEEKS AGO WHEN THE BRIDGE GAVE WAY WITH THE FLOODED RIVER. WE SUSPECT THE SLOW RECOVERY OF MISS ELIZABETH IS THE TRUE REASON. BUT, AS ANY HUSBAND (OR IN THIS INSTANCE, SOON-TO-BE HUSBAND) KNOWS, "HAPPY WIFE, HAPPY LIFE!" BINGLEY'S PLEASING MANNER IS NO SECRET, AND HE LIKELY WOULD HAVE GIVEN MISS BENNET THE MOON IF SHE HAD REQUESTED IT. HE WAS UNABLE TO CONFIRM OFFERING HER LUNAR GIFTS FOR THE WEDDING, OF WHICH, A DATE IS YET TO BE ANNOUNCED.

A GOOD MAN IS A SERVANT
TO THE LADY WHO HOLDS
HIS HEART. MAY WE ALL BE
STRICKEN WITH SUCH A
MALADY.

Darcy's grin was wide, and he realized it had been sorely missed. But certainly not more than he missed his Charles for being so thoughtful and kind towards Elizabeth. But that may mean she had been less than truthful in her letters about how slow the recovery actually has been.

When he read the rest of her letter, the third, he could hear her impertinence and her charm, and it drew him in like a bee to a flower.

He was hungry for more news, so he folded the letter and news article and tucked them away.

With those out of sight, he pushed open the wax seal of the next dated letter. When he unfolded the page, a dried vanilla bean fell into his lap. He brought it to his nose and inhaled the vanilla and caramel fragrance; however, he was surprised that it smelled more of tart cherries and licorice. It was definitely a vanilla bean, as he had been assigned by his tutor to study one early in his youth in order to understand plant anatomy and propagation.

Yes, it was a vanilla bean. One of average length, but the stem was interestingly curved. It must have grown oppressed or blocked a bit from its intended path of growing. The stem had curved up then had a sharp crease. Perhaps a wire had prevented it from hanging, but then pressed up again in similar fashion, only to round out the curve back towards the initial curve of the stem.

The stem was in the shape of a heart!

"How unusual!" he exclaimed.

"Pardon me?"

He apologized for waking Samson, then added, "Have you ever seen anything so remarkable? This vanilla bean was determined to grow, and as it did, it overcame everything blocking it from producing this pod. "

Samson's brows furrowed momentarily, and he just sighed, relaxing his head back down and pulling his hat back over his eyes.

"It *is* a heart," William explained further.

The only response was a deep grunt.

18 February 1813

Dear William,

I was determined not to write again until I heard from you, but I do have one redeeming quality that benefits you in this instance—I am not patient!

I appreciate the book you left in my care. I might be a bit ashamed to tell you that Sense and Sensibility *only makes me wonder how one daughter has no sense and the other, no sensibility. Yet, look at Lydia and Jane! I was so deeply satisfied with Colonel Brandon's calm, easy, but* consistently loyal manner that I reread the book as soon as I finished. He reminds me of the strength of your character, always a bit aloof or even broody.

You may be interested that I heard through the rumor mill that you, or I, or perhaps more accurately, both of us, were caught in a bit of a, let's say, unique small group of two. I will not name Mr. Bingley told me unless you were to point the finger at him. I shan't say I approve, at least not the version Bingley shared; however, I do request a thorough explanation, for I do not recall it happening. I am quite sure that you failed to recall it for me in conversation in the weeks during my recovery, although the timing of the regiment leaving was so foul for our newly made attachment. Does that mean I could not have chosen, even if I had wanted to, any other path than to marry you? I would say you should feel complimented, for I did choose to court you.

Are you still committed to the promise you made me when I woke up at Netherfield? Now that I remember vividly. It keeps me company when my heart and mind drifts north.

I know you must be quite busy with the regiment, but I fear I had not truly known my own attachment for you until I spent four weeks waiting for a response to mine.

A lady's mind cannot be fully grasped, but one thing for certain is that I fear my mind will be much more like my mother's than you remember it being if I do not hear from you soon.

Please, just notify my father that you are well. He will know how to break any other news you feel pressed to share.

Concerned,
Miss Elizabeth Bennett

After reading this letter, William determined he would strangle Bingley when he saw him next. He opened the next letter, but there were only a handful of sentences on it with blotches of watermarks smearing the words. Had she been crying?

2 March 1813

Dearest Lieutenant,

I beg of you to respond. I thought the chest pain I had with the accident was intolerable. One can never stop learning lessons in this life.

Yours truly . . . (Am I?)

EB

Lieutenant Daniels cringed with each letter. Had she not received his letters, sent twice weekly? *Good God! Elizabeth thinks I no longer want to marry her!*

He let out a groan and said, "Let us depart." He heard the hopelessness in his own voice, as did Samson, who slowly sat up but did not make a move to stand up.

"We should leave and find lodgings at the next town."

"Very well. We are not delivering a letter to London for the captain, are we?"

Daniels owed it to Samson for the pace he had made him march for the last five hours. "No, we are not. I shall fill you in. I believe we only have a couple of kilometers before we come across the Horse's Mane Inn. I have stayed there before, and they are very accommodating and inexpensive. We might even be able to charter a horse to continue to London."

"I thought you would never confess why this leave is so personal to you. Was it something in the letters? Or did the letters obliterate your energy. You look like I feel. A far cry from your antsy self four hours past." Samson was prodding kindly and gently, yet he was truly inquiring to Daniel's mood.

His mood had most definitely changed with the reading of the letters. It felt like a windstorm on the Lyme Regis Boardwalk, the part where certain death lay on one side in the rocky ocean cliffs while survival awaited on a sandy harbor on the other.

Reaching out his hand to assist Samson up, Daniels answered. "Both. My intended, Elizabeth, has not received my letters. And it took an enormous amount of time for hers to reach me. She presumes in her letters that I no longer wish to correspond or be associated."

Samson reached his arm out and rested it on Daniel's shoulder. He nodded and replied, "Then you are rightly troubled. So I presume our final destination is Hertfordshire?"

"I am not sure if there is time."

"How much leave do you have?"

"Plenty. You as well, good sir. I requested your company, at first because I need your guidance. You come from the first waters. However, now I understand why I have enjoyed your company these last few years. You pry so little, and yet I have shared the most with you than anyone else in the regiment. I trust you. And I need your help and entrance to society."

They had already started marching; however, upon hearing Williams' words, Samson's pace slowed slightly. "Did I hear you right? You are going to find your family?"

"If I have any. Yes, I hope to claim my birthright."

"Why now? I have never asked before . . ."

"No, you have not. Even if you asked now, I doubt I could explain it. But I shall try. I did search, at first, when I woke up. But there were no leads. No one knew of any kind of shipwreck near the Falmouth area nor did anyone know of anyone missing a son and daughter. I searched Falmouth area for a few months and continued to lose weight and be a burden on the great couple that took me in. But I had to find my way."

Daniels hadn't realized he was twirling the ring on his right hand but looked down at the mud-caked crest. "I . . . I was afraid. I was afraid to look into my parents' eyes and tell them their daughter died in my arms. I had failed to protect my young sister. She was no more than ten years old. I had no memory of them anyway. What if I never gained those memories back? What if I became a bumbleheaded burden to them too?"

"Hogwash. Any parent would have preferred to lose only one child rather than believe they had lost two."

"Indeed, I know that now. I came upon that conclusion about a year ago, but by then I had been missing over four years. What kind of son leaves for four years? Granted, it was not of my choosing, but I *have* chosen to stay away. I have caused them so much pain already. They likely have grieved and moved on by now. I fear that me returning would be incredibly hard to explain."

"May I share with you a story?"

"Of course."

"Do you know the story of the prodigal son, from the Bible?"

"No, I am not a prodigal son. I know the story well, and that man wasted every birthright he had— money, talent, and even his family. Then he came begging to sleep with the pigs. I will not beg."

"This is my story, not yours," Samson continued. "I have a nephew who is nearly as old as I am. His father, my eldest brother and the heir, is over fourteen years my senior. He married young and, for your ears only, he was forced to marry the lady he ruined. Society does not know that part of their blissful marriage, because they ended up a successful and wonderful example of a love match. But my nephew found out and questioned all he ever knew. He ran away from home at a mere twelve years old. I was fourteen, nearly fifteen, at the time. However, I was pulled from my slumber to search for him. All night, all the next day, and on and on and on. With short one-hour naps to refresh ourselves, my father and my eldest brother had every member of the county searching for my nephew. We all fought the elements along with fatigue and hunger. I remember it with a mixture of awe, fondness, and trepidation.

"I was in awe at the intensity and determination I saw in my brother's pursuit. He would never have stopped looking, not for one moment. It was then that I understood that a father's love is infinitesimal, and the needs and safety of his child would never be diminished. But the entire situation frightened me. I was a well-grown boy, one who had been to university for two years already. I was no longer naïve to the world, and I knew that a twelve-year-old boy could be a useful servant but still an ignorant one. Danger was imminent, and the longer he was gone, the harder my stomach knotted. I considered my nephew to be my friend. Eventually he was found, thank goodness."

William considered what Samson was trying to teach. "You assume my father would have never stopped looking for me? All these five years?"

"I am quite sure of it."

"Well, I suppose that it is good that I will be searching the library for the crest this ring represents. I had not known there was a book of family crests until

Captain Echols told me. It is located at the Tower of London Historical Library. Do you know where that is?"

Samson chuckled. "Indeed I do. I remember looking up my own family crest. Our name used to be Samsson, as in the son of Sam, but they shortened it in the early-eighteenth century. Everyone spelled it wrong then, and now they try to put a 'p' in it, like Sampson. But it is just Samson. You just cannot win over the ignorance of the masses."

"Well, I would dearly like to see your crest too. To the Historical Library then!"

"Ah, Daniels, my feet really could use a rest. Perhaps we rest our bodies in the Horse's Mane Inn and start fresh in the morning on horses?"

"Splendid idea. I could use a hot bath. I fear my odor might be offensive with all the marching we have done."

"It is, my man. It is."

Daniels looked sideways at his companion and chuckled hard enough to make him pause in his walking. "Not only do I trust you, but I greatly enjoy your honesty, even if it injures my perspective of self."

"I do have one more question."

Daniels nodded for him to continue.

"Why go to London, when your lady is aching for you under a false understanding that you no longer care for her? Surely the crest research can wait one more day, or perhaps two."

"Then a bath is no longer wanted, it would be required." Daniels' mind drifted quickly to a dreamlike state of seeing Elizabeth again.

"I cannot believe it is nearly the middle of March. Where has the time gone?"

Daniels realized the date was the 12th of March and on the evening next was the Netherfield Masquerade. His smile broadened, and his heart raced. He was actually going to see Elizabeth! He was going to hold her, smell her caramel and vanilla fragrance.

Plans started forming, and his daydreams of holding Elizabeth again warmed him from the inside out.

He cleared his throat and asked, "Samson, do you enjoy dancing?"

CHAPTER 15

Bingley was tired. He had checked and rechecked the music itinerary and menu items. "Are you sure we have enough jelly molds, Mrs. Hankmin?"

The Netherfield cook smiled and nodded. "Yes, sir. And most of them are already made and will be turned just before supper is set. The display will be spectacular, I might add. You will rival the best of the *ton's* balls in London."

Bingley smiled widely, folding his arms over his chest. "Well, then, there is nothing left to do. I suppose I should retire. I am deeply grateful for Jane's assistance in planning this gala. Fine job. She has been an angel and invaluable. Since Caroline left, life has been less, oh, I am unsure how to describe it. Less . . ."

"Complicated?" Mrs. Hankmin asked.

"Spot on! Brilliant choice of words. I feel a sense of contentment. Now there is nothing to do now. Nothing but fall into a deep slumber." He inadvertently yawned with the last word. "And there is the proof I needed. My body must rest."

His cook looked just as tired, but she curtsied and departed.

Maybe I will have one finger of brandy. It will help with the nerves.

He headed towards the Netherfield library, which held no value to him other than a place to entertain his friends and the place of his first kiss with his intended. Since that first kiss, they had found their way to the library on the rare occasion that Lydia or Kitty were willing to accompany their sister. Of course, neither of Jane's sisters had an affinity for books and tended to neglect their chaperone duties. This was not a problem for the couple in any way.

The memory of her kisses, feather light at first, then with a bit of encouragement, melded into a more delightful level of affection.

Bingley poured his glass, drank most of it in one gulp, and started to loosen his cravat and unbutton the vest. He had taken his waistcoat off hours ago, as he pored over and counted the notes from the entire town of Meryton, who were all "delighted and grateful for his generous invitation."

As he took off the vest, he realized that there were still three more responses that had arrived unfashionably late; he had shoved them in his vest pocket when they came at an ungodly hour of nine. One of them was sent as an express!

He would read them on the morrow. He tossed them on the table by the decanter and refilled his glass. But the handwriting on one of them caught his eye.

Why had Daniels sent an express? He emptied the glass and read.

Suddenly he was not tired in the slightest!

William Daniels was coming with Lieutenant Samson by noon tomorrow! He would need a tailor who could assist with a pair of dancing shoes and a fine vest and waistcoat.

This will be the finest surprise for my Jane, Bingley thought. Her favorite sister's concerns will be obliterated. He never subscribed to the fears Elizabeth felt. Elizabeth refuted Bingley's firm belief, and positive encouragement, that the mail was delayed. But now—now she would smile like she did before Daniels had left.

What joy Jane would have!

*****

William Daniels had never pushed a horse harder. He and Samson had been able to secure two fine animals, and the horses seemed to enjoy the pace.

Bingley was on the front grounds of Netherfield to greet them. "Daniels! Samson! What a perfect addition to my masquerade tonight! You are an hour early. Shall I send for the tailor earlier than we planned?"

Both men, a bit sore from the hard marching the day before and then a three-hour gallop, dismounted and simply stretched, first one way, then the other.

Samson spoke first. "An hour of leisure is all I ask for. If William Daniels needs more primping, I will let him speak for himself."

"Primping? How dare you imply I am a lady needing a trained lady's maid to win a suitable match's eye." But his chuckle afterwards betrayed his pretense to sound insulted.

Neither Bingley and Samson had been fooled, and both laughed good heartedly.

"Then come and wash the dust from yourselves, for I hardly recognize that you wear His Majesty's uniform."

From behind them, the men heard an old, gravelly voice, full of bitterness, state with a thick Scottish accent, "The Prince Regent would not know a soldier from a footman."

Bingley chuckled loudly and responded, "Let me introduce you, Mr. Burwick. I see you have brought your apprentice to assist with the costumes."

"Aye, Bingley, you already ken Mr. Nussbaum. What's the matta' wit' ya? But do ya ken he will be purchasing a third of my office every year for the next three years. And then my weary body may be put 'ter pasture. If you ask me, I am not sure I want to see that day come tomorrow or never see that day. You want leisure, aye, boys? Neither of you deserve any more leisure."

Burwick then seemed to revert back to the bemoaning. "Three years! And all I've worked fer will be his!" He motioned to Mr. Nussbaum, who had the decency to look sheepish. "All my life I have used these hands and eyes to create, but I cannot do it forever. I must use my apprentice for the fine work. I will lend my experience and see what he absorbs. As you ken, you cannot lead a horse to water."

Each of the gentlemen waited for him to finish the line, but he didn't. There was a long period of awkward silence as all of them "ken" that was not how the saying ended. One could most definitely lead the horse to water, you just could not make him drink.

The stable men came and took the horses, agreeing to do as exactly as Daniels had instructed: "Treat them well. They deserve a good grooming and perhaps a few sugar cubes."

Bingley forced a polite laugh then introduced everyone before Mr. Burwick started another debatable monologue or politically unfavorable opinion.

The group entered Netherfield, and Bingley directed the tailor duo to the parlor, as most of the other rooms were being decorated and the valuables removed from temptation.

Bingley turned to Daniels. "He is the best tailor in the county. He may not be the most personable, but I trust him with all my attire these days. It is so good to see you, brother!" He took two long strides and grasped Daniels' shoulders, then finished closing the gap, throwing his arms around his friend's chest and pounding hard on his back.

Daniels pounded Bingleys back in return, saying, "Indeed, brother, it has been too long."

Bingley may not have said it, but there was strength in the embrace, and William sensed Bingley was trying to gather his wits a bit before the emotion became observable.

Finally, they both stepped back, and William said, "'Brother. Indeed, I need to secure her first. I like the sound of that though. We will be brothers, if she will have me."

"If she will have you? Daniels, my man, you should have secured her before you left! She fears you will not have her, I am afraid."

"So it is as I feared?"

Bingley took a deep breath and clapped his hands, deliberately changing the subject. "Truly, what do you desire? Anything you want, it is yours."

Samson stepped forward. "Anything but dried crumpets. We are famished."

"An easy request, for our kitchen is well stocked and ready to serve."

Bingley made the requests for a serving of meats and cheeses, a few lemon bars, and fresh strawberries and cream.

"Oh, I love strawberries and cream." Samson's shoulders relaxed, and for the first time, he thanked Daniels for requesting his company.

"Do not thank me until you taste Bingley's version of strawberries and cream," William replied. "You perceive that the cream is sweetened, whipped heavy cream. It is not. I shall not spoil the surprise."

As they waited for the food, the men talked about their troubles on the road, where the regiment had traveled to, where they had been headed, and how beastly the weather had been.

But there was no mention of the eldest Miss Bennet.

William Daniels had enjoyed Bingley's strawberries and cream before, and his mouth began watering when three bowls were brought in. The first bowl had a thick, buttery sour cream, as thick as pudding, and the second bowl held fluffy brown sugar granules, and then the large bowl of strawberries followed.

Bingley knew of William's love for this delicacy, so he asked, "Daniels, will you show our friend how to properly eat strawberries and cream?"

"Take the strawberry by the stem, roll it in the sour cream, and then into the brown sugar. I suggest you try to tame your moaning of delight." Daniels placed the treat into his mouth and bit the strawberry off at the stem in its entirety.

"Sour cream? And brown sugar?" Samson questioned Bingley. He watched Daniels a bit long to ensure there was no trickery in the sampling demonstration.

"Is this a Southern thing?" Samson asked.

"It is a tradesman thing. My grandfather was raised on this delicacy. Our milk would sour, but we learned to use it. This is not something you want to dismiss or refuse."

Samson nodded and followed suit, doing as Daniels did. He hesitated then bit into half of the berry timidly. With a full mouth, he attempted the words, "Oh, good God!"

"You are welcome." Bingley looked proud to have provided such joy to his friends.

Daniels sat forward in his seat, attempting to hide what he had wanted to ask from the moment he touched Netherfield land.

Bingley sympathized. "Elizabeth is well enough and will likely have enough energy to dance as well. She is unaware that you are in town. I wanted to wait until you arrived to send word. I did not think I would be forgiven if your arrival was delayed, and I had led her to hope. Your letter taught me to hope as I scarcely ever allowed myself to hope before. I knew enough of your disposition to be certain that, had you been irrevocably decided against Elizabeth, you would have acknowledged it to me. You would have done so frankly and openly."

"Indeed, but I cannot imagine ever being more decided on something. I want Elizabeth Bennet to be my wife, and soon. Bingley, I must trouble you once more for congratulations. For if it is as you say, her sore heart will be much improved tonight."

*****

Jane put her gentle hand on the small of Elizabeth's back and pushed slightly. Elizabeth sighed, realizing she had paused at the doors of Netherfield's ballroom. She had heard the instruments warming up and tuning from outside as they exited the carriage, but by the time they had been warmly welcomed by several silent footmen taking their outerwear, recognizable music was starting.

She scanned the room, but her mask was not positioned correctly and she was unable to see what was in her peripheral vision. "Jane, I need the feathers farther from my face. Let us go to another room and fix it. I cannot see well on the right."

Bingley startled them from behind. His jovial tones were not hard to miss. "Good evening. I do not presume to know your identity, but I do enjoy a good guessing game. Are not masquerades delightful, my angel?" He winked and bowed deeply to kiss Jane's hand. Turning to Elizabeth, he said, "Forgive me for listening, but I understand you need some privacy? Allow me to escort you."

Both ladies started following Bingley, but then Bingley did something strange.

He dismissed Jane, something he never had done before. "What a beautiful costume; an angel matches your continence perfectly. I shall escort this other angel to a room where she can get the assistance she truly needs and desires."

Jane gave in quickly and departed, almost with a skip in her step.

It wasn't that Elizabeth feared going anywhere with Bingley, but Jane had promised not to leave her side all night. Yet at the first opportunity, Jane disappeared.

Emotion clouded her vision, but Elizabeth was grateful for Bingley's faster-than-normal pace through the growing crowd, all who were eagerly thanking him.

As soon as they turned two or three corners, the tears threatened to escape into sobs. She needed to keep up with him, but her current emotions drained her energy, and she called out. "Mr. Bingley, would you be so kind . . ." reaching her arm out, hoping he would take it.

But he didn't take it.

Someone else did. Somewhat disappointed that a suitor would come at her so directly, even overtly taking a role that was not requested, she removed her hand from the arm of the gentleman, and thanked him curtly. "Thank you, I am recovered."

She hadn't even looked at the man, for she had eyes for no gentleman but one.

The unwelcome guest continued walking beside her, even matching her carefully planted steps. With blurred vision and no idea where in Netherfield Bingley was taking her, or who this persistent man was beside her, or why Jane had deserted her, Elizabeth's annoyance rose.

The costumed man was quite tall, broad shouldered, and walking extremely close to her, her sleeve actually brushing against his elbow at times. Each time it did so, Elizabeth stepped a few inches away, but his next step closed the distance.

When the man leaned in and sniffed her, she twirled around and exclaimed, "I might warn you that I am not known for failing to hold my tongue. One might say that my good opinion, once lost, is lost forever. So if you are desirous for a dance, perhaps stay back a few paces. I insist."

A familiar chuckle escaped her unknown companion's chest, and she saw the lips radiate a joy and happiness that was contagious. She looked harder, taking so long that she doubted herself.

Yes, she knew that chuckle. And she knew those lips, lips she had dreamt about nightly for almost two months. "Is it you? Truly you?" she whispered. She blinked away the tears of what had been frustration to gain better focus. And then she knew.

His hand went to her hair, the curl that Jane had left out, and he twirled it and, almost unperceptively, moved closer.

Bingley had led them left, then right, and through several double doors. And then Bingley had disappeared.

The gentleman in front of her continued to move closer, so close that she could feel his warm breath on her forehead through the black lace mask. Part of her wanted him to confirm who she thought he was, yet the silence between them was tickling her spine. It caused her to stretch to her full height, almost reaching for him.

Instead of feeling like her feet were firmly planted, however, she felt like the laws of gravity had altered in the moment, even altering time itself. The gravity pulled her body closer, her head tilted up as well, and just at the moment when his left arm wrapped around the small of her back, they both closed the distance and connected.

His kiss was sweeter than ever before, while also holding a vast more intensity. It communicated all that she wanted it to confirm.

He missed her.

She kissed him in return to affirm her own lonely longing.

The kiss solidified her desire for more, and his desire, in return, was not misunderstood. No, she could feel his hunger. She reached her hands to his face, feeling hair on the sides of his head underneath the mask. She could also feel his beard had been freshly trimmed but not too short. Just long enough to not prick her skin.

After she pulled him closer, their kisses reached an even higher intensity. His mouth was not just giving her kisses but was pulling her in, asking from her an even more honest demonstration of her longing.

William continued for a moment longer, but then he slowed enough to say, "Sweetie. My dear, sweet E—" He returned to kissing her before he finished.

Even his attempts to say her Christian name increased her own need even more. "Elizabeth," he finally managed, with a heavy exhale.

She didn't remember taking that much-needed breath as they parted. She did, however, notice that she was now actually holding the precious air, trapping it to be a companion to the feeling his voice had sent into her chest, penetrating it to her core.

The alchemy of the heightened air volume, desire, and enormous relief in knowing that he still loved her exploded in an instant, and she whimpered audibly once.

She was not this sort of lady who gave into such intense and dramatic feelings.

She was not like her mother.

But just as she thought it, she felt the onslaught of tremblings and quivers in every part of her body.

Her knees struggled to support her, and she was forced to let the air out of her chest.

Her sobs ravaged her shoulders and would have trembled her entire being, but William had pulled her back in close, supporting most of her weight as her legs rejected the work she was asking of them.

She clung to him, begging the wave of nausea and the spinning hallway to stabilize.

She reached for him harder, but the blackness finally conquered her consciousness.

*****

William shifted Elizabeth's weight just enough to allow most of her torso to be in his right arm. Bending, he lifted Elizabeth's legs.

He could not tell if he was more surprised, or concerned, that she had fainted. Bingley had reported that she was much recovered, so he was almost certain this spell was more from being overwhelmed.

She had certainly been exerting herself. He chuckled at the thought then sobered with the realization that maybe he had caused it.

"Bingley!" But there was no answer. His friend had likely given them some privacy or was attending his guests. William knew most of the upper level but was unfamiliar with the back west hall where Bingley had led them.

He opened three doors before he located a sofa.

Just as he went to place her on the sofa, she opened her eyes and smiled sleepily, bringing her arms around his neck.

It happened so naturally. She pulled him to her, the dazed look in her eyes flashed briefly before she closed them expectantly with slightly puckered lips, almost entreating for relief of their loneliness.

How could he not give her everything she wanted?

He kissed her as tenderly as possible. He could not deny he was a bit concerned that she would faint again. He pulled away briefly, examining her intoxicating eyes, which were once again open and gazing up at him.

"William, please do not leave me again."

Hearing her whisper his name left him momentarily speechless. "My dear, sweetest Elizabeth. I must. I have a lead on who I might be. The crest I have on this ring might be the very clue to finding what my true last name is. I should not—cannot—offer you a false last name. I must investigate it."

"I do not care about that, surely you know that. Indeed I do not. And with all the conversations we have had, I assumed you did not care either."

"But I do care! Not for myself, but for you, Elizabeth. You deserve more than a lieutenant's salary. And if there is a possibility of not earning my breakfast by marching or camping over the winter for long periods without you, I will seek out that option with fervor. Never have I desired money, status, or a heritage until I realized I had none to give to you."

"William," she said, brushing his hair with her fingers, "how long will you be gone?"

"I was granted a month leave."

"A month! You will be gone a month?"

"I have that long of leave. But no, I will not leave your side longer than a few days. Does that settle your concerns?"

"Perhaps a little."

"Please, tell me how you are doing. I cannot discuss my next plans if you are not well."

She arched her back and raised her head to receive another kiss. "I am perfectly well. At least, I am now. I fear the lack of letters was trying on the kind, lighthearted manner that I usually possess. My body is well healed, and days have only been long for lack of word from you, not from fatigue."

He knew he must clear the matter, for she had mentioned his lack of letters twice. "I wrote you twice a week, my dearest. Your letters did not make it to me until two days ago, when I received all of them at once."

Relief flooded her body with an audible breath, and she nodded. "I shall wait for their arrival then. I suppose the same might have happened to your letters to me. It was a very harsh few months. Did you say you have a month leave? How long will you stay in Herefordshire with me? I mean, with Bingley?"

"I have discussed this with Bingley at length. How would you like to come with me to London, to find out the meaning behind my family crest, and hopefully the—"

"But I cannot!" she interrupted him. "It would be improper, even if Jane came as well. That is two unmarried gentlemen and two ladies."

William smiled broadly and took her hands in his, kissing them tenderly. "I believe, sweet Elizabeth, that you have an aunt and uncle in London? It is a short horseback ride for Bingley and me, and a cozy carriage ride for the ladies riding in Bingley's carriage. What say you? I have Samson with me as well, and Bingley has offered his rented London house for all of the gentlemen. Would you like to visit with your aunt?"

"I adore my aunt and uncle, and they would never turn me away. Perhaps I could write and assure they are not away. My uncle is in trade and travels frequently. I was planning a holiday to the Lake District with them in a few months. When are you wanting to leave for London?"

"As ill-timed as this sounds, I feel an urgency, a true need, pulling me there, but I will only go if you are well enough to travel."

"I am well enough, you need not ask again. You must have been truly worried when you received no word."

William kissed her fingers again and whispered, "I was more concerned when I realized you had had no word from me and doubted my regard. My love for you will never be so easy to dissolve as that." He leaned in and kissed her forehead, holding his lips to her head a moment longer than necessary.

CHAPTER 16

It took a lengthy conversation with Mr. Bennet to obtain permission for his two favorite daughters to travel to London. But two days later, their party departed as planned.

The gentlemen each rode a horse from Bingley's stables, and the ladies rode comfortably in Bingley's carriage.

One would think that Elizabeth and Jane had plenty of time to observe their suitors on the four-hour journey. But the truth was, Elizabeth fell asleep minutes after the carriage driver signaled the horses to start. By the time they arrived, Jane's leg was partially numb, as Elizabeth's sleepy head had slowly transitioned from Jane's shoulder, to her chest, to her lap throughout the journey.

Jane began to recognize central London. She knew the plan was to go Bingley's London house first. As she had not been there before, she paid close attention to where they were going. The townhouses they had passed ten minutes ago had been run down, with chipped paint and offering no true beauty. But five minutes ago, she witnessed the transition to more refined, even charming houses. The surroundings continued to evolve as she began to recognize the edges of Hyde Park.

The carriage slowed, then stopped all together at a grand corner house. Jane gasped, stirring her sister. "No, surely he does not live directly across from Hyde Park!"

"Hmm?" her sister murmured sleepily.

"Oh, dear, Elizabeth, this cannot be."

Jane felt Elizabeth stiffen. "Jane? What is wrong?"

Without understanding why, she let out a giggle, which grew just high enough to sound unnatural.

Elizabeth sat upright in an instant. She followed Jane's eyes to the left. "Bingley lives here?"

They watched as Bingley's front door opened, and Jane's future husband was greeted by loyal servants. He removed his hat, grasped the butler by the shoulders, and then released him suddenly, causing the butler to take a balancing step.

Bingley then turned and hurried down the lovely carved steps, two at a time. It took him three more steps to grasp the carriage door, energetically opening it. "Welcome to Bingley House," he declared, looking at Jane. Then with a lowered voice and raised eyebrows, he finished. "Your future home."

Seeing the joy and energy on her beloved's face made Jane's heart speed up to rates she prayed did not make her blush. All of this was an answer to fervent prayers. She blushed and barely whispered her gratitude with shyness as he helped her carefully descend from the carriage.

He then turned to assist Elizabeth.

Jane saw her sister scanning for her own suitor.

"Where are the lieutenants?"

Bingley chuckled and took Elizabeth's hand. "They rode ahead to run an errand. I believe they are arranging a proper chaperone. I trust that this carriage rolling up is exactly that. I presume Samson was able to secure his sisters for the evening. Come, ladies." He offered both arms, one for each lady.

Jane blushed again at how proud he was to share his home.

Samson escorted two finely dressed ladies out of the carriage whom Jane had never met.

Samson had not been the only gentleman in the carriage!

Elizabeth had already taken two steps before Bingley released her arm. Jane watched her sister lift her skirts and hurriedly approach Daniels, assessing him from head to toe.

"Good morning, Mr. Daniels."

He had not even finished exiting the carriage, but he tipped his hat respectfully. It was heartwarming to know that William Daniels truly loved Elizabeth, for he wrapped one arm around her waist, pulling her into him for a brief moment.

"Allow me to introduce you . . ." Samson's words trailed off as he noted that Bingley and Jane were holding back their greetings, not intentionally to be rude but because the couple next to him were standing inches from each other. Daniels had grasped both of Elizabeth's entire forearms. Jane could see Elizabeth's hands gripping his sleeves.

The intensity of their locked eyes grew, and the rest of the party walked ahead, leaving them to their reunion.

Jane thought their actions curious.

That reunion was more than being separated for a few hours called for. Rather, she could see they were trying to communicate something with their eyes. Elizabeth was pleading with hers, while Daniels' eyes looked determined and positive, with a mysterious gleam.

But for what was Elizabeth pleading?

Witnessing their reunion, at least the first moments of it, albeit nonverbal, Jane realized why it perplexed her. She saw no shadows under Williams' eyes. No ghosts behind his look. The lines by his eyes were more pronounced but entirely caused by a warm, tender smile. Jane had a sudden realization.

William was happy; he was at peace.

*****

Elizabeth waited patiently. Her heart raced with excitement, for joy was almost dripping from her intended. He was grasping her arms, almost clinging to them in anticipation, his fingers squeezing and moving in his excitement.

His smile broadened, showing the most charming smile she had ever witnessed. It was extremely satisfying.

Elizabeth could not think of a time she felt more excitement.

"Did you . . . were you able . . ."

He smiled even wider, and the whites of his teeth presented a glimpse into a new level of attraction.

This man's arms she was holding onto, no, clinging to desperately, was the same man she fell in love with. Indeed he was.

"How I desire for you to kiss me, Elizabeth."

His eyes were fine, deep, and inviting. He still smelled like lemon and sandalwood but only lightly, because the current musk was of oiled leather, horse, and road dust. None of which bothered her.

"You know, I will."

And she did.

A thrilling vibration tickled her lips while she kissed him, alerting her to the deep moan that escaped from deep inside his chest. She reached for his shoulders and was surprised when he stepped back, doubling the small distance between them. She made to move closer again, but he stepped back again.

William now was an arm's length away. He dropped one arm, placing it on her waist.

The movement entirely surprised her, for she was expecting a longer embrace. But suddenly her heart started fluttering, its sound echoed in her ears.

He is about to propose! A part of her wanted to just interrupt him and say, "Yes!"

One hundred possibilities of how he would ask battled in her mind.

Oh, dear, he is putting his hand into his vest pocket! Is it the ring? She adjusted her position, trying to catch a glimpse what he was retrieving from the small vest pocket. But then he patted his chest, once on each side, as if he was looking for something.

He took out a folded piece of parchment from the inside of his greatcoat. *Oh, how memorable and considerate to write down the proposal. He must be so nervous!*

He smiled widely. "I have news."

"William?"

He motioned with his hand to step into the Samson family carriage. "Miss Elizabeth, would you like to ride with me to Hyde Park?"

"Oh, bother, I thought you were going to ask me––" Her hand flew to her mouth, covering it with mortification. She had spoken that horribly brazen thought. Her cheeks went hot to the point of discomfort. At the same time, she patted the back of her chilled fingers across her fiery forehead.

William's eyes darted to the open carriage door, adding a subtle tick of his head that encouraged her to get in. As she moved to follow his suggestion, his hand lifted hers and steadied her while she stepped up and entered the carriage.

As she sat down, she saw a basket of packages, most likely bundles of food tied in waxed cloth to keep fresh.

William Daniels stepped up too, rocking the carriage a bit. To her disappointment, he sat across from her and used his cane to hit the roof of the carriage.

After the initial lurch from starting, Elizabeth began to stand to move next to him; however, she was encouraged to sit again in her spot across from him.

"Elizabeth. Elizabeth Bennet, will you . . . tell me your middle name?" William asked.

He was asking what her middle name was? Her name? "Why would you . . ." Elizabeth couldn't finish the sentence, her disappointment was apparent in her voice.

The intimacy and privacy of being together, alone, in an enclosed carriage was thrilling indeed. Even the rocking of the carriage seemed to have mesmerized her until that moment. But now, her disappointment broke the spell, disappointment that turned to anger all too quickly.

She had truly thought he had planned to propose in the carriage.

When he started the sentence, with his deep voice proclaiming her Christian name almost like a prayer, there was no portion of her body or soul that doubted the next words he uttered would be a marriage proposal.

But then he had ended with such a benign. . . nay, ridiculous question!

Elizabeth sat back and folded her arms tightly.

My middle name? He asked me what my middle name is? She had no qualms about telling him that it was Rose. None at all. Her issue was that of unfulfilled expectations. She couldn't believe she had been so naïve!

But Elizabeth had fallen deeply in love during the courtship. She found she needed him in ways that her independent heart fought. Had there been signs that he would not honor his commitment? No, there had not been.

They were not officially betrothed. But they both had discussed their plans with Jane and Bingley extensively the previous two days. Was she overreacting? Perhaps. But perhaps not.

Maybe he had been assuming her acceptance all along? Did he not know that a lady has little freedom in the world in which she lives other than choosing the man she will live with for the rest of her life?

What if Mr. Collins had asked her? Of course, she would have said no. Mary accepted because she was a different breed, and clearly her standards were more pragmatic.

Was it too much to ask for the chance to accept or deny the future she had been imagining with William?

"Elizabeth, did you hear what I said?"

The sound of her name startled her from her thoughts. "Oh, dear, I am afraid I did not. If you do not mind, please repeat it, at least the last part. My mind was preoccupied."

"Indeed, your eyes darkened, even went blank for a moment. Perhaps this was too much to take in all at once. " Daniels sat back, tapped the carriage, and asked them to halt.

"For heaven's sake, I was daydreaming, that is all!"

"Perhaps I was too hasty to share the news. I just had hoped that you would be pleased."

"I am! Or I should hope anything that would please you would please me."

"Quite alright, sweetest Elizabeth. You have hardly been allowed to rest from the journey. Perhaps a stroll through the roses?"

He was offering her a stroll? Her lip began to betray her as it quivered momentarily, but she bit it.

Elizabeth could hear her voice quivering under the stoic attempts to control it. "You obstinate, headstrong boy! Is this the gratitude for my attentions to you last spring? Is nothing due to me on that score?" The anger resurfaced at the omitted proposal. She felt as if her own opinion was overlooked. Perhaps not even considered! "Tell me at once, are you engaged to me?"

His back stiffened, almost unnaturally. The position he took next was that of an ancient sculpture, captured in its torture for all time. "We are not."

The carriage had already been stopped, but with some force, Daniels banged on the roof again as he announced, "To Bingley House."

And those were his final words directed at Elizabeth for the rest of the day.

*****

The Bennet ladies had been escorted to the Gardner's home in silence by Bingley. The exchange of silent expressions between Jane and Bingley had been deafening, but Elizabeth ignored them as best she could. Elizabeth and Jane had been shown to their rooms. They had even begun preparations to retire.

But Elizabeth knew a curious and concerned Jane would not let her older sister truly retire without sharing the story. Jane had patiently waited an excessively long afternoon and evening with their Aunt and Uncle Gardner. Indeed, Jane had allowed Elizabeth to remain silent for a saintly amount of time. She had even picked up Elizabeth's half of the conversation with their relations, who had not been expecting them until that evening.

The two sisters had made all the preparations to retire, even dismissed the maid after she placed the warmers at the bottom of the bed and fluffed the pillows. She and Jane climbed into the bed, Jane facing her back.

After a moment of dreadful silence, Elizabeth asked, "I do not suppose you will allow me to refrain from answering the questions behinds your concerned looks?" Elizabeth let that question hang in the air hopefully, but Jane hardly breathed next to her.

She knew her sister possibly would have waited, at least for the night, but Elizabeth answered her own question. "It is unjust of me to not explain why our feet hardly crossed the threshold of your intended's house before I demanded our departure."

Jane opened her mouth to speak, paused, and then nodded. "You did not have a headache. I suspected that was the case. So was there a disagreement?"

Elizabeth shared the story in a rush. "I had hoped, with all my might, that he would have asked me to marry him before the regiment left. All those weeks of not hearing if he was well were difficult. When I finally saw him at Netherfield, and saw that he had taken great effort to arrive in time for the ball, I knew he loved me. I left no doubt in his mind that I . . . well, you have heard my philosophy before. If a woman is partial to a man and does not endeavor to conceal it, he must find it out. No, I do not think he is under any misapprehension regarding my affection in return."

Elizabeth turned over in bed and finished the story, explaining how she had asked—no, demanded—that he define the agreement between them. She included how the look in his eyes turned dark and partially confused, and how short and limited his direct answer to her forthright inquiry about their engagement had been: "We are not."

"My disappointment rose drastically, to a level I have never endured. My only thought at the time was to depart. I couldn't look at him one more minute. His tight lips, his squared shoulders. The hard, guarded glances at me when he thought I was not watching were unbearable! Jane, it was awful! No, let me correct that. I was awful. And he probably no longer admires me."

Elizabeth fully let go when she voiced the last dreaded fear.

What if William no longer admired her? Her impertinent tongue had done it again.

"Surely he did not realize what you had expected in the moment . . ."

"If he did not, he should have asked me at that very moment. Jane! I shared what occurred as honestly as I could. However, my mind will not stop abusing me for my behavior. What say you?"

Jane had been looking directly at Elizabeth but then looked down at her hands. "Lizzy, I dare not share my feelings."

"I insist! Please, Jane, do not let my mind and heart battle like this without guiding them with your better, more positive, perspective."

"Elizabeth, it might cause strife between us or, worse yet, between you and Lieutenant Daniels. And to be honest, I fear that I do not possess the frankness you possess."

"Help me fix this. I love him, Jane. I love William. I need to be offered hope as I had scarcely ever allowed myself to hope before. I know enough of his disposition to be certain that, had he been absolutely, irrevocably decided against me, he would have acknowledged it. I am quite confident that he loves me too. Truly, be my judge, and if necessary, judge me harshly. I will always be your sister, but if you do not correct me, I might never be his wife."

"You are a proud woman."

Elizabeth laughed and said, "Truly, do not mince words, I must hear the truth. Was I so terrible that I might lose him?"

Jane took a breath. Her words started slowly but then sped up with the rush to say all she felt. "Well, then, I will share with you my disappointment. First, you judge him harshly, then assume he has views of the lesser sex like most of society, as demonstrated on the climb to Rainbow Agate cave, but he proved you wrong."

Elizabeth felt her jaw drop a bit.

"I am not done yet. I shall continue for, Elizabeth, you have made your porridge. You made it quite difficult for him. From the illness to losing faith in him when his letters were innocently displaced, for sure! I say this next part from his point of view."

Jane hesitated ever so briefly before continuing on. "I vow I shall never say harsher words in my lifetime. Your manners, impressing me with the fullest belief of your arrogance, your conceit, and your selfish disdain of the feeling of others, were such as to form the groundwork of disapprobation on which succeeding events have built so immovable a dislike that —"

Elizabeth heard the sharp reproach to her soul.

Do not say it, she begged silently. But Jane did.

"—I am surprised that he had not known you a month before he felt you were the last woman in the world whom he could ever be prevailed on to marry."

*****

Jane held Elizabeth while she cried, which was most of the night. She held her even when the tears no longer came. She reassured her countless times. Jane emphasized that the affection that Daniels had for Elizabeth was not easily dissuaded or eliminated. He was persistent, for sure, but could he truly forgive her and her sharp tongue?

The heaviness in Elizabeth's chest was excruciating. She did not know how to approach William again. Yet she knew she had to! She had to make things right and ask him to propose, or at minimum, she had to make her intentions known. But that was one thing that English ladies did not do. She certainly wasn't French! A lady in this day and age would be considered wanton if she were to pursue a man aggressively, but she would never forgive herself if she did not try.

How do you ask for another chance?

Elizabeth now understood that both she and Lieutenant Daniels were proud. Perhaps neither truly understood how proud they actually were. Jane had said that there was nothing more humbling than seeing how your pride detours you from happiness.

But one doesn't just decide to be humble.

It is a fickle thing, pride. Most assume they are not proud, self-righteously assuming instead that only other people are proud. Many hope they are not prideful, but in doing so, they ensure their pride. Innately, we all desire the praise and affirmations of our worth, or excessive talents, or breadth of our influence in the world. It is our human nature to want what is best for ourselves.

Elizabeth had always wanted to make a difference, to touch lives, or at least be remembered for the good she had done. But now?

She may very well be remembered as an unhappy spinster, for she could not live happily unless she was William's wife. Nothing else mattered to her but William's good opinion.

*****

William had been prepared to depart to the Gardner's townhome in Cheapside for hours.

Bingley had the right of it though. It may be fair to arrive unannounced, but it most certainly needed to be at a decent hour.

Once a decent hour arrived, with hardly a crumb of breakfast, William Daniels hurried Bingley along. "Jefferson, is there no end to your primping?"

Bingley's valet, Mr. Jefferson, assisted both men and had worked miracles overnight with the lieutenant's uniform. His breeches, which had carried all shades of neutral earthy tones—memoirs of his years of marching in the militia—were now spotless white, and the brass buttons on his greatcoat shone gloriously.

He looked as sharp as he had ever looked. He had even dared to remove the beard, allowing the scar on his chin and cheek to reveal itself. Jefferson had taken great care to trim the sides of his head with the latest fashion. He wasn't sure if he had ever used pomade before, but the ointment that the valet used definitely tamed his natural curls.

The fresh look was invigorating. And yet, at the same time, the fresh look was simply a return to who he had always represented.

William looked in the side mirror at himself. He examined how he held himself. With the beard removed, his image felt more familiar, more right, as they should have been all along.

He now knew who he really was. He was not William Daniels.

He was the heir of Pemberley.

Even with the newly discovered heritage, he seemed to be less sure of himself than he had ever been.

He did not care about his past, nor his present and especially not his future at Pemberley if he had just lost Elizabeth!

This person in the mirror now knows who he is, or at least was. Perhaps he could be that person again.

The battle continued, the back and forth between self-recognition of, as well as trepidation for, reclaiming his role as a Darcy. And yet, as prominent as those feelings were in his mind, they did not compare to his angst about what made Elizabeth so determined not to reveal to him her middle name. Now that his mind returned to that rabbit hole, he watched the face in the mirror grow stern and immovable.

He steadied himself and gathered his countenance. He had a lot of work to do if he was to mend things. He caught himself exhaling loudly, and he stopped immediately.

You are a Darcy! For goodness sake, act like one!

William could not help but growl his impatient words. "Enough already, Bingley! Let us depart." His voice was sharper than he meant and bordered on impolite. "Forgive me. I must not have slept well."

Mr. Jefferson did one last brush of Bingley's shoulders and, with a proud smile, stated, "Gentlemen, you look exceptional."

Bingley agreed emphatically, of course. "Daniels, er, I mean Darcy here is like a shiny new penny. He trumps me to everyone else but my angel!"

Samson had arrived from his family home and was waiting in the front entry when the two men came down. The carriage ride was not long; however, the closer they drew to Cheapside, the more uneasy

William's stomach became. He had few people in life who genuinely cared about him, and Elizabeth was the only one that truly mattered. "She does care for me," he murmured, mostly to himself, but Bingley heard him.

"See here, Daniels. . . wait, what should I call you now?"

"Daniels for now. I have not claimed my birthright just yet. I tried to share the news with Elizabeth, but she was in a peculiar mood."

Samson looked perplexed. "So she is unaware of what you and I discovered yesterday at the library about your birthright?

William nodded. "Yes, so call me Daniels for now. I would like to see my family and assure there was no reason that I was placed on that ship. My mother passed many years ago when my sister Georgiana was young. It astounds me how well the mind protects itself from trauma."

Bingley's joyful mood did not abate with Darcy's gloomy one. "Would it not be a wonderful conversation starter if we left our names, mine along with your true name, at the door instead of what Elizabeth knows you by?" Bingley lowered his voice and announced, "Mr.

Bingley, Mr. Samson, and Mr. Darcy are here to see the Misses Bennets."

William just nodded. It was something to consider. Elizabeth may not allow him to be admitted if he gave the name that he went by for the last five years. His thoughts ruminated again on how badly things were now mangled between them.

Her reaction yesterday puzzled him greatly. From what he could decipher in his muddled thoughts last night, she seemed to feel that requesting to know her middle name was completely inappropriate. For she had immediately taken offense, even became intensely emotional at protecting it. The words she had said were not easily remembered; however, her tones of anger and disappointment were seared into his mind.

Perhaps she did not enjoy her middle name or was ashamed of it. So ashamed that she felt he had no right to ask it of her, at least not until they were officially engaged. She had made that very clear. Perhaps he was not allowed to ask her middle name unless they were engaged. Could that be? His heart knew this conclusion was not entirely lucid and tainted Elizabeth with undesirable character traits, ones she definitely did not possess.

Sadly, he was hoping to have proposed in that very moment, but the look of disappointment in her eyes for the impropriety of asking her name had silenced him. He was still baffled at her anger, almost a day later.

Fitzwilliam Darcy, the heir of Pemberley, would not visit his true home in Derbyshire without her. If Elizabeth was not ready to take his true name, then he wouldn't either. If Elizabeth could not share Pemberley with him, he would stay William Daniels forever.

After all, what good is an inheritance if you have no one to share it with?

With firmness of mind, Darcy decided that he would never claim the Darcy birthright unless he could secure Elizabeth Bennet.

CHAPTER 17

Elizabeth always rose with the sun, and Jane needed her beauty sleep. But with the spring drizzle outside, Elizabeth chose to read instead of securing a maid with whom to walk.

Consequently, it was Elizabeth who opened the door to the gentlemen when they called.

The first ten minutes of the three men being at the Gardners was excruciating. Elizabeth had hoped for them to visit, although perhaps had not realized it would be so early; however, she had been ready far longer than her sister. She was quite sure Jane was notified of her intended's arrival while still in her nightdress.

It was entirely up to Elizabeth to entertain the gentlemen until Jane arrived. She ushered them in, signaling for them to take seats on the long sofa. However, William remained standing; therefore, Elizabeth did also.

When Jane finally descended the stairs, everyone stood to greet her. Only when Elizabeth took a seat apart from the others did Daniels take his. The only two available chairs were located by the fireplace and positioned quite close to each other. Daniels, however, positioned them even closer by turning his chair until his knees were nearly touching hers.

He reached for her hands and, predicting what he desired, she met him halfway. Almost instantly their previous doubts disappeared. Their clasped hands were the closest they could come to embracing, and he held on securely. She squeezed his fingers, and he returned the gesture by firmly rubbing hers. He then turned her hands over, caressing the inner wrists, and she arched her wrists to allow him access to her pulse points.

Their hands were clearly enjoying this delightfully enchanting dance between their fingers.

Neither wanted this waltz to end. The energy passing between them healed their hurts and confusion, transforming it into contentment. His touch made gooseflesh rise on her forearms, which he noticed, because he rubbed them gently to smooth them. Regardless of that gooseflesh, often a consequence of feeling chilled, she knew the temperature had risen within the last few minutes. She felt his tenderness and dared to look up to his face, which had been searching hers hungrily.

Once their eyes locked, it was a cascade of wordless communication. Contrition emanated from both of them. Confusion transitioned to understanding in that priceless nonverbal moment. Kindness and considerate apologies poured from both faces. Wordless promises were made and accepted instantly.

Finally, Elizabeth smiled and said, "Rose. Elizabeth Rose Bennet is my full name."

"Meeting you has been the deepest pleasure in my lifetime. I am Darcy, Fitzwilliam Daniel Darcy, of Pemberley."

Her eyes widened. "You jest! You know your name? Is that not near Lambton?"

"Indeed, I grew up but five miles from there. Charming little town."

"You remember?"

"I do now, most of it. At least I remember the important parts. I had a sister, Georgiana. It was she whom I witnessed die on the ship before I too got injured. My mother was Anne Darcy, and she was very much in love with my father, Albert Darcy."

"Is he still alive?"

"The records do not indicate a death date, so I believe so. I have several cousins, one of which is Richard Fitzwilliam, who is apparently now a colonel in the army. Imagine if I had orders to serve under him when I entered the militia? I imagine a cousin my age would have seen through the beard."

"You look very handsome with a beard, but I am finding it hard to look away now that it is gone. I am afraid you have such a classic and yet distinct jawline."

He rubbed his exposed scar and, for the first time since their hands joined, he looked away, but she chased his visual field with her own face. When he met her eyes, the self-doubt disappeared, and he smiled back at her.

Her breath caught in her throat with his smile, for it would have brought her to her knees if she hadn't been already sitting down. "Darcy, is that French?"

"I believe so. Elizabeth Rose, will you show me your aunt's gardens?"

She looked to the windows and smiled. "I adore the rain."

Fitzwilliam Darcy quickly looked to the window too, and then he grinned widely. "We might be forced to take shelter."

"Indeed. I might get chilled."

"A gentleman must ensure the comfort of the lady he escorts."

He stood and offered his arm, which brought an odd silence in the conversation between Jane, Bingley, and Samson. However, the reunited couple were too entranced with each other, and they did not heed the inquiries when they passed towards the rear door.

Fitzwilliam held the door, and Elizabeth Rose passed him into the rain. They walked arm in arm for a few paces, enough to take them away from the house and out of sight. The rain was warmer than she expected, and she looked up at Darcy as he said, "I must speak with you."

But she hurriedly said, "No, please, let me speak first. Allow me this honor, for I behaved abominably in the carriage yesterday. You see, I was expecting you to make an offer for me. So when you began to ask me a question, only you asked my name, I feared that you would never ask me!"

"I had made plans to offer for you, and still should have, but I had never seen you be so upset. I feared you disliked your name, or that I had crossed an unspoken boundary, one where you had secrets or feelings that you did not wish to discuss. For all I knew, you were signaling me to immediately stop with the proposal."

Elizabeth reached for his face. The gentle rain had picked up, but her hand was warmed by his face. She swept away the gathering drops from the hair that had become displaced on his forehead. "I was not finished, William. And I have a few things that I have failed to say in the past. May I say them now? For if I do not, I doubt I shall ever build up the nerve to do so. And it must be said."

Concern crossed his features, but then he smiled, leaning into her hand that was now cupping his jaw.

She took that as encouragement to continue.

Elizabeth chose her next words—and actions—carefully, for there was only one way to communicate the level of devotion and affection she felt.

With genuine happiness, Elizabeth leaned in and kissed him, lingering before pulling away just enough to look him in the eyes as she shared what she felt.

Elizabeth uttered the words that she needed to say: "In vain I have struggled. It will not do. My feelings will not be repressed. You must allow me to tell you how ardently I admire and love you."

Elizabeth took in a slow, cautious breath, holding it for a few seconds. A lady was held to certain societal traditions, and declaring oneself to an eligible gentleman was not one of them.

His smile grew wider with each sentence she spoke.

He stopped her after she told him she loved him, saying. "I know."

"Well, then, I suppose you know how I feel now."

"It was quite brazen for a lady, even for you. Brazen but lovely," he teased her.

"I am probably the last woman you could ever be prevailed upon to . . ." She stopped speaking but winked instead. She knew he loved her. She felt like royalty in his presence.

She wanted her husband to be sincere and know when she was teasing, for she had a natural tendency towards impertinence. She felt much more patient than yesterday, that was for certain. She knew that, as long as he was in her life, her heart was his. He need not ask for her hand in marriage, for she was giving him her whole body and soul, regardless of him asking.

He shook his head, "Yes, definitely the last woman . . ." He paused to get a rise out of her, and her arched eyebrow did not fail him. Then he continued, "That I shall ever have in my life."

Elizabeth said, "I have a surprise for you."

His brow went up, and a single raindrop that had collected on it dropped. "Very well, what do you have for me."

"I believe I made you a promise, or at the very least committed to learn something you requested of me."

Now his features pursed together, the brows, the lips, all of it. He seemed truly at a loss for what she was referring to.

"Close your eyes."

"Must I?"

"Oh, you must, dear sir."

He did as he was bidden, and she took a step away. "I want you to know that I am incredibly grateful that it is raining, because no one shall see my shame if it is an utter fail. Keep your eyes closed."

She watched a moment longer to make sure he was doing as she asked. Then she brought her hand to the side of her mouth and called out, "Ca-ca-coo-coohoo! Ca-ca-coo-coohoo!"

William's eyes opened and looked at her so lovingly that she could not reproduce the sound a third time. "You practiced!"

"Yes, I did."

"It is a perfect replica of the mating call of a blue-laced trigger! I doubt even a blue-laced trigger would know the difference!"

Elizabeth grinned at him playfully then urged, "You should try expressing your heart like that sometime. I do not think I could do it again, even if you asked . . ."

"I have a mind to express myself right now." In one fluid motion, he pulled her into his chest and planted his lips hungrily to hers.

With his lips to hers, their hands were free to find other areas to caress. Her hands were in his hair at one moment then found his firm chest. His pulled at her hips, pleading for her to come closer, and she obliged him.

They allowed themselves the private moment, their heavy breaths fogging the world around them.

It was not a short moment but that only added to its sweetness.

"Now that we have the misunderstanding explained from yesterday, I feel I should try again to share with you the good news."

"Yes! Tell me how you remembered your name! Did something trigger it?

Fitzwilliam Darcy chuckled. "I have heard memory can come back all at once; however, this was not one of those times. Samson and I rode ahead, and Bingley stayed with the carriage. I understand you slept the whole way to London?"

"Indeed, I did! When I woke, I had no idea that you had left at all, as you arrived at the same time as our carriage."

"It was not planned that way; however, I was able to locate the book of family crests easily, in fact it was handed to me when we first made the inquiry. The minute she saw the page of the book we were studying, she gasped. Her name was Mrs. Putnam and she could not restrain herself, for once we understood what the crest on the ring represented, she slapped her hand on her thigh with excitement, exclaiming she knew who I was!

"Mrs. Putnam, is a beautiful elderly lady who adores genealogy. She happened to also assist the *London Times* in editing the societal pages. Mrs. Putnam was very familiar with my family's efforts at finding me. She stated that my father, Albert Darcy, had been searching for his son for years. I listened to her tell me story after story of Mr. Darcy, my father, renewing the want ad month after month. He would always choose half a page, cut no expenses."

Elizabeth couldn't help but sigh. "Ah, you see? Your father is searching, has been searching for you! What blessed news!"

"Yes. However, he failed to renew it this week. For five years he wrote and sent money a week ahead of the deadline for the ad. But last week, the deadline came and went. Mrs. Putnam assumed that I had been found, or at least my body had been. She actually hugged me, telling me that uniting that father with his son was something she deeply desired to witness before she passed. So I have a very important question to ask."

"Yes, I will marry you!"

He chuckled merrily and replied, "I would still like to ask, sweetheart, but I shall not delay it further."

He cleared his throat, took her left hand in his, and kissed the back of her hand gently, lingering a bit. His warm breath sent her skin roiling with sensations. "Elizabeth Rose Bennet, I will give you all that I have, or have not, if you will share with me my future as Mrs. Fitzwilliam Darcy."

She had no idea that words, which really were just tools in communication, could move her to tears. "I shall be honored to be Mrs. Darcy."

"I am so deeply relieved to know your middle name, for Elizabeth Rose Darcy sounds as natural as my own did when I heard it."

"Indeed, it does."

*****

Darcy felt contemplative—no, the feeling was contented—while they walked in the rain back to the Gardner's back door.

Ever since he learned his name and had been reassured that his father was looking for him, William had felt grounded, like the earth had stopped shifting underneath him.

He knew who he was. And shortly, he would know where and when he would be going home.

Home. Pemberley.

The minute he heard the name, he could almost see it, as if he was there already. There was the great entrance, as big as a ballroom, with marble flooring and pillars on the outside that ran the length of the estate. There was an amazing library that he could now smell in his mind.

Elizabeth seemed to sense where his mind was and asked, "Tell me about Pemberley."

"I remember a great deal now, and even more every time I think on it. There was a blue sitting room that held all my mother's, along with her mother's, collectible tea sets. Some of the sets are estimated to be over two hundred years old. You, however, would be more interested in the gardens."

"Is that because they are wild and untamed?"

He patted her hand that was on his arm and smiled at her. "I am afraid that you will enjoy them no matter how they are now kept. What I recall was that there were some nice-sized hills behind the orangery, and the vegetation on those hills are all native plants. I helped the gardener widen the walkway through the hills by laying brick edges to the gravel path."

"I had not realized that you worked the home and land yourself. I supposed from what it sounded like, it was capable of supporting staff to do the work."

"Yes, it is definitely able to do that. I believe it was a lesson assigned from my father. I had to have been about twelve years old. Wickham and I had gotten into some trouble when we—wait . . . Wickham!! I grew up with Wickham!"

The thought was realized in that very moment.

So many questions came with that realization. Had Wickham recognized him? Had he known who "Daniels" truly was all this time? Why didn't he say anything?

"Lieutenant George Wickham? From the militia?" Elizabeth asked.

Darcy nodded. "I believe so. Since the moment I knew my name, and the name of my estate, my memories are flooding back. I see locations and occasionally a face here or there, but I do not recall everything. As you could assess, I just now recalled that I knew Wickham as a child. His father was my father's steward. He left for school around the time that we were forced to lay the bricks on the edges of the path.

"No, he did not just leave for school, he was sent to school! I remember now that my father and his father had a discussion about Wickham's influence on me. My father was a proud man, and I was held to a different standard than his boy. I believe Wickham was sent away because he had a knack for urging me to do things that were less than honorable."

"Truly? I do admit that he was not the hardest worker when the militia helped with the trenches. But do you really think him dishonorable?"

Again, Darcy nodded. "I am afraid so. He had a tendency to shoot mother birds in their nest. He even tortured the cat. . . what was her name?"

"Of whom do you speak?"

"I was referring to the cat. But it does not matter, because it is unlikely she is still alive. No, I am recalling several times where he would try to teach my cat to swim."

"But cats do not like water. They bathe themselves."

"Exactly."

They both pondered that for quite a while, realizing that perhaps Wickham enjoyed the suffering of animals.

Fitzwilliam Darcy turned to Elizabeth. "On a lighter note, I wondered if you could accompany me to see my father. He has been worried long enough. I am anxious to reunite."

Elizabeth tilted her head. "How long does it take to get to Pemberley? Did you say it was in Derbyshire?"

"Yes, it is in Derbyshire. I cannot be certain but likely a few days."

"As for my sister and I, we are at your leisure. Perhaps you should send an express. If it were my father wanting word of me, a single day would be too long."

"Most definitely. Quite right, Elizabeth. I shall beg of ink and paper from your uncle and send it immediately. Then we can depart tomorrow, weather permitting."

With a plan in place, they hurried back to the house where the maid was prepared with dry cloth to assist them from their private frolic in the rain. After they dried their faces and dabbed at their clothing and hair, they returned to the sitting room.

Every conversation halted with their arrival, and every face in the room was intently watching them for news. Elizabeth giggled a bit and looked at her intended to answer their unspoken questions.

"Allow me to introduce you to the future Mrs. Elizabeth Darcy. Oh, how great that sounds!"

The room erupted with joyous celebration. Even Jane let out a feminine squeal that surprised many in the room. After all the embraces and good wishes and blessings were bestowed, the happy couple shared their plan with the rest of the party. Everyone was supportive, and the proper chaperones and traveling arrangements were finalized.

Fitzwilliam Darcy was departing for home tomorrow. The joy in his heart had no equal.

CHAPTER 18

Their travels were not delayed by weather, and the roads had been recently groomed. They made excellent time, with only one overnight stop. Samson rode the entire way on Bingley's horse; however, the other two gentlemen took turns riding with the ladies and a maid whom Bingley had secured.

The party arrived at Pemberley just before dusk, and Darcy's heart sped up with anticipation.

Although his heart sped up, he hadn't realized that he had slowed his horse. Since he was in the lead, showing the way, the entire party slowed as well.

His horse had climbed the hill with ease and seemed anxious to be fed and watered. It was like the stallion sensed their destination was near.

And then he saw it, the beautiful home of his youth.

Pemberley was breathtaking. The front of the yellow pillars seemed to glow and pulse with life when he saw them. His heart swelled with pride and was momentarily overcome. He was home. In moments, he would see his father.

Darcy had chosen to dress in His Majesty's uniform for the last leg of the trip, but suddenly he felt it was inappropriate. He wasn't a soldier and knew he would not rejoin the militia. Not after being with his family again.

The swell of pride and anticipation turned to a brief moment of dread when he realized he would have to share the news that their daughter, their only daughter, had died. William recalled the counsel Elizabeth had shared at the inn the night before.

She had said, "You are not to blame, and your father will have already grieved for two children. With you living, he will be far more focused on a son whom he thought had been lost. Your father will find peace and closure on what was formerly unknown."

"William, are you well?"

Elizabeth must have sensed his discontent again. She had alighted from the carriage and was walking to where he stood, gazing at his home.

"We are home, Elizabeth." He leaned down and kissed her gently then guided her to stand in front of him. Fitzwilliam wrapped his arms around his future wife, and for many minutes, they simply looked at the impressive stone estate. He then started pointing out things, such as the hedge maze on the north side and then the gardens and stables on the south end. "I am remembering so much by just seeing my home."

"Is that the pond where you played with Wickham?"

He had told her about being pondmates earlier while he took a turn riding in the carriage. "I have to admit that it looks smaller than I remember."

"Perhaps from this distance it is, or perhaps it is because you are now a grown man."

He nodded; likely it was both. He was struggling to find words for the turmoil he was feeling. All these years, he had truly never looked for his family or home. He wanted to, but there was always some excuse not to. Not good excuses, he realized now, but what excuse is a good excuse?

He shook away what he was about to say. But when Elizabeth turned around, he allowed himself to say the thing that troubled him the most. She deserved his whole self, not just the brave and stoic sides.

"My sweet Elizabeth, what if I have caused my parents undue stress by not actively seeking them out sooner?"

She smiled sweetly at him and murmured something unintelligible, something along the lines of an "ah ha," but it did not signify what she said, because she reached up for his shoulders and kissed him.

She kissed him until his shoulders relaxed. "Your influence on me is shameful."

"Then shame on me. But I can say the same for you too."

"I am as shameless as a man can be if that is how you measure love."

"You are most shameless, but I do not feel any amount of guilt for causing that smile on your face now. Shall we?"

"If you are ready, I am."

*****

As they entered the gates, which were unusually wide and unattended, Darcy felt some concern. His father always employed a manservant to be at the gate to escort any visitors to the front of Pemberley. He was amazed at the speed of things he was remembering, but this memory was not comforting.

Could the family be away? The thought disappointed him greatly, until he saw the bustle of servants in the front loading a carriage. He searched the crowd for someone he recognized, but there was no one—until his eyes found the most distant servant standing to the side of the open door. The elderly lady was standing still, looking at him while he trotted closer.

He knew who she was, and it appeared she was watching him intently as he neared. He slowed his horse, and one by one, the servants who had seemed to be in such a hurry, stopped and stared as well. The previous chaos was immediately replaced with the ten or so servants all standing as still as portraits. While he couldn't recall the names of those standing so still, he was very familiar with the elderly woman.

Fitzwilliam dismounted, then adjusted the uniform collar and assured that he was presentable. He walked towards Mrs. Reynolds with careful steps, her eyes intently focused on his face.

As he approached, the eyes of Pemberley's housekeeper widened even further, and her stillness turned into three tentative steps forward. He continued forward, narrowing the gap between them, and once he was close enough, she reached out her hands to his face, and examined him.

She murmured something in Irish, and Darcy smiled, replying with tenderness and longing for the woman who was nearly a mother for both him and Georgiana. "Mrs. Reynolds, I am home."

Her first words were muttered, but they gained strength and emotion as she said them. "Master Darcy. Master Darcy? How? Where? For God's sake, son, give me a hug! Welcome home, Fitzwilliam!"

He embraced her and held her tight. She stepped back, ensuring her eyes did not imagine him. She turned his chin one way and then another, rubbing her finger along the scar on his chin. "I have a cream that will help with that scar."

"Of course, you do, Mrs. Reynolds. It is so comforting to finally be home."

She shook with emotion, as did her voice. "Pemberley's heir is home! The master of Pemberley is home at last! What joy! And just in time too."

The rest of the servants put down any supplies they were holding and lined up to greet Darcy. They took turns bowing and offering the deepest of curtsies.

Mrs. Reynolds smiled proudly and began to lead the group indoors; however, Darcy stopped them and said, "Let me introduce you to the future Mrs. Darcy, Miss Elizabeth Bennet of Hertfordshire."

"Oh, sir, what wonderful news at such a difficult time."

Darcy paused at the entrance and looked around for a few moments while Mrs. Reynolds rattled on in her usually comforting Irish accent talking about how she never believed she would ever see him again. She told of how his father had remarried and what a sweet lady Mrs. Darcy is. She explained that there were two children from Lady Anne Darcy and his late father; the children were his half-brother and half-sister.

The marble flooring that he hadn't seen for five years no longer held his interest.

"Pardon me," he paused, looking directly at Mrs. Reynolds. "My *late* father?"

She seemed to choke on her words now, but no sound escaped.

He waited an entire minute before he was finally able to repeat his question. "My father is dead?"

Fitzwilliam knew the answer, and he knew that he had returned home too late. His father was dead. He took a steadying breath and asked, "Where is my cousin, or I suppose she is now my stepmother. Where is Mrs. Anne De Bourgh Darcy?"

Mr. Reynolds, the butler, cleared his throat and rescued his wife from answering. "Master, I am afraid that she has eloped with George Wickham."

CHAPTER 19

Elizabeth could not believe it, but apparently Fitzwilliam could. She had never heard his voice filled with such angry passion.

"That bastard! So that is why he left the militia and asked for more leave. He did know who I was all along! That blasted man has no honorable bone in his body. Ready my horse immediately. Bingley, Samson, I will need a second, for this man will not survive five minutes from seeing the fury in my eyes. I could strangle him myself. God help me, I will."

The butler cleared his throat. "Yes, sir. The arrangements are underway as we speak. We were undergoing preparations to rescue her. If you will, I can fill you in while you prepare for the journey to Gretna Green."

"William?" Elizabeth asked carefully. "May I come as well?"

"Certainly not!"

Elizabeth was standing behind him. She couldn't say she waited patiently for him to turn around because she was most displeased.

He continued to give orders to the servants who dared to seek to please him. He cursed Wickham a time or two as well. When those who could be commanded had left his presence to do his bidding, he finally turned to Elizabeth and the remaining party.

When his eyes landed on Elizabeth, she unfolded her arms, placing them on her hips.

"Is there something amiss, Elizabeth?"

She shifted weight onto one leg and then the other, raising her eyebrows. "Certainly not?" She asked, "Are we not to be partners in everything?"

Darcy was preparing his rebuttal, but Bingley walked to his side and placed a hand on his shoulder. Darcy took notice of the cautioning look on his friend's face before he exhaled and said, "Elizabeth, we will be traveling as quickly as possible . . ."

Bingley gripped Darcy's shoulder harder. He turned back to Bingley and almost spoke, but Bingley shook his head again.

"Mr. Darcy, perhaps you are prepared to leave me at an estate I have never been, in a county that I have never travelled to, but you will not leave me again. You promised," Elizabeth declared.

Recognition of his promise—and how easily he was ready to break it—dawned on Darcy as if in slow motion. He bowed his head. "You are correct. However, it is dangerous, even for me."

Elizabeth folded her arms again with determination. "You obstinate, headstrong boy."

Darcy slowly smiled. "I love you, Elizabeth. I cannot lose you."

She unfolded her arms and stepped nearer. Reaching for his jaw, she said, "I love you, William. I cannot lose you."

And that was how Elizabeth tamed the tiger in Darcy. It wasn't anger, or stubbornness, or even logic that won over Darcy; it was pure, unadulterated love.

*****

The trip to Gretna Green was a bit brutal. The speed was that of a charioteer, but Elizabeth and her maid simply held on. Thankfully, they were traveling only as fast as the lanterns would allow them. Darcy had not wanted to wait until dawn to depart.

Darcy had the right of it though; they had to arrive before the brief marriage ceremony at the blacksmith's, so speed was of the utmost importance.

As Elizabeth watched him, she felt a pull to him, knowing that his cousin, Anne de Bourgh, was misled enough to consider eloping.

Darcy had ridden his horse for most of the day with only a short, one-hour break at Pemberley. Consequently, he decided to ride in the carriage next to Elizabeth for a spell. With him beside her, Elizabeth finally allowed herself to relax as well.

Her eyes must have betrayed her, because they would not stay open. It was as if purse strings were pulling them taut, closing them against her will.

Darcy took her heavy hand and kissed it. "You must be very fatigued, Elizabeth."

"I am, forgive me. You are likely just as tired. I suppose you are blessed with more will power." She lifted her head with exerted effort and stretched. "How much farther?"

"As you know, I have sent scouts on horseback to search for fresh tracks and ask around. The first report came just before I entered the carriage. They have been sighted on this trail, not more than three hours before we arrived. At this speed, we should come upon them shortly, perhaps under an hour. "

"William? May I ask a personal question?"

He pulled her head to him and kissed her forehead. "Yes, my sweet. I cannot deny you anything."

"Were you close to your cousin Anne?"

"Very close. She and my other cousin, Colonel Fitzwilliam, and I were as close as siblings, although perhaps not as close as you and Miss Bennet."

"Perhaps I did not ask that question the way it should have been. Were you affectionate with her? Or perhaps, did you have certain marital hopes with her in mind?"

Elizabeth's heart was beating as hard as it ever had. This concern had occupied her mind ever since she saw his vehement reaction to hearing Anne had eloped with Wickham.

It took great courage to ask the question at all, but she had wanted to be prepared for however he answered. She truly thought that she was ready for the truth; however, she was unprepared for Fitzwilliam's response. He laughed!

"Many years ago, perhaps when we were thirteen, we shared a clumsy first kiss. It was child's play, and I was to blame. I recall her mother, Lady Catherine de Bourgh, insisted that she and my mother intended Anne for me. Lady Catherine, in her officious voice, would declare that we were intended from infancy. I doubt either of us ever had plans to unite families. But she did marry my father, which is an interesting twist. I wonder if my aunt pressed her will in that relationship too."

Elizabeth forced a smile, for he had given her the truth. She did not enjoy hearing that the woman they were racing after to save from a disastrous marriage with Wickham might actually desire the man that was intended for Elizabeth.

Or was it the other way around?

Her cheeks began to ache from the unnatural cheer she maintained for longer than natural. Mr. Darcy stared off out the window, first ahead of them, then behind, and then up to the sky as well.

"Now, Elizabeth, may I ask you a question? We will be stopping at the next inn to allow you and your maid to rest. Will you please not press me to beg of you to do so? I have truly been troubled since I agreed to bring you with us. I cannot imagine you being in the midst of . . ."

She did not wish to fight tonight. She didn't even allow him to finish the sentence before she nodded. "Yes, Mr. Darcy, I understand. It was imprudent of me to have pressed you so hard to allow me to be at your side. I am quite certain that you shall prevail. Now that we know we are on their heels, and you will not be hours away if you were to be injured, I will wait for you at the inn."

"Then we are in agreement. Excellent. I must say, seeing my servants was extremely invigorating. I know I said that memories were flooding back before we arrived at Pemberley, but that is nothing to the barrage of thoughts, faces, and events that are playing out again as if it were yesterday. Better yet, I shall be able to lay eyes again on Anne, my own family!"

She wasn't sure if she wished to hear any more about Anne, the bride of choice for Darcy by both his and Anne's mothers. But as they rode, he shared one story with Elizabeth about his cousin Anne de Bourgh, which led to another, and then another.

He continued to ramble on from one story to another until the carriage slowed and came to a halt. The sky had brightened with the promise of a gorgeous sunrise. There had been a beautiful crescent moon dodging in and out of the clouds all night; however, the dark black skies were now brightening into a bluish-grey in the east. Elizabeth chose to focus on the fast-moving clouds as the skies began to grow pale lavender, with a brighter center in the east where the sun would eventually rise and light their path.

As she looked at the sky, her mind was restless. Anne may have been Darcy's first kiss, but Darcy, or Lieutenant Daniels, was Elizabeth's first kiss. However, would his affections shift when he saw Anne? Or had they already?

Although Elizabeth felt uneasy about the next few hours, she knew that Darcy loved her. What Elizabeth did not know was if Fitzwilliam Darcy loved his cousin, Anne, more.

*****

Darcy had full confidence in his man, Roberts, the groundskeeper of Pemberley, whom he had chosen to watch over Elizabeth and her companion. He walked them to the room that they would be staying in and embraced Elizabeth, whispering in her ear while at the threshold. "I will be back for you."

"I know, Fitzwilliam. Please hurry, but more importantly, be safe. I do not wish to be denied my winnings."

Reaching to the flowers pinned in her hair, he asked, "So now you have *won* me?" Darcy continued to fiddle with the flowered hairpins, almost curiously.

"Most definitely, and I shall not give you up without a fight." Her tone was light and playful, but there was a distant darkness that he searched to understand.

He continued the playful banter she had started. "When was the contest, my dearest?"

They both heard heavy footsteps in the hall, so they withheld further remarks until they faded. Then Darcy asked, his question again. "When was this contest?"

"Oh, the contest was won the day you hid the book from me in Netherfield's meadow. You tried so hard to be discrete, saying the book was not of any importance. However, you most definitely held your place in the book. I knew I had found a man who cherishes books the way I do, and that is no minor thing, but you also independently chose to read outside, alone, as I do. Most gentlemen read in studies or their libraries. I cannot tell you how often I have read in nature myself."

"Truly? You observed I was holding my place in the book?"

"It was hard not to miss the secreted book, held gently but protectively as well. You held your place the entire time we talked. Well, perhaps until I said you had fine eyes!" She winked and pursed her lips. He was all too willing to oblige, bending down to kiss her impertinent mouth.

"What a minx you are."

"But I am *your* minx. I do have one more question though, William. Tell me at once if your affections have changed since the fall."

"Indeed you are. I am so blessed, but you, my dear, are the prize. Except there was no contest. You were and always will be the only one for me. Now go dream of being Mrs. Darcy in a few weeks."

"A few weeks?"

"As soon as they read the bans. I shall not delay Pemberley a mistress any longer than necessary." Darcy kissed her again and moved to leave, but she had a firm grip on his shoulders. "Elizabeth? Are you well?"

She smiled again in that strange way she had in the carriage, as if she were holding a secret, or perhaps more afraid than she was letting on. After a lengthy pause, she finally answered him. "I will be, as soon as you return to me."

Darcy embraced her tightly, smelling her hair and then kissing her forehead.

"Three weeks, Miss Elizabeth Bennet. Three weeks, and you shall abandon that name forever."

"I am so proud to become Mrs. Elizabeth Darcy."

He pulled out one of her flowered hairpins and slid it into his vest pocket. "The Darcys possess complex characters."

"You have always been Mr. Fitzwilliam Darcy in character. So I am quite familiar with the character of a Darcy."

Darcy leaned in and placed his large hand on the base of her neck, gently pulling just enough for her to look up at him. A deep, baritone growl came from his chest, and he said, "I have sides of me you have not witnessed."

"I shall anticipate you showing me this—how shall I describe it—this animal side of you."

He chuckled warmly and kissed her, then pulled slightly away. "Do not worry yourself, I do not bite."

"That is a shame."

Fitzwilliam Darcy tossed his head back in laughter then brought her to his chest for one last embrace. "Elizabeth, you will always keep me on my toes with your impertinence."

*****

Elizabeth made excuses to her maid and Roberts, claiming she was chilled and needed another blanket. When Roberts turned to retrieve the blanket himself, she firmly insisted she needed a brief walk.

It had only been ten or so minutes since William had left her room; however, her stomach was in knots. Her only method of coping was walking. She would not go outside. No, she would do as she had said and obtain the blanket.

She rang the bell, and the innkeeper moved a curtain just enough to see who was disturbing his sleep once again. "Forgive me, may I have another blanket?"

He let the curtain drop, but she heard him slipping on his boots. She had no idea that he slept behind a curtain at the desk! She felt selfish now in her desire, and she added, "Take your time. I am in no hurry."

Elizabeth walked away from the counter and looked outside to examine the sunrise, but she saw far more than she expected.

With the early-morning sun shedding its light on the world, she observed two people exuberantly embracing, just as she and Mr. Darcy had earlier. The sight almost brought a smile to her face until she recognized the red coattails flying behind him as he twirled a lady in a black-laced dress.

He found her.

Darcy had found his Anne.

Hot tears burned her cheeks. Elizabeth lost repeatedly at attempting to look away. She watched as the two separated a few inches, only for Anne to grasp his face tenderly and kiss his lips. At least she thought it was his lips. He leaned down and picked her up again, his face joyous. There was no broodiness or reservation in his happiness. Not in any way.

Behind her she heard a low voice whisper with a snarl. "Miss Elizabeth, what a pleasure it is to see you again. Or should I ask if it is Mrs. Darcy? From my perspective, it might never be."

She quickly began to turn but was abruptly stopped as the voice behind her shushed her in a sickly, cooing fashion.

But even without turning, she recognized the voice of Mr. George Wickham. "No, no, no. No need to confirm who you think I am. Now do as I say, and I won't put a bullet through Darcy out there. I am assuming from your goodbyes that I overheard that those are jealous tears running down your cheeks. They should be. Darcy and his cousin were intended since birth. Now move slowly and tell the innkeeper that you changed your mind about the blanket and that you are retiring to your room."

Elizabeth did as she was instructed, politely refusing the blanket. "I am afraid that this blanket smells like the grass at Netherfield. I cannot take it. I have changed my mind about needing a blanket that smells like the meadow of Netherfield."

The innkeeper dismissed her with an indecent gesture and colorful words.

Wickham pushed Elizabeth gently to the right. However, instead of going up the stairs and back to her room, she was forced to head through the servants' quarters and out to the stables.

"Mr. Wickham, you are wasting your time. I have nothing you could need or want."

He wordlessly directed her to get into a waiting carriage. After looking over his shoulder to make sure they were not seen, Wickham followed suit, and the driver took off immediately.

Elizabeth started whistling casually in quiet tones to see what Wickham would do, and since he seemed to allow that, she took a deep breath and let out the call of the blue-laced trigger over and over again as loud as she could.

"Ca-ca-coo-coohoo! Ca-ca-coo-coohoo! Ca-ca-coo-coohoo!"

She was only able to start the fourth one before Wickham placed a muffling hand over her mouth. His eyes were dark and threatening. He had much of his weight on her body as the carriage bumped, and he fell onto her.

As he regained his balance, Elizabeth removed one of the flowered hairpins from her hair, tossing it out the window as she called one last time, "Ca-ca-coo-coohoo!"

Wickham growled menacingly. "Stop that!"

"Or what, Mr. Wickham? Do you really fail to understand that you are being hunted by the most powerful and richest man in Derbyshire?"

"So he knows who he is now, does he? How much has he told you? Did he tell you that his father loved me like a second son and that I was to inherit a living when his father died? Imagine me, taking orders! That will be the day that I cut off my right hand!"

"Interesting analogy. Did you know that in some countries they cut off the right hand for thievery?"

"I am no thief. Do you dare call me a thief for claiming what is rightfully mine? I have stolen nothing, nothing at all."

"I see." Elizabeth halted all communication at that moment and looked out the window.

The carriage was heading farther north at an incredible speed. She assumed Wickham would take her south, away from Gretna Green. So she continued to drop petals from her hair.

Just as Elizabeth expected, Wickham did not wait long to respond. "Pemberley should have been mine! It would have been too! My father, the steward, made sure of it in Mr. Darcy's will."

Elizabeth did not know if what he said was the truth or not, but she glanced at Wickham and rolled her eyes dramatically.

"You do not believe me? Do you think I tell tales regarding my livelihood? I am the rightful heir because Mr. Daniels, as Darcy went by in the militia, was not here for the funeral. Why did he go by that name anyway? And did he truly not recognize me?"

She narrowed her eyes and glared at him. "Mr. Wickham, you have not the character of Darcy nor do you carry the heritage. Your father was nothing but a paid servant. If the late Mr. Darcy, as you say, loved you like a son, why then did you just claim he offered you a living? A living that likely carried with it an excellent income, if you ask me. A parson could earn anywhere from three to four thousand pounds a year working for the Darcys."

"You aim high. The living is just short of three thousand a year. What is three thousand a year, compared to twelve? I am impressed that, through the grief of his son, the late Mr. Darcy was able to maintain an excellent watch over the estate and increased the income by twenty percent in five years. I have seen the books these last weeks. "

The carriage slowed again, most likely as it passed another carriage.

"But you will never be a Darcy. Darcys are strong, inventive, insightful, and proud, yet not vain.

"They are proud! But you are wrong, they are very vain. I was born to be a Darcy, perhaps not in blood, but I was raised like his son. For no reason at all, Mr. Darcy sent me away. Right at the moment when young Darcy was showing that he was no different than me. Young Darcy was conniving and mischievous and had a dubious nature."

Elizabeth fixed her hair a bit more and said, tossing a hairpin out the window, "I had no idea that you were so insightful to your character."

Giving her no more warning than he had upon her kidnapping, Wickham slapped her, knocking her unconscious.

CHAPTER 20

Darcy had walked his cousin Anne up the stairs, where they found the door not only ajar but without Roberts posted at the entrance.

He stilled Anne by putting pressure on her arm and then stepping ahead of her. He still had his pistol at his hip as well as the bayonet over his shoulder, and the hair on the back of his neck prickled.

Anne must have sensed his concern and heightened awareness, and she stepped back, going down one or two of the stairs. Darcy nodded his approval of her new position and inched forward toward the door that was ajar.

He heard nothing and, from his position, would see nothing until he got to the frame and peered around into the room. He checked his pistol, positioning it in front of him. He made one attempt to look inside, but there was no one in sight.

Where was Roberts? He was supposed to be posted at the door!

Darcy pushed the door open just a bit more, wide enough to side step through, his pistol leading the way.

With one quick examination of the room, sweeping every corner, he found the maid they had brought with Elizabeth, sitting but slumped over on the bed, as if asleep. Her legs were still over the edge of the bed, and the coverings of the bed were neat and tidy around her.

"Nancy, are you well? Where is Miss Elizabeth?"

His words startled the maid, to the point she alighted from the bed immediately, trying to smooth her apron in desperation as she prattled. "Pardon me, sir. I mean, Master Darcy, sir. I was not fully sleepin'. I was only resting while Miss Bennet finished speaking with ya. I had no right. Forgive me, sir . . . it ain't right, and I shall never leave her side . . ."

It was then that she looked around in a panic. "Where is Miss Bennet?"

Darcy's eyes narrowed. "I believe I asked you that question a moment ago. You do not know where she is?"

"Honest, I was only restin'! Mr. Roberts, where is he? Oh, dear me, I should be strung up, hung, drawn, and quartered! If she is harmed, I shall take full resp—"

Darcy was furious, and he left her in mid-sentence. Once in the hall, he yelled so loud that Anne flinched. "Roberts! Fetch me my horse at once! Roberts! Where the devil did you go?"

He heard hustling feet and then a loud ruckus that sounded as if someone had bumped a table with tea settings out.

Roberts' anxious words were nothing compared to his tone as he asked, "Did you find Miss Elizabeth?"

"Did I find her?" Darcy bellowed. "When did she disappear? It was your job to protect her!"

"She went for an extra blanket from the innkeeper. When she didn't return immediately, I set out to find her. I just came from the innkeeper, who states that she asked for one, then refused it saying it smelled like the grass of Netherland Park."

"Netherfield Park. When was that?"

By this time, Darcy had reached Roberts, who swiped the hat of his head and held it in both hands in front of him. "Sir—" he hesitated.

"When?" Darcy bellowed at peak volume.

"Near a quarter of an hour, Mr. Darcy."

"Wickham! Elizabeth would never venture out on her own. He must have seen that I had found Anne and gone for Elizabeth. Prepare our horses immediately, but mine first! I should have never taken her with me. Damn!"

Darcy followed after Roberts, who was sprinting to the stables. Darcy's stride was that of a near run, slowed somewhat as he attempted to replace his pistol in its holster before finally simply tucking it behind him in his trousers under the flaps of his greatcoat. He would need his hands to race after Elizabeth.

Suddenly he stopped. In the early light, he saw something shiny a few yards to the north, past the stable door. His heart sped up as rushed over, reaching down for the object.

Sure enough, his suspicions were confirmed. He picked up Elizabeth's hairpin, brushing off the dirt on the white petals.

One moment he cursed Wickham's name, and in the next, he sought and mounted his saddleless horse. The stallion was tired and still wet from the reckless speed they had traveled through the night. But Romeo did not fail him. The horse responded to the tangible energy from his master and seemed to catch maximum speed in remarkable time, but then again, there was no heavy saddle on its back.

The stable hand must have only had time to remove the saddle but not the bridle. The heat and moisture from the night's journey seeped into Darcy's trousers as they rode.

Most anxious to please his troubled rider, the horse invested itself in the direction Darcy led it. Darcy allowed the creature to find a rhythm and then leaned his torso down close to the animal's neck, holding to the mane, whispering, "That is right, Romeo. Let us get there in time."

Darcy worried if a quarter of an hour was too long a head start but reasoned that he was on horseback, practically bareback. He prayed that Wickham had not taken Elizabeth by horse but rather by carriage. There was no true way to know. Since there had been no rain recently, the road had tracks from every carriage and horse that had passed through this resting station for the past three days. Darcy wasn't the best at tracking anyway, but one thing he knew— Elizabeth had left that hairpin for him to find.

Romeo snorted, but the rider and horse melded well in their flight to save Elizabeth.

Darcy searched both sides of the trail for more signs left by Elizabeth, but he had not seen anything for over a kilometer. Did he miss something going this fast? Is there any way that they turned east or west at that last intersection? He soothed the horse, but the horse was intent on sprinting. He felt some trepidation at Elizabeth's whereabouts; however, in the minute or two that he was attempting to slow the horse, he saw the second hairpin.

Without stopping to pick it up, he pressed on, encouraging Romeo in his sprint forward. He could buy her more hairpins, but he could never replace Elizabeth. He had never felt such energy racing in his blood now that he had received confirmation that he was still going the correct direction.

A few minutes later, he could faintly make out a dust cloud ahead from what could only be a carriage going at dangerous speeds.

He called out one more time to spur the horse faster, and Romeo exceeded his expectations. He had ridden Romeo endlessly before the shipwreck, and now the horse remembered all of his master's subtle nonverbal cues as they rode as one to save Elizabeth.

As they neared the speeding carriage, Darcy used his cravat to cover his mouth from the dust. The driver of the carriage looked behind him and whipped the two horses he was driving even harder, but the heavy carriage was rocking at dangerous levels. Darcy was gaining ground on the carriage, and as he got closer, he guided the horse to the left of the carriage by a few yards. Wickham recognized him, and Darcy spurred Romeo even faster with his heels. The horse was as obedient as ever.

Romeo was parallel to the driver now, and in just a few paces, Darcy inched the horse close enough that the driver could hear him.

"Slow the carriage now, or I will slow the carriage after I shoot you between the eyes!" The fury in his voice was that of his father, demanding respect and obedience from anyone within earshot.

The noise of the horses was exceptional, but he still heard the gun fire from inside the carriage and felt the bullet narrowly missing him.

Thanks to Wickham and his poor aim, most likely because he never cleaned his weapons or gave them the respect they deserved, Darcy was not injured. But the gunfire made the decision for the driver, and he pulled with all his might to slow the carriage, pressing the wheel brakes with committed effort.

Darcy directed his own horse to slow, swinging one leg over the animal as he commanded, "Closer, Romeo. That is right."

The carriage was nearly stopped when Darcy lunged from the horse onto the driving platform, hitting the driver with his fist. The driver protected himself by jumping and rolling onto the ground below. Darcy called out to him when he got to his feet, but the driver had only made it a pace or two before he weighed the options Darcy yelled out. "Run, and I will find you. Stay, and you shall have my respect forever. Choose wisely."

The man turned around and nodded, swiping his hat in submission. His eyes darted to the carriage and alerted him that Wickham had climbed out and was running.

Darcy pulled his rifle from behind him, cocking the gun and taking aim. It was done so quickly that Wickham had not moved more than five paces from the carriage and slowed.

"Do not run, Wickham, or I swear I will take out one knee at a time until you are crippled, never to run again. You will be begging on the street for the rotting food that could not be sold or fed to animals."

Wickham slowed further, clearly assessing his options, then turned with his hands in the air. "Ah, come now, Darcy, surely you would not murder me. I am unarmed!"

"Where is she?"

"Somewhere safe."

Darcy pressed the butt of the rifle harder into his shoulder and aimed again, removing any doubt Wickham may have had about his intentions.

"Hold up now, Fitzwilliam Darcy, it was just a little prank between pondmates. Elizabeth is in the carriage, sleeping, no doubt." Wickham got on his knees and looked submissive.

Darcy glanced to his right but heard nothing. Returning his suspicious eyes back to Wickham, Darcy commanded, "Driver, remove the lashings on the side of the carriage and tie Mr. Wickham. I shall inspect your work, so do not deflect back to a man who has no chance of surviving the next ten minutes."

He looked directly at Wickham again, who had lifted one leg from the kneeling position. Darcy gave him a hard look.

"Move. I dare you."

The driver halted momentarily but then realized that Darcy was speaking to Wickham. Darcy kept his rifle aimed and watched as the driver mumbled to Wickham, "You couldn't pay me enough to save your hide. I wouldn't have moved an inch if I had known that you only thought of doing harm to Pemberley's heir."

Darcy was surprised at the loyalty in the driver's words but then realized that the years had been less than kind to whom he now recognized as his childhood riding teacher. He wore moth-eaten rags and a hat that neither held shape nor offered much protection from the elements, considering all the holes.

"Daniels?" Darcy asked. "Is that you?"

"Aye, Master Darcy. It is I."

Darcy alighted from the carriage seat and walked slowly towards the two, cautiously examining the fine binding that Daniels had done.

"You were like a father to me."

"I could never be so humble to claim you as my son, but yes, I hurt as bad as your father did when we assumed you had died. Drank a wee bit more than I should have, but the master of Pemberley kept me on, knowing how close we had been. Forgive me, Darcy. I tied him as best I could."

Darcy could see that the bindings were very tight, but he checked them anyway.

Wickham scoffed, and with upturned lip, he snarled, "Is that not par for you, Darcy? You take what I have, what is mine, and claim it as yours. Daniels, did you know that I served with this idiot, and it took me a few days to figure out he could not remember anything about his youth, not even his own name. Do you know what name he chose for you? Shall I tell him, or do you wish to tell him?"

Darcy still did not know the answer to that, but there were not two words he would trust coming from Wickham, so he played along. "Wickham, I remember all of it. I remember leaving, and I remember your character was something that Daniels would never follow willingly. You are nothing to him. You will never be anything but a servant for the rest of your life."

"You cannot sell me, not as an unpaid servant. It is no longer legal in England."

Darcy smirked and, before hitting him with the butt of the rifle, stated, "I own you and the debts you left in Hertfordshire, or I will within the week. Oh, yes, Wickham, I know you. I know your character. I had not known you a month before I knew you were the last man in the world who I would ever be prevailed upon to grant clemency. I will have gathered enough evidence of your debts to put you away into debtors' prison. There is not one man in the militia who did not see you for the scoundrel you are."

Wickham readied to spit at him, but Darcy followed through with his threat to hit him with the butt of the rifle.

Daniels removed his belt and immediately tied up the unconscious man's feet, then stood and proudly saluted. "Sir!" Daniels then relaxed and asked, "Did you really use my name when you couldn't remember you were a Darcy?"

"I did, Daniels. Looking back, it felt like the name of my family but never exactly right. Now I see that I really did think of you as a father. After all, it was you that taught me to ride, not my father."

Daniels bowed his head, "My condolences to you. Bless his soul."

"Thank you, Daniels."

Darcy's mind now returned to searching for Elizabeth. He looked back at the carriage and saw her reddened face peering out the carriage window.

He handed Daniels the pistol from his trousers, instructing his newly remembered friend to shoot Wickham if he even thought about moving.

Daniels's reply was one of strict obedience.

Darcy's legs could not carry him faster to Elizabeth, but as he got closer, he realized the reddened face was only on the left side, and there was a decent abrasion on her temple. "Elizabeth! Oh, my sweet, are you well?"

She smiled and said, "I am, my dearest, I am. I knew you heard me."

"Heard you?"

"Yes, I called out to you, the call of the blue-laced trigger."

"That was you? I had not realized that was you. I heard it and most definitely thought of you, which promptly ended my reunion with my cousin Anne. She wants to meet you in the fiercest way."

"How is Anne Darcy?"

He felt some confusion, for her tones seemed cautious perhaps even laced with a double meaning. "I suppose she is well. I left her to come after my future wife. Is there something amiss?"

"I love you, Darcy. Tell me at once, are we engaged?" Her deep-brown eyes were wildly searching his for something.

He gave her every assurance and climbed into the carriage with her. He did not take the bench across from her but rather the one next to her. When she adjusted to offer him more room, he inched closer, then closer still.

"Elizabeth, do you remember the morning you woke after the accident? When I asked you to enter into a courtship with me?"

She nodded, her eyes getting wet with emotion She did not, however, break eye contact with him.

Fitzwilliam Darcy smiled and said, "Never will you have a more devoted servant than you have in me. My will is yours to command. My life is yours for the taking. I gave you all of me without you asking, but I ask you now to take it in its entirety. Marry me, Elizabeth. Marry me as soon as we possibly can."

Darcy heard Daniels clear his throat behind them, but he would not risk looking away from Elizabeth until she answered.

Even through the noise of the rest of the party catching up to the carriage, Elizabeth's response was heard in his physical ears, and every other corner of his soul.

"You could not have made me a better offer. For you are all I desire; you are all I need."

Fitzwilliam Darcy was no longer lost. He had found his home, right there in the carriage with Elizabeth. The only witness was Daniels, the horse trainer, who was peering inside the carriage.

Daniels, the horse trainer, who was also a blacksmith!

He pulled away from Elizabeth and asked, "Do you trust me?"

"I do! With everything," Elizabeth said excitedly.

"Daniels!"

"Aye, sir?"

"If I am not mistaken, you are a true Scotland blacksmith! Are you still certified to—"

"Absolutely!"

"Now?"

"Here?" Daniels asked uncertainly, glancing at Elizabeth for approval.

Elizabeth nodded as soon as she understood what was happening. "I want to return home as mistress of Pemberley."

"Well, then, do you, Fitzwilliam Darcy, take Elizabeth Bennet, to be your lawfully wedded wife?"

"I do."

"Will you, Elizabeth, take Fitzwilliam Darcy as your husband?"

"I do."

"Will you both hold onto each other, both in body as you are now, and in spirit, from now until the end of your time on earth, and no one else?"

They both spoke in unison. "We do."

"Then by the certification which I hold, I, Frank Daniels, declare you married as of this moment. You may kiss . . . ah, I see you anticipated my next comment. Very well. I shall leave you to your musings."

Darcy devoured Elizabeth's face with his lips; their joy was evident through their smiles and passionate exchanges for many minutes to come.

During the shortened ceremony, many of the rescue party had arrived and clapped joyously when they realized what had taken place.

Darcy had little recollection of the ride home with Elizabeth safely seated next to him, or even how Wickham was transported to the Derbyshire magistrate's office. And neither Elizabeth Rose Darcy nor Fitzwilliam Darcy cared to ask any questions about either event during their whole wedding trip to the Lake District.

Darcy learned two things about the Lake District. First, the inn was quite comfortable, and second, that he need not show Elizabeth the sights outside their bedroom.

Elizabeth had once told him she always wanted to see the Lake District; however, regardless of extending the wedding trip twice, she never did.

The master and mistress of Pemberley found their way back to their home in Derbyshire several weeks later than they had originally informed Jane and Bingley of, but Jane and Bingley had no hesitation in exploring the many nooks and crannies of the estate and even those of the neighboring estates. Not more than a day before the return of the newlyweds, Bingley signed a lease on the estate just short of three kilometers on the other side of Lambton. Knowing full well that he and Darcy would forever be best of friends and, perhaps more importantly, that they could never part these good sisters, he opted for a permanent residence eight kilometers from Pemberley.

Hardly a week passed that the couples did not dine together. When there was a ball to be thrown, the two couples jointly extended the invitations.

Pemberley's heir had found his way home, and a short three months later, Elizabeth shared with Darcy news that the next generation of heirs would be joining their family.

"William, it has been nearly four months now that we have been married. I loath to release you from your promise to be my personal servant, but I know better than to deny you the chance to spoil our child."

Awareness dawned, and he grinned. "Are you truly with child? Do not jest with me. Am I to be a father?"

"No more than I am to be a mother."

"But how?"

Her only response was to raise her eyebrow impertinently.

He winked and smiled. "Perhaps you can show me how this happened?"

"Perhaps, or perhaps you can show me that thing you do again."

"I am not playing coy with that offer. Well, Mrs. Darcy, I must do as you bid. Your wish will always be my duty."

"Speaking of duty, you never shared with me how you were discharged from the militia."

"Colonel Fitzwilliam, my cousin, a horrible man, you would hate to meet him," said Darcy with a chuckle, although his smile belied that statement as he continued. "Colonel Fitzwilliam arranged it as soon as he and his parents were notified we had run off to elope."

"We did not run off and elope!"

"I believe we did. I followed you all the way to the borders of Scotland, very nearly into the heart of Gretna Green. And we came back married. Not a single ban was read, and our marriage is documented in the Daniels Stable book of records."

"A decision that I will never regret. You have done your due diligence with me, William Darcy. But I warn you, as devoted a man as I know you to be, this child will have you wrapped around her fingers in a fraction of the time you fell in love with me."

"It is not possible. I am still falling in love with you. Every round inch of you."

She playfully laughed and rubbed her hands over her nonexistent abdomen. "I am afraid the saying is 'every square inch of you.'"

"You are as soft and sweet as ever, my Elizabeth. Whatever shape you take, I will be glad to have more of you to love. Now let me partake of your shape as I did in my mind at Rainbow Agate Cave."

"You did not! As far back as the trek up to the cave?"

Darcy kissed her soundly then whispered, "I was in the middle before I knew I had begun."

THE END

About the Author

Jeanna Ellsworth Burrill had many detours in life before she "got it right" and found her Mr. Darcy. She is so proud of her three daughters and the three children she inherited through marriage, all of whom have supported her through her writing, and have always been her inspiration.

She absolutely loves her chance to influence lives as a neurological nurse navigator, helping people cut through the red tape of the medical system.

Her other hobbies include polishing rocks and selling the gemstones at a farmers market, gardening, and learning about anything that interests her. She finds great joy in her many roles she juggles, but writing especially has been her therapy.

Jeanna fell in love again with Jane Austen when she was introduced to the incredible world of Jane Austen-inspired fiction. She can never adequately thank the fellow authors who mentored her and encouraged her to write her first novel.

Other books by Jeanna Ellsworth

Pride and Prejudice variations

Mr. Darcy's Promise
How can an honorable promise become so vexing?

Pride and Persistence
At some point, a good memory is a bad thing.

To Refine Like Silver
Our trials do not define us; rather they refine us.

The Hope Series Trilogy:

Hope for Mr. Darcy
Hope is all they have left, will it be enough?

Hope for Fitzwilliam
For two destined to be together, hope is their only defense.

Hope for Georgiana
Hope has become vital—*especially* when it comes to love.

Regency Romance

Inspired by Grace
What started as friendship has evolved into something quite tangible.

Buying the Duke's Silence
Eventually Evelyn learns that Silence is golden.

PEMBERLEY'S HEIR

Made in the USA
Coppell, TX
27 February 2024

29497787R00267